THE BREEDING TREE

J. Andersen

Brimstone
Fiction
Lighthouse Publishing of the Carolinas

THE BREEDING TREE BY J. ANDERSEN
Published by Brimstone Fiction
An imprint of Lighthouse Publishing of the Carolinas
2333 Barton Oaks Dr., Raleigh, NC, 27614

ISBN 978-1-941103-98-2

Available in print from your local bookstore, online, or from the publisher at:
www.lighthousepublishingofthecarolinas.com

For more information on this book and the author visit: www.jandersenbooks.com

This is a work of fiction. Names, characters, and incidents are all products of the
author's imagination or are used for fictional purposes. Any mentioned brand
names, places, and trademarks remain the property of their respective owners, bear
no association with the author or the publisher, and are used for fictional purposes
only. Brimstone Fiction may include ghosts, werewolves, witches, the undead,
soothsayers, mythological creatures, theoretical science, fictional technology, and
material which, though mentioned in Scripture, may be of a controversial nature
within some religious circles.

Brought to you by the creative team at Lighthouse Publishing of the Carolinas:
Courtenay Dudek, Rowena Kuo, Eddie Jones, Meaghan Burnett, and Brian Cross.

Library of Congress Cataloging-in-Publication Data
Andersen, J.
The Breeding Tree / J. Andersen 1st ed.

Printed in the United States of America

PRAISE FOR *THE BREEDING TREE*

A captivating, twisty dystopian that kept me on the edge of my seat and left me craving more.

~Rebekah Purdy
Author of *The Winter People*

Compelling characters. A world from a vivid imagination. J Andersen masterfully uses her dystopian society to address the issue of "life"…and who gets to define it. *The Breeding Tree* is a gripping, worthwhile read.

~C.A. Wolcott
Author of *Call to Arms*
Staff Writer with Worldview Warriors (www.worldviewwarriors.org)
Speaker at The Colorado Christian Writers Conference

Fiercely addicting and refreshing dystopian that had me white-knuckling my iPad into the wee hours of the morning!

~Rachel Van Dyken
New York Times bestselling author

J. Andersen weaves what at first might appear to be a fantasy world but which quickly turns into a world that could become a stark reality with chilling consequences. An energetic and suspenseful novel with a smidgen of romance that will keep the reader turning pages until the last word is read.

~Martin Wiles
Author of *Grits & Grace* and *God*

Despite the fact that this compelling, well written novel takes place in the distant future, the killing of defective unborn babies to achieve the perfection of the human race sounds amazingly like something from today's headlines. No matter how fictitious the story, it couldn't be more relevant to life in contemporary America and the blasé attitude many people have about abortion.

Readers need to be careful, though. Although this story is in no way a pro-life "sermon," it is powerful—an arrow shot straight from the gut to the heart. Watching Kate come to grips with the fact that what has always seemed normal and desirable is actually evil and undesirable might result in some changes of heart.

I pray that it does!

~**Roger E. Bruner**
Author of *The Devil and Pastor Gus, Found in Translation, Lost in Dreams,*
and *Yesterday's Blossoms*

A unique vision of a dystopian world. J. Andersen's characters jump off the page!

~**Robin Brande**
Award-winning author of *Evolution, Me and Other Freaks of Nature*

I tried to put *The Breeding Tree* down a few times but couldn't force myself to stop reading. Instead, I finished it in one day. This story draws you in and makes you care. In a few places, I'm pretty sure I forgot to breathe. Definitely one I want to read again.

~**Kelly Martin**
Author of *Betraying Ever After*

Characters and suspense that grab the heart and make it think and feel. This is a book to read as we ponder the direction of our future values.

~**Dottie Rexford**
Author of *Cora Pooler*, recipient of the first place Writer's Digest
Self-Published Inspirational award.

The Breeding Tree is both an entertaining and evocative read you'll want to finish in a sitting.

~**Elizabeth Seckman**
Author of The Coulter Men Series

J. Andersen has written a book that will capture the reader's attention and hold it 'til the last page of this dystopian story. Be prepared to keep turning the pages until the end. Fantastic book, and I heartily endorse it!

~**Carole Brown**
Award-winning author of *The Redemption of Caralynne Hayman*

DEDICATION

To Ian, Eliza, and Gemma
I'd choose you a million times over.
~Mom

ACKNOWLEDGEMENTS

WRITING IS A SOLITARY endeavor. Thankfully, I'm surrounded by several amazing people who have encouraged me through this journey.

To Todd, for letting me chase this crazy dream of writing … again. I love you.

To the incredible team at Brimstone Fiction, a Lighthouse Publishing of the Carolinas imprint, including: Eddie Jones, Rowena Kuo, and all the others. I am humbled and honored to have worked with such a talented crew.

To my editor, Courtenay Dudek, for making me rework, rethink, and rewrite those clichéd scenes; for letting me bounce ideas off you; and for liking my edits the first time around … mostly.

To Meaghan Burnett, for walking me through this process and answering all my questions a thousand times over. You are more patient than I would ever be.

To my agent, Steve Hutson and his team at Wordwise Media, for sticking with this no-name from Podunk for so long. I'm grateful to call you my agent and my friend.

To Bri Katilus and Jeanine Bailey, for being my biggest cheerleaders, for giving the first feedback, for brainstorming and squealing at just the right times, and for fighting over the roles in the future movie. *wink*

To Deb Bailey of Phoster Images, for making me look halfway decent in my author photo. That is a talent that cannot be rivaled.

To Brandi Meacham, for taking on the book trailer project with gusto. I'll hire you again and pay you double next time!

To my writing group, The Write Circle, for cheering me on and never letting me doubt. Friday mornings are a delight because of you.

To my amazing betas, Wendy S., Danielle R., Jeanine B., Brianne K., Debbra B., Abigail B., Alexandria B., Jen P., Tracy H., Mom, Jerry M., Rell J., Penny R., Michelle T., Karen H., Meagan M., Brittany S., Elizabeth D., Jessica H., Alicia H., Brandi M., and anyone else whose name eludes me, thank you for your insight and for catching those typos.

To Mom and Dad, for always believing that everything I write is amazing. I'm sure if it's not too heavy, this book will be pinned to your refrigerator. I love you.

To God, for teaching me patience and for continuing to give me stories to tell.

ONE

THE ANNUAL PARADE AND OTHER REVOLTING PRACTICES

Code of Conduct and Ethics: The Institute—Sector 4, USA
Section 9 Article 3.8: Community celebrations must be attended by all indi-
viduals, regardless of age, gender, or physical capacity.

THE PARADE OF VALUES is my best friend Taryn Black's favorite event of the year, and every August 2nd she shows up at
my door bubbling with energy, dressed in something fabulous;
strawberry blonde hair waving in the breeze, and ready to nag me into
leaving early.

Too bad I detest this day with my whole being.

For her, it's a holiday. For me, it's duty. Even if we were allowed to
miss the event, I wouldn't, because no matter how much I hate it, I go
to support Gran. At least there will be one person there who knows the
truth.

Taryn knocks at my door with an hour to spare, wearing a white
sundress.

"Why aren't you dressed yet?" she shrieks at me in her breaking
soprano.

1

"We don't have to be there for another hour, Taryn. Chill, would you?" I pull myself out of the recliner and shuffle my fuzzy pink slippers across the tile floor to the sink.

"Katherine Dennard! Get your butt upstairs and put on something presentable this instant! We need to leave in five minutes to get a good view." She stomps her foot like an angry child.

I clink my cereal bowl against the porcelain sink and sulk my way upstairs. "Yes, Mother," I tease. Every year she forgets about my preferred seating … having family involved and all.

We leave twenty minutes later, and by the time we make it to the main attraction, a mob of people cover the lawn of The Institute. I flash my ID badge to the guard posted at the edge of the preferred seating and worm my way a little closer to the stage, bypassing the common seats. Taryn follows.

We find two seats in the fourth row and settle ourselves. Mom and Dad are already seated a few rows ahead, having arrived early. The tension in Dad's neck is visible from where I sit.

At precisely 5:00 p.m., Dr. Fishgold, head of The Institute and leader of the eastern sectors, steps to the lone microphone at center stage. Normally, having the leader of the entire eastern sectors speaking in front of you should be a big deal, but since he chooses to live and work in Sector 4, his presence here is nothing new. He doesn't even have to call attention to the crowd. Instead, he stands in front and straightens his suit coat. The people feel his presence, and a hush works its way to the far corners of the crowd.

"Welcome to the 56th annual Parade of Values."

Cheers well up from the multitude, but he quiets them with a single motion of his hand.

It's the same each year: a history of our medical advances and how everything is hunky dory now and how one day we'll bring the perfected races together again to form the flawless human race. I try to let my mind wander a bit, but sitting so close requires me to at least pretend like I'm paying attention.

"It is my duty and honor to officiate this year's celebration of our community. Nearly a century ago, the races segregated themselves into the sectors we know now in order to wipe out maladies specific to each race. Breakthroughs in medical science allowed our people to eradicate many diseases of the past. The introduction of the first Microchip Implant for Health helped destroy illnesses such as cancer and heart disease, all the while increasing the longevity and quality of the lives of our people. One day, we will once again join together to create the most perfect human race in the history of mankind.

"It is these advances in technology and medicine that we celebrate today."

I lean into Taryn. "Think he'll add anything new to the speech this year?"

She shrugs. "Probably ..."

Suddenly, Dr. Fishgold raises his hand in the air, and the crowd follows with the same gesture. "Success and health for all," we chant.

He cuts us off. "Do not forget how frail our bodies were in ages past. Without the evolution of our medical practices, you would be like the last generation of Natural Born, whose bodies and minds are left to chance as they age, deteriorating to mere nothingness. It's the natural development of life without advances like the MIH."

My stomach twists. It's my great-gran he's talking about.

"Today, we present them to you as a reminder of what once was and of the blessings we now have of superior mental and physical health." He makes a sweeping gesture and steps back. "This could have been your fate."

"Here they come." Taryn points offstage to the line of silver-haired people. Only three of the ten can still walk by themselves, aided only with canes; the others are pushed toward the stage in wheelchairs. One of them is my gran.

My fists clench the sides of my chair. Every morsel of my body hates that they parade Gran and her friends before the masses like a circus sideshow. I have to restrain myself from running toward the stage to stop them.

Dr. Fishgold may have told part of our story, but he left out the most important detail—that they killed thousands of Natural Born when

Gen 1 took over, and then tried to finish the job when the rebellion took place.

My great grandmother and the few others standing beside her are the last of the final generation of Natural Born allowed to live in our society.

Taryn must notice the look on my face because she says, "Kate, it's no big deal, you know."

I nod. "I know." But Taryn can't understand. She doesn't have a Natural Born relative being paraded in front of the entire community, much less one who's entirely lucid. And I can't tell her about Gran. No one can know about her clear mind or about what she's told me.

Dr. Fishgold steps to the microphone again. Just seeing the movement makes my blood boil, and I brace myself for his next announcement.

He gestures to the row of people in front of him. Three of them are drooling, and almost in unison, assistants reach around with rags to wipe the saliva from their chins. One woman stares into the clouds with a blank expression. And Gran's friend, Henry, keeps shaking his head and saying, "No, you're wrong," over and over.

I wonder who he's talking about.

Gran allows her chin to drop and her eyes to glaze over. Years of practice allowed her to perfect the look of dementia.

"This, my fellow citizens, would have been your fate had our scientists not chosen to make the sacrifices they did for the good of our society. But now, you all benefit from the MIH."

In unison, the crowd calls, "Success and health for all."

"Not all." Fishgold's sharp voice stops the people's chants. "Not all."

I look at Taryn, who has the same confused expression I do. She shakes her head and shrugs her shoulders at my silent question. Everyone around me is looking to their neighbors for an explanation. No one knows what's going on, so we turn our attention back to Dr. Fishgold for clarification.

"There is one group of people that will not benefit from our successes. Those who work to destroy the progress mankind has made. From the raids of years ago until now, there is one group that seeks to undermine further growth and development for our people: the Natural Born Rebels."

Whispers rise through the crowd and soon turn to gasps. From the far corner of the stage, Institute workers carrying weapons emerge. Two in front, two in back and between them a young man in handcuffs and ankle chains. The soldiers lead him onstage next to Fishgold where a folding chair awaits. One soldier forces the man to sit while another withdraws hair clippers and presses them to the man's scalp. There's silence as the soldier shaves the man's head, revealing to the crowd the community identification tattoo at the base of his neck. (A barcode with identification numbers.) It looks the same as the rest that come with the MIH we all receive at birth. But it's not.

"This man tried to infiltrate our society. He was caught attempting to upload a virus into the latest batch of MIHs. Tried and failed." Fishgold then withdraws a scalpel from his pocket, letting it glint in the August sun. He snaps rubber gloves around his hands and holds the knife with expert precision.

"Let this be a warning to any of those who dare to join the rebellion. You will be caught. Treason such as this will not go unpunished."

He turns toward the man as the soldiers step forward and grab the rebel by the arms, forcing him to stand.

"Any last words?" Fishgold asks as a soldier holds the microphone in front of the man.

"Long live the rebelli—"

His cry is replaced with a shriek of pain that echoes through the silent multitude as Fishgold presses the scalpel against the man's neck. In a few swipes, he's removed the thin layer of skin where the tattoo was. The man tries to pull his head away from the knife, but his chains and the soldiers restrain him. Fishgold makes one more cut, fully removing the tattooed section of the man's neck.

From my seat, I see the blood run down the back of his neck, soaking into his shirt. Taryn clenches her eyes shut. I wish I could, but I can't stop staring. This can only mean one thing. The man is a Natural Born. His tattoo is a fake, and he'll most likely die for his cause.

TWO

....

FOLLOWED

B Y THE TIME WE leave the parade, it's nearly dark. My parents
stay to make sure Gran gets settled back into her room at the
center. Taryn has met up with a few classmates to continue the
celebrations after the parade, but I don't feel like celebrating. I'm still
sickened by what's just happened. The reminders of who is in control
linger around every corner, and public displays and checks by the soldiers keep the people frightened. Torture is never easy to stomach.

Maybe taking a quiet walk through the park will calm my nerves a
bit, and I'll actually be able to sleep tonight.

The paved walkway leads through the middle of the town park
that divides the business district from the residences. It's lined with
hand-planted flowers, and the grass is trimmed into neat rows on either side of the walk. A few trees decorate the grasses, thicker in some
areas, creating groves of maples. It's picture perfect. No fallen leaves, no
nuts or branches littering the ground beneath the massive trunks. All
cleaned by the arborist students. This path is a shortcut to my house.
Tonight, with the warm breeze, it's a perfect respite to clear my mind.

My feet scrape the cement as I make my way down the path, avoiding the flowers on either side of the landscaped walkway. The trees, off
to the side, wave softly in the breeze. Ahead is a group of huge maples,
and I wander off the path and into the cool air of their shadows. I'm

almost through the grove when I hear a scraping noise behind me. Not again.

My muscles tense, and I freeze, listening to the sounds of the evening. The crickets chirp in the distance, and the wind snakes its way through the leaves and brushes against my skin. Goose bumps rise on my arms when I hear footsteps trudging through the dirt. My goose bumps aren't from the breeze.

Willing myself to turn around, I pray there isn't someone there. *Please let the pathway be empty.* Slowly, I twist my head back, my body following, and peer into the shadows of the trees. When I don't see anything, I relax. But then a movement a hundred yards off catches my eye.

It's nothing, I tell myself. *An animal or tree branch.* But when the fluttering of a long coat flies out from behind a tree trunk and a pale, bony hand slithers out to control it, I know it's happening again.

Someone's following me. *It's nothing*, I tell myself, but that nervous knot in the pit of my gut tells me to be careful, to watch my step, to peer over my shoulder.

Sure, it could be anyone going for a walk at night, but why would they hide?

"Hello? Is anyone there?" Maybe they'll answer. But after a long pause with only the whistling of the wind through the trees, I can draw only one conclusion: whoever it is doesn't want to be seen.

I don't waste any time sticking around. If someone *is* following me, I'm going to get as far from here as possible. I fly over the patch of land, my feet skidding through the mud-covered lawn. The summer rain made the ground soft, and it nearly swallows my shoe with each nervous step.

Pumping faster and faster, I force my muscles to work against their will. *Come on! Move!* Through another grove and over a patch of brush, just a little further until I can round the bend and slip behind a tree. Once I reach the safety of the massive oak, I press my back against the trunk and suck in a deep breath, attempting to calm my tittering heart. The rough bark digs into my shoulder blades with each desperate breath.

I only have a second to rest. If I wait too long, he'll find me.

For weeks, it seems, as I walk home each night, someone has been following me. Eyes peering through leaves. Footsteps tapping on the sidewalk behind me. But every time I turn, I see nothing. Only the night wind whistling its lonely tune, taunting my fear. But tonight is different. Tonight I saw something.

Someone.

Tomorrow I'll avoid the park. Take the long way home through the bustling streets. Even if it takes twice as long. Yes, definitely. My shaking hands confirm this idea.

Maybe whoever is there has given up by now.

I'm not taking any chances. Until I'm inside my house, I'm not safe.

Pushing my hands against the bark of the tree, I shoot off, dodging the branches that scratch at my arms.

Just up ahead, I see the clearing and the widened path, where the light from the streetlamp casts its dull glow across the sidewalk.

Another ten steps, and I'll be safe.

BAM!

Out of nowhere a blunt force knocks me sideways.

"Whoa!" a deep voice echoes.

Large, pale hands grab my shoulders and pull me upright.

"No!" I cry, flinging my arms out. I'll hit anything that comes close. "Stay away!"

When I right myself, I peer into the face of a boy a little older than me. Eighteen, maybe twenty. He looks familiar.

"It's okay." He pulls his hands back in mock surrender. His soft, gray eyes gaze at me with concern through a mess of black hair. I peer nervously over his shoulder. He must notice my fear. "You okay?" he asks. Then he tries to lighten the mood. "In a hurry?"

I'm not amused. "Um, yeah … heading home." I toss another look over my shoulder to the darkened path behind me. "Just wasn't paying attention … Sorry." My breathing is shaky as I try to calm myself.

Someone is still back there.

Waiting.

Watching.

"Okay, well, be careful." The boy looks across the street toward my house.

He looks so familiar, but I still can't place his face. I know I've seen him before; I just can't think where …

"Thanks." I point to the lighted windows. "I'm almost there." I glance once more behind me.

Nothing. No long jackets quivering in the breeze. No snake-like fingers reaching through the brush.

Stepping onto the street, I march to my home. My trembling hands reach for the doorknob, but thankfully, within seconds, I push myself safely inside and latch the deadbolt behind me. With my back to the door, my breathing steadies, and when my heart slows, I draw back the curtain and peer outside.

The boy is still standing there.

Staring.

Our eyes meet across the distance.

Then he disappears down the path.

THREE

....

GRAN

The Code of Conduct and Ethics—The Institute—Sector 4, USA Section 3 Article 5.4: All citizens must conduct themselves in a manner worthy of The Institute. Misconduct is closely monitored and will be dealt with swiftly.

EVEN AFTER MOM AND Dad arrive safely home and settle into their evening routine of tea and reading on the couch, I still feel agitated. Sleep eludes me most of the night, and what little rest I do get is filled with dreams of pale fingers clenching my neck.

When I wake the next morning, still groggy from the restless night, I determine to see Gran later, to tell her what's going on. But after a day of studies, I decide not to bother her with one more thing to worry about. Instead, I'll just visit. Gran has a way of lifting my spirits even if she's not purposely trying to take my mind off something scary.

"Afternoon, Gran!" I say as I stride into her room at the retirement center.

Her bed, bolted to the floor, is covered with thin white sheets. Gran's deteriorated legs lay like twigs under the threadbare blanket. She stares at the far wall, the one with the only splash of color in the sanitary, white-washed room. It's a Van Gogh print. *Starry Night.* The swirls hypnotize me whenever I look at it for too long, but she seems to like it. Stares at it for hours.

I take a small rag out of my back pocket. It used to be hers. The initials E. L. D. are embroidered in purple thread on the corner of the handkerchief. Emma Lin Dennard.

I try to envision what she was like when this scrap belonged to her. Young. Vibrant. Feisty.

A fighter.

She still is. Only they don't know it.

I wipe the pool of saliva gathered at the corner of her mouth with the hankie. "Wanna go for a walk today?"

She answers with a groan, and her tiny body rocks gently back and forth.

I glance at the video camera in the corner. It's recording.

Always paying attention.

"Hang on, Gran. I have to get someone to help me."

I find a young worker at the check-in desk, and he helps me move Gran's fragile body into a wheelchair. I fold the thin quilt and place it over her legs and wrap a sweater around her bony shoulders.

"There, much better." I turn to the young man. "Thanks. I can take it from here."

He nods and heads back to his station.

"All right, M'lady. To our usual spot?"

Her soft grunt is confirmation, so I pull the chair toward me and spin it around. Halfway down the hallway, I stop and sign the appropriate papers.

"Afternoon, Kate," Nurse Peterson calls. "Taking your great-grandmother for a spin?"

"Yes, don't worry," I say, as I sign my name. "I'll have her back by dinner time." I push the clipboard back toward the nurse and grab the handles of Gran's wheelchair.

"Sounds good," she says as I head past the security guards and out the door. The workers are used to seeing me. I've visited since I was little, first with my parents, then, when I was old enough, on my own.

Gran loves the outdoors. She relaxes as soon as the sun hits her face. No one else would be able to tell, but the corner of her eye hides a twinkle, and the way the corners of her mouth pull up ever so slightly tells me she likes it.

We've learned to communicate without words.

The wheels of the chair bounce along the walkway as I cross the paved path. Nearby, soldiers in training are practicing attack drills. Must be the newest recruits to The Institute's militia. Soon they'll be out on the streets practicing their newly learned techniques on the people, who by some chance, forgot to follow some minute rule. The new recruits tend to be overly ambitious. In front of the neat rows of soldiers stand two men. They're rather young, from the looks of it, but their straight backs, stiff gaits, and scowls boast their power. The one, a tall, broad-shouldered guy with short-cropped hair, glares at me from across the grass, eyes following as I push my grandmother up the path. Then suddenly, his glower morphs into a tight-lipped line. Almost a smirk, but not quite. I look away.

For a few moments, we walk in silence except for my heavy breathing. Pushing the chair is my workout for the day. It's too hard to make small talk; besides, what I really want to talk about can't be said where listening ears can hear.

"Almost there, Gran. I thought we'd go near the waterfall today."

Her body lurches forward. She wants me to hurry.

I scan the yard. A groundskeeper digs through the landscaping near the building. Another worker has three residents outside enjoying the sun, and a few soldiers patrol the far edges of the main field. But there are more eyes watching us that I *can't* see.

"I know, but I can only go so fast without attracting looks. Be patient," I whisper.

Gran's facility lies at the edge of town near the river. Well, more of a creek. Most people follow the paved pathway downstream where they can sit on benches overlooking the water. Gran and I like to travel in the other direction. Not all the way to the fenced border, but enough to feel like we aren't being watched. But it means I have to push her and her wheelchair along a dirt path and over the grass.

The walkway ends, and I lean closer to her chair to allow my legs better traction.

Leaning forward, I whisper in her ear, "We need to find a new place to talk. This trek is killing me!"

She lets out a muffled hoot, and I know she understands.

I struggle through the soft grass as I press further upstream, glancing every once in a while over my shoulder to see if anyone notices us. No heads are turned our way. Soon, I see the clearing.

We reach the spot where the tree-lined path thins, and I drag the wheelchair up close to the jutting rocks. It's there I sit, staring across at the Outer Lands. Behind us is civilization. It's never far.

Always watching.

But here, as I look out over the river, past the fence that runs its length on the far side, the land seems freer. Like uncharted territory. Safe.

"How was your workout?" her tiny voice whispers above the rush of the water. I can barely hear her, but that's how it has to be. No one can know.

I smile.

"Fine. Seems like you've lost a bit more weight," I say. "You need to eat."

"They serve crap down at that place. I can barely choke it down. Nothing like when I used to cook. They don't even know what 'from scratch' means. I can't remember the last time I had real potatoes. With gravy. Lots of gravy. I miss that."

I try to picture my great grandmother bustling around a kitchen, complete with a checkered apron tied snugly around her tiny waist, her brothers and sisters of all different sizes and shapes gathered around her. It's a description she's told me a thousand times, but I still can't quite picture it.

I turn my attention to her. To look at her, you wouldn't be able to tell she *isn't* sick. She still stares over the river—always careful—but the look in her eye is different. And she sits a little taller, but not much. Because if anyone came this way, they'd have to see the Gran everyone else sees. The one they believe is failing mentally and physically.

I know otherwise.

She turns her head toward me the slightest bit, her blue eyes blazing. "Are you still being followed?"

Darn it! I wasn't going to talk about that with her, but she has an uncanny way of reading my mind.

I nod. "Don't worry, Gran. I'm safe. It's probably just someone from school trying to pull a prank."

It's a lie, but there's no need to worry her. I don't tell her about the rustling and footsteps I hear behind me whenever I'm in the park. The ones that I can never attach to a specific person. Nor do I tell her about the glimpse of a coat I saw the night before. It could have been anyone walking home from the parade. Yes. That's it. But I can't ignore that feeling in my gut that tells me otherwise.

"Katie-Did," Gran uses the nickname she came up with when I was an infant, "they *know* something. You can't bring me out here anymore. We can't talk like this. I'm not going to be the one who causes them to put a tail on you."

If only it were that easy. But I'll admit, I need to be more careful.

"Gran, I can't give this up. You're the only one who understands. Even Mom and Dad have no clue what's going on."

Gran flashes me a quick look.

"Well, Dad knows some things. Suspects stuff." Of course he would. He's her grandson, and there's no way he could have gone his entire life not knowing about his own grandmother, especially after what happened to his parents.

Gran understands my predicament. It was her generation that began our way of life. Some of her friends discovered the genetics that brought us where we are today, that decided to separate the races and improve our bodies in the first place.

They had good intentions, really. Less disease. Longer life, better life. And once all these things were accomplished, they intended to gather everyone together again, to blend the human race once more, this time with superior beings. But in the process of the improvements, the restrictions came. And Gran was sent to that facility, kept like a rat in a cage, only to be let out to make a statement about how the Natural

Born are so inferior. For the good of everyone, she has to play along with the ruse, but it's exhausting. It's why we come to the river to take a break from it all.

"You haven't told your folks about the park and the footsteps?" she whispers.

"No."

"Probably for the best. They'd pitch a hissy fit and hire someone to look after you. If they did that, it'd be the end of our little chats in an instant."

"Maybe it would save The Institute from having to put a tail on me since Mom would follow me everywhere." I laugh, but it's not funny. Not when it's entirely plausible that I could be tailed right now.

"Be careful, okay sweetie?"

"I will, Gran. I promise. And I'll stay out of the park tonight." I press my back against the mossy rock wall. "So, what's the news with you?"

Her face hardens, and she looks like she doesn't believe my promise. She continues anyway. "You should have heard what they said today." Her lips pull back, revealing a perfectly straight line of false teeth. Dentures. She scrapes one ridged fingernail over the surface of her front tooth, which makes the entire line of them fall away from her gums. She pushes the denture back in place with her tongue. It's so strange to think an old person could lose their teeth like a child.

When I was little and Gran was able to interact more without raising suspicion, she used to play tricks on me. "Look, Katie-Did," she'd say. Then she'd flip her teeth upside down in her mouth and smile a crooked, upside down grin. Sucking them back in place, she'd smile again, and the light would flash off her single gold-capped tooth.

I realize I haven't seen that metal tooth in a while.

She doesn't smile much anymore.

Today, her silver hair is brushed away from her forehead and secured in a tight braided bun at the base of her unmarked neck. She raises her arm and brushes a hair that came loose in the breeze a little too quickly. Glancing around, she eases her arm back into her lap.

"What is it this time, Gran?"

She turns her face to the sun and closes her eyes.

"They're going to discharge Mr. Ross."

"Henry?"

"Yes." She folds her hands together on her lap.

"They say he's gotten too bad." Her face turns sad, and her eyes well up with tears, but she won't let them spill over. "It's true. He is. But it's too soon. It's always too soon." She sighs. "They're making an announcement on Friday."

I reach out and tuck that lock behind her ear again. As I do, her face tilts into my hand, and her skin feels thin and brittle against my palm.

"You're the only one who touches me like that, Katie-Did."

I give her a soft smile and pull my arm away slowly.

"So, a discharge isn't any news, Gran."

"It is when it puts the Wombers down to nine. Nine of us left, Katie-Did. Not only that," she grasps my hand in hers and draws me in close to her. I smell the rosewater they bathe her in. "They've planned to discharge the rest of us once a month until we're gone. I'm the last on the list because I'm the youngest of all of them."

Gran leans back. My skin goes cold, and I can't breathe. Holding her fingers between my hands, I stare deep into the ocean of her eyes.

So alive. And no one can see it. She can't let them see it. If she did, they wouldn't wait nine months.

They'd kill her now.

FOUR

·····························

PARANOID

Code of Conduct and Ethics: The Institute—Sector 4, USA
Section 2 Article 1.1: Be truthful and honest in all interactions with your
fellow man. Lies and secrets will bring about harsh retribution.

I T's EARLY. NOT QUITE six. But if I'm going to be on time for the career assignments they're giving today, I need to get moving. Being late is not an option. By the time I leave the house and stop by Meg's Café for my morning coffee, the line reaches around the corner. I know I'll have to jog the few blocks to The Institute to avoid being tardy. Gotta love year round career preparation. In undergraduate schooling, we had a few months of respite before heading back to school, but not anymore.

Any demerits will mean closer surveillance of my movements, perhaps even a personal escort, and right now, I can't afford that. Not after sneaking around with Gran. I always have to be extra careful after my visits with her.

It's at least a ten-minute walk to The Institute and another ten to the Education Department. The buildings are all interconnected, just like the people here. At least, that's what we've always been taught in all our classes. Our community is an extension of The Institute, the living, breathing organism that mimics its stone counterpart.

The campus spans most of the city with a branch for medicine next to the education section. All the shops and eating houses are located within its borders, and all the residents work within its factories or subdivisions. The library, the research facilities, and even Gran's retirement home are considered part of The Institute. It's a massive construction, surrounded by a three-foot high brick wall along its boundaries. The only things outside The Institute are private residences and a few roads leading to other communities like ours. If you travel far enough, you'd arrive at other sectors. I've never been outside the borders. Most people haven't. One must have special clearance to travel to another sector.

Even the far boundaries are surrounded by high fencing. *To keep us protected*, they say. And then there's the Outer Lands. But few venture beyond the boundaries of our community, and then only for purposes defined by The Institute.

It's a dangerous place out there, and The Institute wants to keep us safe.

Grandeur is a key component to the construction of our society. The buildings, with their massive peaks and ornate carved stone, leak beauty from every corner. Often, I find myself distracted by the curling stonework along The Institute's edges or the endless patches of flowers littering every corner, yard, and tree base in our town. On more than one occasion, I've had to rush to class so as not to be late.

The people passing by me on the walkway are as well constructed as the buildings. We're all bred that way. The Institute pours all its creative energy into the outer face of its facilities, leaving little variation and beauty for its people. Sure, we have strong bodies and sound minds, but our outward appearance is steadily growing more and more identical to the next. One massive sea of brown haired, brown eyed, light skinned, average-looking people. At least in Sector 4. Some days I wish I could gain the clearance to travel to the other sectors to see what the other leaders have done for their people.

The main gates squeal in protest as I yank them open and race along the pathway past the library and a block of shops. I pass the retirement center and enter through the main doors of the hospital, which is linked to the research center. At the far end of the research center are doors leading to the education department. This is where I need to be in less than seven minutes.

The good thing about having everything interconnected is that I can get from one place to another from either inside or outside.

My classroom is at the far end of the hallway, past the Creation Unit laboratories. That's why I come this way. Passing those doors daily is a constant reminder to stay focused on my goals. If I'm ever going to be chosen as a Creation Scientist, I need to do well in my studies. It's one of the most prestigious careers available to our people. And I want it.

With a few minutes to spare, I take my seat in the second row of my classroom and pull out my compact. One click and it lights up. I flick my fingers around the screen. Closing out a notice about one of the original Wombers dying and an old news article about a teenager mangled in a car accident I used for research.

I focus instead on the research project due today. "The Unviables: Progress of our Kind."

Clicking on the file opens it, and I scan the document for any glaring errors. Not that I would find any in the three minutes I have before Professor Limbert arrives.

After scanning over two pages, I give up. Why am I even trying? If it's not perfect by now, it's never going to be. With one tap of my fingertips on the screen, I send my project to the class server where it will be graded, analyzed, and sent to the professor's compact.

Hopefully, this will get me into the lab apprenticeship.

I still remember my dad's reaction when I told him what I wanted to do with my life. "A lofty goal," he said, "but one that can be attained if you work hard enough." Being a research scientist in data collections himself, he was glad his only child was following in his scientific footsteps. My mother, on the other hand, wanted me to go into the justice field like she did, but dealing with criminals all my life seems like too much of a downer. No. I'd much rather have the wonder and excitement of creating human life. That is the ultimate job.

A few other students have gathered, and soon the classroom is bustling. Professor Limbert rushes in, slapping his compact on the desk at the front of the room. He seems a bit frazzled.

"Take your seats," he calls. Everyone sits, opens their compacts on their desks and folds their hands in their laps while they wait for his instructions. The screens and keyboards provide even more light to the bright room.

His compact beeps as it receives a message. He glances at the screen, then steps away from the desk, pacing up and down each row as he does each morning. It's a technique used to intimidate us. To show his authority to his students. But it's unnecessary. We wouldn't dare cross a man of his stature.

"I see a few of you waited till this morning to turn in your projects."

I blush as he slows his pace and places a hand on my desk.

"You should be thankful," he continues, after tapping his index finger on my table twice, "for the immediate feedback from our data systems." Then, as any good teacher of The Institute would, he reminds us of our advancements at the hands of science. "If we lived a few generations ago, you would have had to wait to receive your homework. I would have had to read through each project individually and decide on your assignment and placement after much deliberation. Your future would hinge on my decision."

A silent understanding fills the room. We're all thankful Professor Limbert isn't the one deciding our fates. Imagine the chaos of putting our futures into the hands of one or two people. It's a crazy thought.

"But now ..." He steps forward again, moving into the other row. "Thanks to The Institute's efficiency, I have your apprenticeships ready."

A nervous hush falls over the class. We've been waiting for this day all semester, and we all look around, wondering if our weeks of work will pay off ... if we'll get the placement we've dreamed of since we were children. Some will. Some won't. And we'll be able to determine who does and who doesn't by the looks on their faces.

All at once, multiple beeps sound, indicating a new message from The Institute.

I press the open button, and the seal of The Institute appears. The icon moves, and the envelope graphic opens. It unfolds, and I read the words on the screen.

Congratulations, Katherine Dennard,

You've been assigned to the Creation unit.

Yes! Awesome! Everything is falling into place, and I'll finally get my chance to see if the things Gran says are true.

***

"Units one and three, please move to the back of the classroom," Professor Limbert says. "Your lab technician will be here shortly. Professor Donovan will be overseeing your progress from here on out. That's not to say you can't come to me for anything, but Professor Donovan is also an unending source of useful information for your studies. Unit four, follow this young woman. She'll show you down to the horticulture unit."

I wrinkle my nose. Why anyone would want to study plants is beyond my comprehension. But I suppose it's useful, knowing how to create the food that sustains us. To me, it would be my personal hell having to rummage around in the dirt. As they leave, I say a silent thank you to the computer system that decided my future.

A line of my friends march out behind a twenty-something woman, and I turn my attention back to the professor. He'll be calling unit two, my group, momentarily. When I turn back, my skin grows cold.

Sweat breaks out on the palms of my hands, and my heart thumps so loudly, I swear people around me can hear it. *Nervous anticipation,* my mother calls it. She says it happens to her whenever she's awaiting a judicial decision.

"Unit two," Professor Limbert says, "this is Micah. He'll lead your group." He points to his side where a tall, lanky guy stands. "He'll be taking you to the Creation lab and showing you around for the next few weeks."

I look at the guy again. The same black hair. The same gray eyes.

The boy who ran into me the night I was followed. He glares straight at me with a look that could kill. And my blood runs cold.

He was the one following me.

....

FIVE

CREATION UNIT

Code of Conduct and Ethics: The Institute—Sector 4, USA
Section 7 Article 3.9: In all interactions with your superiors, listen and
learn. Conduct yourself with the utmost restraint. Respect your superiors.
A quiet, thoughtful presence is best.

I PACK UP MY compact and move to the front of the room behind Taryn. We've sat next to each other since kindergarten. When we reach the front of the room, she whispers in her high-pitched sing-song voice, "Yikes! He's a hottie."

I stare at her as she runs her eyes from the top of his head all the way down. I'd like to be able to admit how much of a turn-on his broad shoulders and gray eyes are. Or how I'm intrigued at how he stands out from the rest of us. Taller than average. His jet black hair, light eyes and olive skin are an anomaly. Add in the long nose and square jaw with a speckling of stubble covering it, and it's hard to deny. He's extraordinary. Even the way he stands with his arms crossed and a serious look on his face can't hide the fact that he's handsome.

Not that his features don't happen occasionally in the Creation Unit. They're just rare. Like Taryn. Her hair is a little too light for her to look exactly like the others, and her tiny frame stands out from the rest. But she's still in the normal spectrum for our society with her brown eyes and average build. Not like Micah. I guess these differences are to be expected ... until the spectrum is narrowed. Our scientific advances, when it comes to breeding, are still young. It hasn't been perfected yet. There are still differences in hair color and eye color, even in skin tones. But it's still weird. That's why it's part of our job as creation specialists to reduce these anomalies. In a few generations, we'll all look the same. No one person better looking than the next. It's best for our society. Less competition on a personal level creates a greater focus on our community at large, something that will benefit the whole. Then one day, during a generation I will never know, they'll combine the sectors and their perfected human beings together again. It'll be the ultimate human race. It's all explained in the Code of Conduct and Ethics.

"Follow me," he says. His voice is deep, too. Not the mellow tenor of most of my classmates.

A line of about seven other students walks silently behind him. He doesn't give any introduction to our duties until we arrive at the Creation Unit. I'm forced, instead, to observe the way he ambles with a sway in his stride like his long legs have too far to move to take the next step. He rolls up the sleeves of his lab coat, revealing defined forearms covered with the same black hair that glistens on his head.

He turns to check on the group, and the light catches against his fierce cheekbones and squared jawline. He looks harsh. Demanding. Dangerous. And incredibly stunning.

We pass what seems like miles of sterile white walls before we stop at a set of double doors. Above the door is a sign, *Utero*. The windows are tinted, so we can't see what lies inside, but we know. It's our future.

It's here we will study the science of genetics. We will create life and rid our community of disease and difference. We'll create the next generation of Sector 4.

The future will literally be in our hands.

Micah bursts the bubble of our excitement. "Today, you won't participate in any lab procedures. For the first few weeks, you'll observe and learn." His eyes scan the small crowd of anxious first-year residents, resting on me for a second longer than anyone else. "At the end of the tour, notes will be sent to your compact. You're expected to have all terms and tools memorized by Wednesday's lab."

As he speaks, a wave of hair falls onto his forehead and sways in the tiny breeze of the air conditioner. His hard features soften for a millisecond. The change mesmerizes me, and when he turns his back to us and pushes through the heavy, metal doors, I realize I have no idea what he's said.

Everyone around me sets their compacts to low light as we enter the darkened room, so I do the same. Micah must have mentioned something about this. Lining the walls of the room are locked glass cases filled with shelves of Petri dishes. Each is labeled with a date. I scan the labels as we walk past. Batch 1. Three weeks old. Work tables line the center of the room, and in the far corner is a supply closet. Just above that, attached to the ceiling, is a small dome with a blinking light. Surveillance. Amazing I even notice these things anymore. They're everywhere.

Micah stops a few steps ahead. "We keep the lights down and use black bulbs to mimic the conditions in a natural womb. Here you'll notice the beginning of life." He peers into the case of Petri dishes in various sizes. "Each of these zygotes was created recently, and by the end of the week, we'll transfer these specimens to the growth unit."

Taryn gazes into the microscope attached to the wall cases. "Isn't this amazing?" I look through the eyepiece and see the cells rapidly dividing. "Yeah," I answer, breathless with wonder.

It's remarkable. These containers hold the lives of the next generation. Some are a mere gathering of cells, already moving in rhythm. Heart cells. We've studied this in class. They aren't developed yet, but when they join, they'll form the heart muscle.

Others, in slightly larger containers surrounded by a thick liquid, are all alien-looking with minuscule spines and bulbous heads and tiny blue veins creating roadmaps over their bodies. I use the stylus to jot down what I see on the note screen of my compact. Flipping it to the other side, I'm able to sketch out a quick drawing of a preformed human to add to my notes.

"Follow me, please. I'll show you the growth unit." Micah heads toward the back of the lab and pushes through a dividing door. "Let's get everyone in here before I explain what you're seeing."

It's uncomfortably warm, and as I cross the threshold under Micah's arm, I inhale a whiff of his clean, woodsy scent, like the outdoors. Meanwhile, I've already started to sweat.

This room holds aisles of cylinders connected to the table and ceiling at either end by countless tubes. It's still dark, but we can see each other with the help of the black lights, which make our lab coats glow an eerie purple.

Micah walks up one aisle and stops at the end. "Once the zygote grows too large for the dishes in the previous room, they're transferred here with a Batch 2 label. It's a delicate process that you'll learn to perform in the later weeks of your studies. It's even more delicate than the actual birthing process, which is why you'll learn it last. Transferring embryos, because of their fragile state at that point in time, requires great skill. Skill I'm sure you all have since you've been chosen to study as Creation Specialists. Congratulations, by the way. The embryos who survive the transfer are then labeled as a Batch 3. Making it this far is a huge accomplishment. These are usually the strongest of the bunch; however, the numbers will still have to be narrowed down."

Everyone is enthralled by Micah's explanations. I, on the other hand, am more interested in the Petri dishes. It's difficult to grasp that the next generation is developing right in front of us. The way he explains the process does show off his impressive brain power. To have attained his assistant teaching position, he must be pretty smart.

"If you look in the capsules to your right, you'll see the various stages of human life. These two aisles are dated within the later weeks of the first trimester. The rows against the far wall," he motions that way with his arm, "hold fetuses within the second trimester."

The steady hum and pulse of the machines make it hard to hear what he's saying, but I can tell he's used to talking over them.

"Feel free to look around. I know you may have seen pictures of developing life throughout your studies, but seeing it first hand is pretty incredible. Whatever you do, don't touch anything." His lips pull back, revealing a row of glowing teeth, and his harshness disappears into the shadows. He looks happy.

Instantly, my initial fears about him subside, and I can't stop looking at him.

When he smiled, I noticed his teeth. How the one in the front sits just ahead of the other. They aren't straight. They aren't perfect.

I must gasp a little too loudly because Taryn nudges me. "What's wrong?"

I shake my head. "Oh, nothing. No, it's nothing."

Micah backs up against the wall and watches as we slowly work our way around the lab.

Liquid flowing into the metal-capped cylinders suspended by tubes and wires distracts my suspicious mind. The darkness, the warmth, and the sound. The scientists left nothing out. Except the human host. There's even a synthetic placenta on the bottom of the cylinder. Even the containers are made of a pliable material that can stretch when the baby stretches.

It's astounding. To think a hundred years ago, none of this was possible.

I step up to one of the cylinders. Inside is a fetus about sixteen weeks old. A tiny thing, only about the size of my palm. Its skin is translucent so I can see the inner workings of its body, the heart pumping the blood through tiny vessels. His eyes blink, and he brings his left thumb to his mouth to suck.

"A lefty." Micah's heavy voice startles me.

He's uncomfortably close. So close I feel his breath on my cheek.

"They say you can see which ones are going to be left handed by observing what hand they suck while in utero."

"But we don't have any left handed people here." I look up in confusion into those glowing gray eyes. In the light, they're lilac-colored.

Without blinking, he says, "Unfortunately, they'll schedule this one's discharge as soon as they notice. Then again, they usually wait until further along in development to see if these tendencies will change. So this little guy might be with us for a while longer. Good for research purposes," he adds.

"Oh," I say, not sure what he wants to hear.

He moves his attention from me to the rest of my classmates, who are examining and frantically scribbling notes in their compacts. We'll be tested on what we observe during our next lab.

"Finish your observations, people. We'll move into late development in about five minutes."

The Third Trimester Unit is just as astonishing as the previous two. The room itself looks basically the same as the Second Trimester room, but it's obvious the fetuses are nearly fully developed. Only, there are fewer of them. By this stage, the weak or disabled have been identified and disposed of. But there are a few who make it to the last few weeks before an elimination is decided.

I count the capsules. Forty-five. Five of these humans will be discharged soon. They'll probably decide based on birth weight, which they can determine within the artificial womb.

Micah brings our attention to a table at the front of the room that holds a tray of silver tools. "These," he begins, "are what the scientists used to birth the generations before our scientific advancements took over and made them obsolete. Be sure you know their names and uses by our next class."

A boy named Johnny speaks up. "If we don't use them anymore, why do we need to learn them?" He slaps his hand over his mouth as if immediately realizing his mistake. We may wonder these things in private, but voicing such a question can lead to disciplinary actions. *No one* is allowed to question The Institute.

But Micah takes this inquiry without a reprimand. "It's part of the history of birth; therefore, we need to know and understand. Personally, I find this part the most fascinating." His soft smile eases the boy's anxiety, but we all wonder if Micah will turn in John for his outburst. "Now please, if you would make sure you have the instruments noted in your compacts ..."

If he's going to report John, he's at least not doing it immediately. Perhaps Micah is more kindhearted than I first assumed.

At the same time, ten heads drop to their compacts and type or scribble in the necessary information. It won't be difficult to memorize this information. We're used to it. Our brains are specifically designed to take in and hold information in short periods of time. The enhancement microchips help, too. Not to mention every few years we're brought in for upgrades to our chips. They'll enhance our mental capabilities and make other adjustments. Some say they start to suppress any desire for the opposite sex, but that hasn't been confirmed. Taryn thinks it's true. "There's no need for sex if The Institute procreates for us," she says. But all of that is just rumor. Most upgrades deal with keeping our bodies and minds in pristine condition. I'm due for enhancements next year.

Micah continues, "This is my favorite room because it's possible to interact with the preborn." He moves to a table in the front corner. "Let me have your attention up here, please."

Taryn grabs my arm and pulls me to the front of the crowd where we have a front row seat to the show and to Micah.

"He. Is. So. Cute," Taryn whispers again. "I'd totally do him in a heartbeat!"

My eyes grow wide, but I can't avoid the little snicker that escapes my lips. "Taryn!"

"What? We have to live while we can. Another three years and our chip enhancements will start to minimize the desire."

I give her a look.

"You may not believe me, but look at how pathetic our parents are. They don't even like each other. I swear it's because they never want to have sex. It's not like we'll get preggers or anything."

"Taryn!"

She laughs and steps a little closer to Micah, then looks back at me and winks as if being extra attentive will score her flirting points. "You know it's true." Her lips press out in a sexy pout even though he's not paying any attention to her.

"This fetus will be birthed at the end of the week," he says. "Some of you will have the privilege of observing that process. But that's not what I wanted to show you." He steps around to the side of the table and places his hands on either side of the flexible tank. "At this age, fetuses are able to interact with the outside world. Watch. When I press against this capsule, the child will move, sometimes squirming away from my touch, sometimes kicking in response."

He presses his hands together, one on either side of the container. Instantly, the child responds, kicking against his hand.

"Wow," I whisper.

Micah looks at me and smiles. I smile back.

"That's all we have time for today, ladies and gentlemen." Micah steps down from his post next to the fetus. "Now, if everyone will please check your compacts, you'll find a completed set of requirements to study before Wednesday." He pulls a tiny device out of his pocket and taps the screen a few times. Instantly, everyone's notebook beeps in response. We've all received his message.

***

Once everyone is packed up, we're dismissed. It's the perfect opportunity to head home, grab something to eat, and begin studying my notes. If I start now, I can have them completely memorized by Wednesday morning.

Taryn walks part way with me before turning off toward her house.

"Tell me he was totally hot, Kate," she says.

"I'm not saying he's not. But don't you think it's weird that he's so different?"

"You and your pessimism. Always looking for the worst in people. Give the man a break. That's what makes him so interesting." She twirls a lock of her hair around her finger. It's a habit she's had since we were kids.

"Don't let The Institute hear you say that."

"I know. 'Success and health for all.'" She rolls her eyes and pumps her fist in the air like we used to do in grade school. "I've heard the motto my whole life, too. But don't you wonder what our lives would be like if we were different? I mean, more different than we are."

"You should talk." I point to her hair, which is glistening a bright blonde. The glow from the street lamp gilds it a shade lighter.

"You know what I mean," she says. "Just think about our lab leader, Micah. Black hair and light eyes."

It *is* unusual. People who look like Micah rarely exist in our society. I used to ask Gran why her generation decided on the specific look to give all the following generations. "If you all look the same, Katie-Did, you'll focus on your studies instead of each other," she told me. It's true. When one boy looks like the next, it's easier to pass him over, but every once in a while, there's one like Micah. Different. Interesting. Gorgeous and not like the rest of us. And it would make us all wonder why he or she was not considered one of the Unviables. Gran explained that it was still hard to determine hair color at birth. Often it would change with time. They attempt to manipulate the genes, but since The Institute has only worked with four generations so far, they're still perfecting their procedures. They try not to dispose of fetuses for unusual traits. Not until they have the genetics perfected. But by my children's generation, or maybe one after, the anomalies will be eliminated. And it'll be my job to do it.

"Yeah, it's interesting," I say. It's conversations like these that make me wonder if Taryn knows a bit more than she's leading on.

"Interesting and boring. I'd prefer to stare at specimens like Micah all day."

"Pretty sure that's the point of making us all look alike."

There's a scuffling sound behind us, and I turn to see what it is. No one's there. *Strange.* I know I heard something just then.

"Here's where we part." Taryn switches her compact from one arm to the other. "I'll meet you at the coffee shop before second session?"

"Sure. See you then."

As she treks off down the path toward her house, her blonde hair flutters in the breeze. I like Taryn. Probably because we think so much alike. We both have questions about how The Institute runs things. But the thing I like the most about her is that she voices those questions. Maybe not aloud to everyone like that kid in our lab group, but at least to me. I'm glad I'm not the only one with doubts.

There it is again. That scratching sound. Like someone shuffling along behind me. Not again. I take off and cut through the park. I know

I've promised myself I'd never go this way again, but it's shorter, and the only thing on my mind at this moment is how fast I can get home and lock the doors behind me. Every few steps, I glance over my shoulder.

My heart speeds up, and my palms sweat when the tail of a long jacket tucks behind a tree a few feet away from me. I see a foot jutting out. Someone's there. The man with the skeleton fingers. I wipe my hands on my pants and quicken to a jog. No need to stay and meet my demise. A few more steps and I'll be through the park and to my street. Just a little faster. *What have I done to deserve this?*

One more glance over my shoulder reveals a shadow. Without a doubt, I can make out the shape of a person, legs elongated in the moonlight. The body is covered by a long coat and atop the figure's head sits a fedora. My eyes follow the shadow to the source. This time, he doesn't hide, stepping out from the tree so I can see as clearly as the darkened night sky will allow. He pulls his hat down over his eyes to shroud his face. He stares at me then tucks his hands in his pockets and slithers away.

I stumble backward, nearly tripping over my own feet before I turn around and gain my balance again. Heart racing, I run to my front door and fumble with the keys. My parents are both at work, so I'm home alone, but at least I'm inside. I press the door closed and flip the deadbolt lock. Then I move to the windows and make sure those are locked before drawing back the curtain enough to look out across the street.

I can't see anyone, but the brush surrounding the opening to the park where I emerged minutes before is swaying as if someone was just standing there. There's no one now, but the thought that someone stood there watching me enter my house sends a shiver up my spine. I close the curtain and head upstairs to my bedroom. I want to study. I *need* to study, but with my nerves the way they are, there's no way I can concentrate on memorizing medical terms. No way. So instead, I lay back and stare out my bedside window into the darkness wondering who would possibly want to follow me and why.

SIX

....

THE BOOKS HAVE EYES

Code of Conduct and Ethics: The Institute—Sector 4, USA
Section 6 Article 4.7: Education is a top priority in any young person's life.
Free time should be devoted to studies and further learning.

"**K**ATE, ARE YOU PLANNING on seeing Gran after your classes today? She'll want to hear about your apprenticeship. She'll be so proud of you. We all are." Dad glances at me over his cup of coffee, and I know by the look in his eye he's heard something. It's probably not relevant to anything, but Dad and I have always shared a love for the forbidden. Any little tidbit of information we overhear gets our adrenaline pumping, and each night, while my mother is off finishing up her last minute work papers, we trade any secrets we heard throughout the day. It's not like we don't love The Institute. We do. But Dad and I still love to hear the little snippets that make life a little more interesting.

Mom gets up to refill her mug. "Honey, you know your grandmother will just become more confused if Kate starts telling her these things. I don't know why you insist on sharing these sorts of things with her. It'll make her more upset."

"Just because she can't fully understand everything we tell her isn't a good excuse not to spend time with her. She's my grandmother for goodness' sake."

Dad leans across the table to whisper. Normally, he doesn't talk over a meal. Too difficult with my mother hovering around. The conversations would crisscross. "What'd you find out?" he'd whisper. "Well, I saw ..." "Pass the potatoes, sweetie," my mom would say. "Later," I'd say to my dad. "No, now please," would be my mother's response. It would become thoroughly confusing.

The fact that he is telling me this now means it must be big.

"They caught another rebel yesterday." He takes a bite of his toast. "Think he might be connected with the one they displayed at the parade."

I don't need to ask where he got this information. More than likely, he found out at the Station where he works. It's where all the computerized data is collected and stored on huge databases. But since it's a Justice Department issue, Dad could've overheard my mother during one of her confidential phone conversations. He's pretty sly about his eavesdropping, but I worry when he tries to listen in on Mom. He could get in huge trouble. Doesn't matter that she's his wife. Many wives have been known to turn in husbands for lesser offenses. The rewards for revealing anyone who might be a cause for concern are much too high for anyone to pass up. I hope my mother isn't one of those people; I believe she isn't, but it's hard to be sure since she never lets her guard down.

I want to tell Dad about the man in the park the other night, but Mom turns around before I have a chance. There's no need to worry him, I guess. He'd probably accompany me to my classes, and that is an embarrassment I'm not willing to endure.

Dad straightens up as I grab a peach from the bowl on the counter and cut thin slices over my oatmeal. "Not sure if I can make it to Gran's, Dad. I'll try."

"Just message if you are." He slowly sips his coffee and takes a bite of his peanut butter toast as my mother sits down at the table beside him.

"Make sure you record your meals," she tells both of us. This is my mother. Always doing the right thing, following all the rules. The Institute's rules. It's that true-to-country spirit that put her at the top of her field in the Justice Department.

Appeasing her, I open my compact and click on the food icon to record breakfast. Food isn't rationed here like it is in some parts of the country. They make us record our food to make sure no one has too much or too little. Because if someone ate more than what their body could handle, it would alter the average look and weight of the people here. And The Institute doesn't want people to stand out if they have any control over it.

We can pretty much eat what we want as long as we record it, and they allow us each our favorite treat once a day. For my dad, it's the jelly doughnut he's biting into now that he's finished his toast. The jelly squirts out the other side and lands on his plate where he wipes it up with his finger and licks off the sticky stuff from his skin. He uses his teeth to squeegee the red jam off his finger. He's always done this. Meanwhile, my mom makes a face.

"Do you have to do that?"

"What?"

"That," she points to his fingers, "with the jelly."

"Of course, my dear. How else would I get the jelly out from under my fingernails?" He flashes me a wink, knowing it'll make his wife roll her eyes, which she does as I laugh.

To her, it's disgusting to stick your fingers in your mouth, and she never allows me to do it, but curbing my dad of the habit is another story.

"Be careful," he says to me. His daily mantra, which I know really means, *watch your back.*

"I'm probably heading to the library after my sessions," I add, scraping the bottom of my bowl and shoving the last spoonful of oatmeal into my mouth. "I have to study for my lab tomorrow." I address my mother, who is stacking the dishes neatly in piles while she fills the sink with hot, soapy water. "Don't count on me for dinner. I'll grab something at the café."

Before she can protest and go on about how the food at the café isn't healthy, I pick up my compact, slide it into my bag, and head out the door. "Don't worry, I'll record it." As I step out the door, I hear a quiet chuckle escape my dad's lips.

***

Sessions for today don't include lab work. That's every other day, so after another *thrilling* lecture by Professor Limbert, Taryn and I head to the library with a quick stop at the café along the way for my indulgence of choice: a pumpkin scone and coffee with cream. I've consumed them both by the time we reach the front steps of the library, except for a final swig of my coffee, which I swallow before tossing the cup in the garbage can on the sidewalk.

The library is an old building, built with ornate stonework masonry and rustic brick. It looms out from the street front with its giant pillars, and lampposts light the long stairway leading to the building's massive doors. This building is obsolete in this day. We have all the information we need or want at the touch of our fingertips, so the structure is used more as a gathering center or museum than a place of learning or research. One giant piece of nostalgia in our ever-evolving, technological world.

Taryn and I skip up the steps and tug the door open. Just past the marble-tiled floor in the entryway, a group of our classmates lounge on couches in the sitting area.

It's Chase and Devin with a few younger-looking girls I don't recognize. Normally, I wouldn't mind hanging out, but Devin has been a little extra friendly lately, and I'm not interested. I'd rather not give him any ideas if I can help it.

"Wanna join them?" Taryn asks, adjusting her study bag on her shoulder.

"Nah. You go ahead. I've got some work I need to finish."

She shakes her head at me and tugs at my shirt. "Study later. You've still got time before the lab tomorrow."

"Thanks, but I'd rather get it done now. No need to procrastinate."

She shoots me a look. "You love to procrastinate. Remember what I've always said? 'Kate, Kate, procrastinate. Turn it in a little late.'" Taryn's eyes light up as she recalls our little chant from childhood.

"Yeah, well, I'm trying to change my ways. You know, the life of a Creation Specialist and all."

"You're not a Creation Specialist yet." She smiles. "Go ahead, then. I'll catch up with you later." Taryn heads toward the group, swings her bag off her shoulder and sets it to the side of an overstuffed chair. I glance over my shoulder as I round the corner to the research room and catch the look of disappointment on Devin's face. It fades quickly when Taryn flops down in between the two boys and flashes them each a brilliant smile. She has the ability to turn anyone's head. Heck, I wouldn't be surprised if she could convince them to do whatever she wanted with merely a grin and a wink.

I prefer to be alone when I work. It helps me concentrate. There's a couch in the far corner of the research room nestled between a few bookshelves. My fingers brush the wooden spines of the book inserts as I pass by. The shelves almost reach the ceiling and were once filled with titles. Now, each holds either a canvas with painted book spines or wooden blocks carved to look and feel like books on a shelf. But it's all a façade. What use is there for books when any information is given to us through the city's database system? Even the stories read to young children or those used for entertainment purposes are found in our database. This library is merely for show. A place to gather. Like they didn't know what to do with the building when they started eliminating the literature, so they kept it to keep a few things normal when so much else was changing.

My corner is tucked between two rows of shelves covered in the wood carvings. I prefer these to the canvas paintings for the mere fact that I can run my fingers along the edges and wonder what mysteries these books held. The titles written on the spines don't match those in the database of literature. Years ago, when our community was just forming, certain books were deemed unworthy of storage and eliminated from society altogether. *1984*, by George Orwell. *Hamlet*, by William Shakespeare. *The Crucible*, by Arthur Miller. Stories long gone except for a title and author. Nothing left but a name on a piece of wood. I wonder if Gran ever read these books. It's something I never thought to inquire, but I now make a mental note to ask. What was so horrible about these stories that they ended up as rubbish?

It makes me wonder what my grandchildren will decide to destroy of my earth. Of my life.

I settle myself onto a worn cushion and take out my compact, pressing the button to bring it to life.

I love it here because I'm alone. After all the time I spend in the lab with my classmates, I seek any opportunity I can afford to find solitude, even if it means walking at dusk through a creepy park or hiding in the corner of an ancient building with only the dust and ghosts of writers past as company.

Glancing over the screen, I take a moment to read through the announcements that pop up. A write-up about the recent Womber death. I glance through it and slide it into a folder of announcements to read. Then I click to my own notes of that first lab observation. The pictures I've drawn are primitive, but my notes are thorough, and soon, I have lists of terms stored into the memory chip implanted in my neck. You'd think if a society was going to implant enhancement chips at birth, they'd at least make it easier to absorb information. Who cares that it's programmed to shut our brains down when we're one hundred and twenty? I'd like a few more benefits now, please. It'd be nice to click a button and send the terms and studies to long-term memory, but our chips are still being developed. We can retain much more information at a faster rate, but we still have to put forth some effort. At least we get healthy bodies from it.

I'm not sure how much time has passed when I hear a noise around the corner. No one comes back here on purpose, so I know it must be Taryn looking for me. "Over here, T."

There's no answer. Odd. I thought for sure I heard something. I ignore the thought until I hear a soft scraping a few feet away. "T, I'm in my spot." When she doesn't respond, goose bumps stand up on my skin.

Maybe she can't remember where I am, so I get up and walk halfway down the aisle. To my left, I see a space between the façade of book spines. It's small, but I'm sure there weren't any empty spaces here. In other parts of the library, on other shelves, yes, but not here. Here they pack the shelves solid to simulate an old-fashioned library. It's all for the ambiance. I've passed this place so many times I know each crack and crevice. This one didn't exist thirty minutes ago. I peer through the crack, but all I see is another shelf of fake books about four feet away.

The flash of movement crosses my line of sight causing a prickly heat to spark on my skin. My gaze sharpens, watching for the slightest change. Leaning a bit closer, I slide the wooden book ends over, pressing my forehead against the shelf so I can see.

What I see causes me to jump. "Ow!" I jump back and whack my head on the jagged metal shelf. I rub the spot. There's no blood, but a bump is already forming. I turn around, and my back presses against a cold, metal divider and I slide to the floor, staying there until my racing heart slows to normal.

When I can breathe normally again, I press my hands on the floor and work my way back to a standing position. The space is right next to my head, so all I have to do is turn around and look, yet I stand there frozen, building my courage.

Finally, when I can't handle it any longer, I tuck the waves of hair behind my ears and turn to peer through the space.

Gray eyes look back at me then disappear.

"What the h—!" Lunging to the end of the stacks, I round the corner, expecting to see a body attached to those eyes. But the aisle is empty.

This is creepy. I must be going insane. I know what I saw, and I know whose eyes they were. There is only one person who possesses the gray-blue eyes that studied me through the books.

I find the space between the books again. Only this time, it's not empty. Sitting on the shelf is a tiny piece of paper. Real paper. On closer inspection, it's not just any paper. It's a page from a book, and it's folded into the shape of a fish.

Turning it over in my fingers is strange. The feel of the paper. Its smell. The yellowing color. I've never seen anything like it. I know I can't show it to anyone. Something like this would be forbidden, so I gently tuck it in my back pocket until I can put it someplace safe.

Still, I don't know why anyone would take a risk like this. What if I hadn't found the gift, if that's what it is? And the idea that someone is watching me totally freaks me out.

***

I pack up my stuff and head toward the common area where Taryn is turning on her charm. She's snuggled between the two boys with a grin the size of Sector 4. When she sees me, the smile disappears and a glint of concern replaces it. She can tell I'm upset.

Pushing off the boys' legs, she crosses to me. "You okay? What happened?"

"Nothing. I'm fine. I just thought I'd join you here." It's a total lie, but I don't care. It's not like I'm scared. I'm not. Definitely not. I know who it was, and I'm *mostly* sure he's harmless, especially since he left me a gift. At least, I think it was a gift and not an omen.

We return to the group where Taryn pushes Devin aside, making room for me. I don't care for Devin. I especially don't like his loose hands, but I'm so dazed that being anywhere near people is good. Devin's arm quickly slides off the back of the sofa and stops centimeters from my shoulder. But that's not what causes the hairs on my neck to stand out again. It's what I see when I look toward the door.

A group of people clog the exit in an attempt to leave at the same time. But on the far side is a taller boy with a mess of jet black curls tucked underneath a baseball cap. He doesn't look toward me, but inside I know even though I can't see them, beneath a line of dark lashes are eyes of gray.

"Kate?"

"Huh?" I look at Taryn. She doesn't finish her question, but the look on her face asks if I'm okay again. I manage a weak smile and a nod as I look back toward the entrance. The congestion has dissipated, and the boy is gone.

I know who was staring at me through the bookshelves. I just don't know why.

SEVEN

GIVING BIRTH

Birthing class begins this week. As soon as we get to class on Monday, Micah takes us to the observation deck. It overlooks the birthing area where a group of third-year residents are awaiting the doctor assigned to the case. They've already scrubbed in and are becoming visibly impatient.

I sit down at the end of the bleacher with Taryn on one side of me and Micah standing at the edge, so close I can smell his cologne. He looks especially nice today in a fitted black T-shirt beneath his open lab coat, and I have to look away when he catches me staring. I wonder if he knows I found his gift in the library. I won't tell him. Not now. There has to be a reason he didn't stop to talk. I'll see what I can find out first and in the meantime, I convince myself it's okay to appreciate his physique.

"Be sure to remain silent. This is the first time these residents are assisting a birth, so your distractions are not welcome. You'll notice the process is fairly easy and doesn't take long because there's no need for lengthy human labors," Micah says. He steps in front of the group to give instructions and then moves back to his spot by me and leans against the wall. As he passes, he brushes my leg.

"Sorry," he whispers, holding my gaze.

I barely hear him over the tingles that flow through my body where he touched me.

"Why do they need—" a guy from the back row asks, but Micah cuts him off.

"For now, if you have any questions, write them down in your compacts. After the birth, we'll have a debriefing session. You can ask me anything at that point."

I turn my attention to the room below me as Dr. Donovan, our other professor, enters dressed in scrubs. He ignores the group of us gathered in the spectator section and addresses the three residents ready to help with the birth. "Good afternoon, students. Shall we begin?" They nod silently and take their places around the table.

A fourth resident wheels in a cart with the fetus still in the capsule. She's fighting with the wires still attached to the tube as she rolls the cart closer to the work area. Donovan reaches over, untangles the tubing, and helps her slide the birthing capsule onto the table.

"As you know, the child in front of us has been created from DNA reserved from each parent. Nine months ago, they applied for their own child to be created. This is the culmination of that process. The first step is to open the capsule." He turns to the girl who wheeled in the baby. "Go ahead."

She reaches over and releases the clasp, lifting the top of the canister off its base. Donovan continues as she works. "It's important not to disconnect the tubing until after the fetus is born. Doing so too soon can result in oxygen deprivation, which may cause birth defects. If this happens, an emergency disposal will be necessary, and we'd like to avoid that when possible." Donovan's words are practiced, like he's said this a million times. "Johnson," he continues, "please ready the suction and cleaning cloths. Ms. Moinihan, are you ready?"

The shortest of the group nods her head.

"All you need to do is reach in and remove the fetus from the surrounding liquid. Pass her to Mr. Johnson, who will begin cleaning the child."

As Ms. Moinihan steps toward the capsule, I lean closer to the edge of the viewing area. This is it. The moment of birth. It's fascinating and wonderful and makes my heart pump faster.

The med student reaches her hands into the gelatinous liquid and grabs the child behind the neck with one hand and under the leg with the other, lifting the baby out. She hands the baby to Johnson, who's waiting with outstretched arms covered in blankets. As soon as the infant touches his hands, Johnson rubs the baby's body and suctions out her nose and mouth. She screams and shivers at the touch of the cool air on her skin. It's a beautiful sound, and hearing it relaxes me enough to sit back into my seat. The fourth student clips the umbilical cord, detaches the tubing and wires from the container, and scrapes the residue from the sides of the pod. He removes the placenta from the base of the container and places it into a bag, labeling it with the date and time. It will be saved for further research.

The area below is busy with movement. Cleaning up this and that, weighing, measuring and swaddling the baby. Turning off pumps and reorganizing the tools. Seeing the process hasn't been quite as exciting as I anticipated. Open the capsule; take out the baby. Big deal. Nothing like the stories of my great-gran's day when there was rushing to the hospital, hoping to arrive on time. Battling weather and physical complications. It must have been so much more thrilling then.

But our scientific evolution is better. Easier. Safer.

Once everything calms down, the group below me meets near the birthing table again. Professor Donovan hands a syringe to the resident who rolled the child into the room. "Ms. Lindquist, you'll implant the MIH after Mr. Kater applies the tattoo. Then, since this fetus is female, Mr. Johnson will be responsible for removing the eggs."

Now it's getting interesting. I'll bet they never tattooed a newborn in Gran's day. The rest of my classmates must agree because we all lean forward together like we're one large, connected organism. Even Micah, who's probably seen this procedure a hundred times, leans over the edge of the viewing area to get a better look. For a moment, he's wide-eyed with wonder. He glances back at the group to make sure he's not in anyone's way and catches my eye. Tossing his eyebrows up in a quick acknowledgment, he smiles and scratches his stubble before turning his attention back toward the group below. I tuck a lock of hair behind my ear and glance at the floor before turning my attention to what's going on below.

Ms. Moinihan holds the swaddled baby on her stomach, exposing the child's neck. Meanwhile, Mr. Kater programs the laser device which will imprint the tattoo on the baby's skin. It looks like a scanner cashiers use at the café. "Citizen number 1285692," he says as he presses the numbers into the device. Mr. Johnson repeats the numbers and punches the information into The Institute's database through his compact.

Kater then presses the flat edge of the device against the child's neck and depresses the trigger. It beeps and flashes. The baby whimpers, but settles almost immediately. This part of the procedure doesn't cause pain, just a burst of warmth, we're told. Kater pulls the tattoo machine away from the baby and reveals a black barcode imprinted on its skin. Moinihan works quickly, having already programmed the microchip with the ID number and placed it into the embedding syringe. She slides the needle under the skin right next to the tattoo and sets the chip into place. By the time the baby screams, she's already removed the needle.

"Nice work, Ms. Moinihan," the professor says. "Looks like you've been practicing your technique."

She grins proudly at his affirmation.

I can't help it. My hand brushes over the tiny bump in my neck where my MIH sits. I press it, fingering the lump with my fingertips. The thought of something foreign embedded under my skin is kind of gross. Then, out of the corner of my eye, I see Micah looking at me. His hand rests on his own neck, and he gives me a sheepish smile before he looks again over the railing toward what's happening below.

They move the child to a small operating table where they place a mask over the child's face. "This administers a gas that will subdue the infant for the egg removal procedure. It will not render her totally un-conscious but will anesthetize her enough to do the procedure without pain," Professor Donovan explains.

From my vantage point, I can see the child relax under the drug. Her eyes close, but her breathing is still quick and even. Ms. Lindquist presses an ultrasound scope against the child's abdomen, and Johnson, who holds a syringe much like the one used to implant the MIH, studies the screen until he sees the ovaries come into view. Since the image is projected onto a larger screen for us to view, we can see every detail as he plunges the needle into the baby's stomach directly hitting the ovary. He moves it until he's suctioned the eggs out of the sac. Working quickly, he repeats the process on the other ovary, rendering the infant barren. Like all women in our community. Johnson then places the eggs into a storage container for future use and labels them with the baby's ID number.

After bringing the child out of anesthesia, Dr. Donovan instructs the residents to bring the baby to the nursery before finishing any administrative work. That's Micah's cue to gather us together and head back to the classroom, and as we move into place behind him, he's still rubbing the spot on his neck where his MIH chip is.

....

EIGHT

DATE WITH A POTENTIAL STALKER

Code of Conduct and Ethics: The Institute—Sector 4, USA
Section 5 Article 2.1: Interest in a person of the opposite gender must be re-
ported to parents within two weeks.

D AD ALWAYS TELLS ME to watch and observe. Glean information. Never confront anyone because you don't know where
the real power lies. So I have no idea what possesses me to
confront Micah during our next lab.

He's set another lesson in observing. No procedures yet. Not until
we've gone through all the proper observations. Boring, if you ask me.
I'm more of a hands-on kind of girl, but I suppose it's necessary. We
wouldn't be able to do a birthing procedure like what we saw yesterday
without training, after all. We're given assigned pairs and sent to a developmental station where we're supposed to gain a baseline for observation. Our studies will progress from there.

"Katherine Dennard, since there are an odd number of students in
class, you'll be paired with me." There's no emotion in Micah's voice or
face. The total opposite from yesterday in the observation deck when he
seemed to be watching me every chance he got.

Taryn elbows me. "Wanna trade?" She raises her eyebrows in a tease and licks her lips. "He's so yummy. I don't know why you're so paranoid. I'd let him follow me anywhere."

Okay, so I told her. I probably should have kept my mouth shut, but I had to tell someone other than Gran about being followed. I figured if I told Taryn, she could tell me that I'm *not* a total raving lunatic. Unfortunately, she confirmed it instead, and she's been hounding me ever since.

"Think I can get him to follow me to my bedroom?" she asks through a grin.

I can't help but laugh. Maybe it's her teasing that lightens my mood, but within the last thirty minutes, I've decided to refuse to be wary of Micah the lab guy anymore. I can't try to interpret his every scowl or smirk. If I did, it'd take up most of my day. An easy, *I don't suspect anything* approach will work much better in my opinion. A little trust can go a long way. Hopefully, he won't know that I've suspected anything, and I can show him the normal, sane me … sort of.

The pairs of my classmates go off to their stations while I wait for Micah to gather his things and join me at the batch of embryos we're supposed to study.

"Looks like you're stuck with me," he says, crossing his arms over his compact, which he holds against his chest. He looks almost shy standing like this, but I've seen his confidence in these lab procedures. He's not fooling anyone. *Note to self: Stop interpreting his every look!*

"Could be worse."

His head cocks in question.

"I could be stuck with Stewart." I thumb over my shoulder where, without even looking, I know Stewart stands. I can tell by the nasally voice, which is sure to annoy his female partner.

"Tonya, look at this!" Stewart says.

I swear I hear him snort when he sniffs.

A half snicker escapes Micah's lips before his stone face returns. He removes a piece of tissue from the pack on the counter and wipes the microscope clean before he presses his forehead against the scope and looks through the lenses. "Give yourself a few moments to watch before you note anything."

Right. We're supposed to be studying. This is a lab for my Developmental Biology class. Somehow standing next to Micah with my heart speeding and my palms sweating makes that fact hard to remember.

Placing my eyes against the scope, I inhale his clean scent still hanging in the air. Not looking at him gives me courage to say what's on my mind. Perhaps it's a moment of bold idiocy caused by his presence, but it comes out before I can think too much about it. "So, I've seen quite a lot of you lately. If I didn't know any better, I'd say you were following me." He isn't. I know he isn't. I hope he isn't. But all the talk from Taryn has it stuck in my subconscious, and it slips into my speech before I can tie my tongue.

I hold steady but can see his hand leaning easily on the countertop, clench into a fist.

Oh crap! No way! Maybe he was.

However, his voice is steady as he says, "Following you? I didn't realize I was." He changes position and leans against the table, fiddling with the lens paper.

I keep my eyes on the embryos under the microscope. "Sure, you know. That night last week when I ran into you near the park. Then the other day at the library when you spied on me through the bookshelves in the old section. And now this lab partner deal you have going on. Slick. I mean, if you wanted a date, it would've been easier just to ask, don't you think?" *Wait. Listen. Don't look at him yet. Oh, my goodness, my mother would kill me if she heard me say this.*

I pull my gaze away from the lenses and look at the tiny smirk on his lips. Like his front teeth, it's slightly crooked. Sure, he's a little different from the rest of us, but in a way, it's endearing. He's cute in a not-like-the-others kind of way, but it's more than that. Rugged, perhaps. A little rougher around the edges than most guys I know. And the stubble that constantly rests on his chin lends to that wild, sexy thing he has going on. I wonder if he knows it.

He relaxes and twists and folds the tissue as he speaks. "I can't help it that we happen to be in the same places occasionally, Kate. We live in the same town. Study at the same facilities. It's bound to happen." His serious face returns, and I can't tell if he's joking or not. Even so, my heartbeat quickens when he says my name. It's like he's rolling it around in his mouth for a moment.

Now it's my turn to cock my head. I'll give him credit. He didn't deny it. And his answer settles my mind and entices me at the same time. It's true. It could be a total coincidence to have ended up in the same places, but Gran always tells me there's no such thing as coincidence. And it doesn't explain away why he didn't just round the bookshelf at the library and say hi or how he seemed to disappear into thin air when I went to look for him.

He interrupts my thoughts. "As for the lab partner bit, it's a perk of being the lab assistant to be able to pick the smartest girl as a partner."

I feel myself grow hot, and I know my cheeks are crimson. So I turn back to the microscope to hide. "Hmm."

"But as long as you're asking. I'd love a date."

Wrenching back in surprise, I bang my head on the cabinet. "I didn't ask—"

"It's okay," he snickers, lips curling into a mischievous grin. "I'd be afraid to ask me out, too." He leans close, and I catch another whiff of his skin. "Being your lab leader and all. It must be awkward for you." His smile widens when he sees my mouth agape at his explanation. He thumbs over his shoulder. "I think your friend, Taryn, might be jealous, though."

Over to my right, Taryn eyes us. Her brows are furrowed, but when she sees me watching, she smiles and winks. I know she'll catch me after class and quiz me about everything Micah said. She'll want all the juicy details, which means I'll have to tell her that Micah and I apparently have a date.

"And where and when would this particular meeting of the minds be?" I ask.

"Ah, and she gives in." He shakes his head and clucks his tongue. "I thought you'd be one to put up more of a fight. It must be my charming personality. Impossible to say no."

"Unless you weren't interested. In which case, I could easily find something else of value to do, instead of wasting my time wandering through the park or catching a flick with my lab partner. Or is your idea of a date more of a study session?"

"Coffee at the café and a walk by the river," he says without hesitation. "Friday at six. I'll pick you up."

"Sounds like a plan." I smile at him.

"So you don't forget." He presses something into the palm of my hand then calls the rest of the class together. "Let's hear what you've observed so far. Finish up in the next few minutes and meet me back in the classroom."

When he's no longer in sight, I open my palm. In it is a tiny folded butterfly. I tuck it into my back pocket and turn back to my lab notes, wondering how I went from suspecting him of stalking me to setting up a date.

······························

NINE

DATE NIGHT

Code of Conduct and Ethics: The Institute—Sector 4, USA
Section 5 Article 2.2: Relationships between two persons under twenty
years of age shall be strictly monitored by the parents of both individuals.
Curfews must be honored. Failure to adhere to curfews will result in de-
merits. Three demerits results in loss of privileges.

RUSHING TO THE BATHROOM, I cling to the toilet and dry heave. I'm dizzy when I stand up. I've never been this nervous for a date in my life, not that I've been on a ton. *What have I gotten myself into? And why am I such a nervous wreck?*

"Katherine, you okay?" My mom is putting the finishing touches on a well-cooked meal by peeling back the sealant and warming it up in the microwave. Mom claims to be a master chef, but we all know if this were true, she would've been selected for the food service careers. Since she turns up her nose at that type of job, I'm thinking she couldn't even boil water if she had to.

"Yeah, Mom. Just getting ready for my date." I pull my hair back off my neck and wrap an elastic band around it. A wet washcloth dabs the sweat off my neck and face, and I pat dry with a hand towel. Better. The nausea has subsided, and with a pinch of my cheeks, I'll look normal again. I hope.

Once a little color has returned to my face, I give myself a once over in the full-length mirror behind the door. I turn my back and look over my shoulder, running my hands over my hips. These jeans make my butt look fantastic. For a while, I contemplated something a little nicer, but I figured with a walk near the river, comfort and convenience was essential.

With my hair pulled up, I can see my ID tattoo. Normally, my hair hides it, but pulling it back reveals the barcode pressed into the base of my skull. 1-2-0-5-9-0-1. My number. Complete with a tiny bump under the skin, the microchip programmed to make me as perfect as possible ... Staring at mine now, I fight the urge for my stomach to heave again. There's something about it that indicates my body isn't fully mine. And I guess, if I think about it, it isn't. Once I do actually die at exactly one hundred and twenty years from my date and time of birth, my body will be returned to The Institute for study, just like everyone else's.

It's this sort of thing that makes me jealous of Gran. At least there's a little mystery for her. When she'll die, how she'll go. Not so for me, unless I meet with some terribly unfortunate accident. I'll know the time and day, and I'll even be able to plan the place. It's too nice and neat for me. A perfect little life-sized box. This thing in my neck is a constant reminder of the spontaneity I'll never have.

The thought disgusts me, and as I give the elastic a tug, my hair falls over my back, covering the black carved lines. I'll deal with the heat.

Mom stands at the door, leaning on the frame, a cup of coffee in her hands. "So, who's this boy you're seeing? You did record this date into the database, right?" She's trying to be serious and concerned, but I recognize the way the corners of her lips pull up the tiniest bit. Secretly, she loves the fact that I have a date, as long as she approves of the guy.

"My lab partner, Micah Pennington. And yes, it's recorded."

"Micah Pennington?" my father asks. "Isn't he one of the assistants in the Creation Unit? How would he be your lab partner?"

"There were an odd number of students, so I got stuck as his partner."

"An assistant to the assistant. Impressive," Dad says as the look on my mother's face brightens. "Way to work yourself up the ladder. It's all about who you know." Dad's anxious for me to have an *in* with the higher-ups. He feels the more people like us who secretly resist The Institute and its power, the better. My dad, the undercover rebel.

"That's not what this is, Dad," I urge, knowing what he's thinking. "It's a date. It's personal."

"Mmm hmm."

Okay, so I suppose dating the guy in charge doesn't hurt my chances of being placed at the top of the group that's vying for the few openings as Creation Specialists. But I'm not interested in filtering information for some underground rebellion I don't even know exists.

It doesn't matter how much she tries to hold back, my mother can't hide her excitement over the prospect of my date with someone higher up in the Creation Department. Her smile is practically reaching the back of her head.

"Okay, okay," I say, escaping their stares by heading to my room to grab a jacket. "He'll be here any minute. Can you two please behave yourselves?"

When I return, Micah is standing inside the front door. I attempt to make introductions, but he stops me. "We've already become acquainted while you were upstairs."

I sigh and roll my eyes at my mother to which she replies, "We behaved. Just made polite introductions."

"It was nice meeting you, Mr. and Mrs. Dennard." Micah holds the door open for me.

"Bye, Mother, Dad," I say, closing the door behind me.

"Bye, Katie-Did," they reply in unison.

"Katie-Did?" Micah asks when we step onto the front porch.

"It's a nickname. Like the bug."

A light smile plays across his lips, but he says nothing.

The driveway is empty of a foreign vehicle. "Didn't you drive?" I ask, zipping up my jacket in a fight against the cool of the air.

"I figured we were going to walk by the river anyways, so there'd be no need to drive."

I plunge my hands deep into my pockets. "To the café then for something warm?" It's a good thing we have to walk a bit. At the very least, it'll warm up my extremities. Despite the sunlight, the late summer air carries a chill.

At Meg's Café, I order my usual: pumpkin scone and coffee with cream. I skipped it this morning in anticipation of this date. Otherwise, I'd receive a notice that I've exceeded my limit of innutritious foods for the week. The rigmarole and paperwork associated with that is a pain in the neck, so I'd like to avoid it at all costs if possible. Micah gets a cranberry orange scone, a choice that surprises me at first, and when I give him a questioning look, he says, "What? Can't a guy like cranberries?"

"I guess so. I just expected you to be more of a bagel with cream cheese or jelly doughnut type of guy."

"Well," he says, holding the door wide for me. "There's a lot you don't know about me, Kate."

"Like your ability to create animals from tiny pieces of paper?" I expect a subtle smile when I look at him, but his face is the stone mask I'm used to seeing in class.

O-kay. Maybe this dating-the-lab-dude wasn't such a great idea, after all.

"Let's keep that between the two of us, okay?" he says, rubbing the back of his neck.

"Um, yeah. Sure. Sorry."

"It's fine. It's something I do to keep my hands busy, but if anyone knew I have a paper folding hobby, I'd never hear the end of it."

Instantly, his demeanor lightens, and he's chatting about work and the Creation Lab. With mention of the Utero Lab, he relaxes.

"So," I ask, "what made you want to be a Creation Scientist?"

"I dunno. I guess I found it challenging to create something new, something perfect. Besides, it's the closest thing I could think of to becoming a father."

"Father?"

"Or brother."

"You don't think you'll be a dad someday?"

"Maybe, but I have to find the right girl first." He picks up a twig and snaps it, tossing tiny pieces on the grass as we walk.

It's odd to think that at nineteen, Micah has thought about being a father. We can't even apply for children until we're thirty, so planning so far in advance seems odd. The thought of raising my own children is so foreign to me at seventeen, it seems like a lifetime away before I'll ever have to consider those life choices. First, I have to focus on getting my degree, then finding a husband.

"A girl who will put up with your stone face, you mean?"

"Stone face?"

My face slides into a serious look. "Yeah, this one." But trying to hold it without laughing is impossible.

His eyes glitter in the moonlight, but he doesn't laugh. "You've named it my stone face?"

"Maybe."

"Huh, and here I thought girls went for the serious brooding type."

"Oh, yes. We do." I mock his stone face again.

When he practically glares at me, his eyes icy, I wonder if I've gone too far. This is our first time together. Maybe my teasing is too much.

Thankfully, he breaks into a grin. "If you're going to make fun of it, you at least have to do it right."

"Right. Well, I'll have to practice."

"You'd be surprised at how useful a straight face is. Everyone thinks you're mad, but really, you can hide away, listening to the action around you. I've gleaned a lot from being that quiet face in the corner."

Now I'm curious. Maybe, being so far from the center of The Institute, Micah will open up a bit. "I'm sure you have. Tell me something juicy you've heard."

He pulls his hands from his coat pockets and wipes them on his jeans. I'm sure he's going to reveal something interesting, but instead he clears his throat. "We're almost there."

So much for deep conversation. This is only the first date. I'm sure neither of us is ready to reveal our deepest darkest secrets. Or any secrets for that matter. It's too bad, really. I'm sure Micah has an interesting one or two.

A break in the walkway leads down river, and Micah suddenly turns right. I've traveled this way many times, pushing Gran through the thick grass to our secret clearing near the riverside, but in all the times I've been up this way, I've never known anyone else to come through here.

"Mind if we wander through the wilderness a bit?" Micah asks. "I know of this really cool spot. I go there sometimes to eat lunch."

"Um. Yeah. Sure." Oh dear, what if it's the same place? Does he know about it? About me?

Another ten minutes through the damp grass, and the dew from the afternoon rain has soaked through the canvas on my shoes. The squishy sensation I feel between my toes every time I place my foot is of little concern with my thoughts on Micah and his mysterious persona. I'm intrigued by where he's taking me, wondering with every stride if it's the same clearing I take Gran to talk.

"Hold on." Micah moves forward and brushes aside some branches, revealing the clearing. My clearing. The one overlooking the waterfall. How have we never bumped into each other here in all the times I've snuck away to this very spot? If Micah comes here, too, he must have seen me at least once or twice. The odds of *not* running into me are very slim. Yet, I can't remember a single time I've seen anyone lingering around here. I thought I was alone. Safe.

He holds out his hand. "Here," he says, "let me help you."

The weeds have grown over since I brought Gran here last, but there's still a little worn path leading to the edge of a cliff, evidence that someone has frequented this spot. I settle myself against *my* rock and nibble the rest of my scone. He's looking right at me with some sort of anticipation.

"It's beautiful. Do you come here often?" I ask.

"Now and then. Very few people know about this place, I think." He settles himself on the damp dirt next to me. His elbows rest on his knees, and his coffee cup hangs loosely in one hand. Sipping lightly, he steals a glance at me before surveying the river below. "I found it one afternoon on a walk. It was crazy; this one day, instead of taking my usual route along the fencing of The Institute like I normally do, I decided to brave the wilderness. Found this place. Now, it's kind of my secret spot."

Picking up a rock from the ground, he tosses it into the river. "I've never brought anyone here."

"Wow, I feel special."

"You should." His eyes twinkle, but his face remains steady. "I figured you might be an outdoorsy kind of girl."

He's right; it's nice to get away every once in a while. Be alone. "Yeah, there's not much alone time when you work for The Institute. You know, with all the cameras and surveillance equipment everywhere." *Dang! Why did I just say that?* It's not like I don't know better. You're never supposed to admit anything to anyone around here, yet I go and open my big mouth. It's like being around Micah opens the doors to my innermost thoughts.

I glance up at his knowing eyes. There's something about the way he looks at me that makes me want to spill my guts to him. It's a tug-of-war with my secrets. Stay hidden deep inside or come to the surface to rest on Micah's listening ear. I know I should be careful of every word I utter. I want to trust him, to tell someone the secrets I know. But I can't. Not yet.

"Kinda nice to get away from all the hustle and bustle of The Institute. There aren't any rules and regulations to follow here, you know?"

"Don't you like to follow the rules, Micah?" It's a joke, but as soon as I say it, I regret it, and I can't tell if the look on his face is fear or something else. Whatever it is, it makes me regret it even more. "Sorry, that's not what I meant." *This is the strangest date ever.*

"No, it's okay." He fingers his coffee mug and then scratches his cheek. "Yeah, I follow the rules just like everyone else, but sometimes being here, listening to the water run over the rocks. It's peaceful. Makes me wonder if anywhere else is different."

"Different how?"

"Different from Sector 4."

"It's all the same. I'm sure of it." For a moment, I feel like I'm talking to Taryn. We've had this conversation a million times before.

He looks up but doesn't say anything. Suddenly, I feel like I must have worms crawling over my face or something. Who am I to make such a statement anyway? I know nothing about the other sectors. It just sounded like the right thing to say to get back to that playful side of him I saw on the walk here.

Finally, he breaks the awkward silence. "Don't get me wrong. I love it here. I have a great job that I love, food to eat, a roof over my head. What more can I ask for? I mean, The Institute is only interested in our well-being, right? 'Success and health for all.'" His attempt to sound enthusiastic falls short.

"So, do you have a secret place? Somewhere you can go to be alone? Get away from the rules."

Now I wonder if he's brought me here to test me somehow. Maybe he's some sort of spy for The Institute, hired to track down dissenters or sympathizers. He *sounds* like he might have doubts about the way things are run around here, much like I do, but no one goes around talking about it to strangers on the street. Okay, so maybe I'm not a total stranger, but it's not like he knows me very well. We've just started working together. I could totally report him for suspicious language against The Institute. But I won't. Somehow, I assume, he knows this.

But what if I've been noticed acting strange and someone is checking up on me using Micah to do it? *Oh crap.* All he'd have to do is to bring me to my own secret hiding spot, pretending to be a sympathizer himself and strike up a simple conversation. He could even be recording it right now. Then he goes back to The Institute, perhaps even to Fishgold himself, and tells him what he's found out. It's as simple as that. My future would be destroyed in one conversation.

Don't say anything more. Give him nothing to analyze or tell anyone else. Do not, under any circumstances, give yourself away.

This date is a disaster. I should have known better.

As if reading my mind, he says, "Kate, you can trust me, you know." I nod. Of course I can't.

It's the closest we both come to revealing anything because I quickly change the subject.

"So, what do you like to do in your free time?"

He takes another sip of his coffee and stares across the river into the darkness. "Honestly, I don't have much free time. Most of my day is spent in the lab. When I'm not working with your class, Professors

Limbert and Donovan fill my time with menial tasks so it looks like we're accomplishing something with our research. But when I do have time, I'm usually home alone."

"Aren't your folks ever around? What do they do?"

"They're dead."

Insert foot into mouth. "Oh, I'm so sorry. What happened?"

"Car accident when I was fifteen. I became Sector 4 property until three years ago."

"Wait, were you the kid who was mangled in that crash? I was just researching that for my paper for Limbert's class. You were the only survivor."

Micah makes a sweeping motion with his hand and half bows from his seat on the ground. "Yours truly."

"Wow! I'm sorry. About your folks, I mean. That was big news at the time."

"Mmm hmm."

"So, what happened?"

"The doctors fixed me up. I got a new face. End of story."

He's obviously uncomfortable, fidgeting with a pile of twigs near him.

"Well, they did a great job."

He looks at me, confused.

"Your face," I continue. "They did an awesome job. You can't see any scarring or anything. It's perfect."

A small smirk appears on his lips, but it disappears almost instantly. His hand scratches through his stubble and feels along his jawline for what must be a hidden scar.

I stumble over my words. "I mean, you know, your face. It's nice. Handsome." As his grin grows bigger, I become more agitated. I must like him more than I originally thought for me to be this flustered. "I mean, if I had a doctor like that, I'd get a new face."

"You don't need a new face." The way he's looking at me makes me nervous.

"Sure, I'd fix my nose. I hate my nose. And my chin is too small. Maybe someday they'll fix the chins. Make us all look the same. At least that way my great grandchildren won't have to have this chin."

Suddenly, his fingers brush my chin. The feeling of his chilled skin on my face sends a shiver down my spine. I can't move, my eyes glued to his gaze. "I think your chin is perfect." Smiling lightly, he lets go and looks out over the water.

The moon has risen above the horizon and with it brings a crispness to the air that makes me pull my jacket tighter around me. Micah starts to move, so I stretch my legs and stand up. When I move forward, however, my foot lands on wet leaves and mud that has clustered near the ravine bank, taking my leg out from under me. My hands flail, trying not to let my body fall over the edge and into the river, and I reach out for anything to grasp onto. Micah's arm is the closest thing. Before I know it, he has both arms wrapped around me, pulling me from the edge of the chasm.

"Whoa, there. Let's not fall into the river tonight. That'd be difficult to explain to your parents." He smirks.

Right. Very funny.

His hands, which just a moment ago had a steady hold on my upper arms, slide gently to my elbows. His eyes pore over my face, searching for something as we hang, suspended in time. I feel myself melting into him despite that tiny voice of caution. It's like some magnetic pull. Stepping into his body, I give in to those searching gray irises. His lips hover just over mine, and the air sparks between us. He leans forward.

I break our gaze and look at my feet, not knowing what stops me.

Taking a quick breath, Micah licks his lips. "Right. Sorry. Too soon," he says, letting me pass. "Maybe I should get you home."

"Sure. Yeah." I tuck a lock of my stray hair behind my ear. "Good idea. It's getting cold anyway."

We walk back to my house in silence, his hand wrapped around mine. "Kate," he whispers. "I had a nice time tonight. I'd like to do this again soon if that's okay with you."

I snicker to myself on the inside. That might be the sweetest lie a guy has ever said to me. If only he knew what went on in my head. That pull between wanting to trust him and thinking he might turn me in. If he knew, he'd most likely not be asking for a second date. I let it slide as I shift my gaze between the road and his face. "Yeah. That'd be fine."

With that, I say good-bye and walk into my house. From the window, I see him linger for a minute before he heads down the street.

TEN

SET UP

MY PHONE RINGS EARLY on Saturday morning. I glance at the screen. Taryn. You'd think after being my lifelong friend, she'd know better than to call before 9:00 a.m. on a Saturday. I clear my throat and flip open the phone. "Hey," I say groggily.

"Did you just get up?"

"No. I was sleeping. Not up yet. Not everyone has the abnormal amount of energy you do, Taryn. You're like a chipmunk on caffeine."

"Well, get up and get moving. You need to get all your work done early today because we're going out tonight."

"Oh, really?"

"Yes. And wear something sort of sexy. I hooked you up with a guy from my political science class."

I let out a groan. "Taryn! Why do you do that?"

"Oh hush. He's fine. You two will get along great. Besides, he's hot, and so's his best friend."

"Lemme guess, you asked the friend out."

"Yep. I considered dating them both at the same time, but I thought you might like a break from studies. These guys are definitely a good distraction."

"Fine. What time?" I don't tell her about my growing interest in Micah. We've only been out once and awkwardness seems to follow us everywhere, but that isn't a good reason to give up.

"Seven. Meet us at the diner for some grub."

By the time seven rolls around, I am ready to head out in a pair of jeans and a camisole. Taryn will probably frown on my outfit the moment she sees me, but I'm not up for impressing some guy I don't even know. I throw a ruffled scarf around my neck, slip on a pair of earrings and examine myself in the mirror. It will have to do.

"Where you headed, Katie-Did?" Dad asks as I lace my shoes.

"Out with Taryn."

"And …" He gives me a questioning look.

"And some guys I don't know. Friends of Taryn's from class. Don't worry, I'm sure it's recorded in the database."

"Just be careful."

"I know."

Dad is always telling me to be careful. Most of the time, I ignore it and let it fly out of my head.

At the diner, Taryn, flanked by two guys, waits at the bar. One has his arm around Taryn's shoulders—her date, obviously—and the other leans with one elbow against the counter. His back leg crosses at an angle, giving him an ultra-casual look. When he sees me walking toward them, he straightens up and smiles.

"We're getting it to go, so hurry up and order," Taryn says sweetly.

I draw my ID card from my pants pocket and slip it into the computerized menu. A second later, choices that fit my body type, caloric intake, and weekly allowances pop up. I select a sandwich, figuring it'd be easier to consume picnic style than a messy plate of pasta. The whole time I watch out of the corner of my eyes to see Mr. Casual examining me with interest. I might have been disgusted by the way his eyes rove over my chest, but when my order comes, and he offers to carry it for me and even opens the door like a gentleman should, I give him the benefit of the doubt.

"I'm Saul," he says with a shy grin.

"Kate."

"Nice to meet you." He holds the door as I pass through.

Dodging under his arm, I notice someone sitting in the far corner of the diner. Micah. He glowers when Saul takes my hand. As we walk outside, I can't help but glance over my shoulder to see if he's still looking at us through the window. He's not. Instead, he stomps out the front doors and to a car parked across the lot. I hope he's not mad. Though, by the look on his face, I'd venture to say he is. It's not like we're exclusive or anything. Heck, we've only gone out once.

I turn my attention back to Saul when he says, "Taryn talks about you all the time, so I'm glad I can finally put a face with a name."

I glance at Taryn, who clings to her man's arm. "What? I only say nice things, I promise," she says.

"I don't believe you for a second," I say.

She laughs lightly as she introduces me to the guy standing beside her. "This is Cameron Jenkins." She pats his chest with her free hand.

"Cam. Please. Just Cam. My grandmother calls me Cameron."

I don't have time to respond because Saul opens the door to the car, and I slide in. Cam and Taryn take the back, and I know from her flirty giggles that she'll probably be spending the night in that back seat. I hope Saul isn't the type who minds sharing his car for such a purpose.

"So, where are we headed?"

Saul's dark, cropped hair gives his face a severe look, but his eyes are soft, like melted chocolate as he smiles at me.

"You'll see."

A few twists and turns down the main streets and Saul pulls the car into a parking lot of a small building near the far edge of The Institute's official grounds.

"Where are we?" Taryn asks as she steps out of the car, Cam not far behind her. "You aren't gonna do anything to us out here, right? Because we all know you Institute Military men are a little crazy!" She giggles.

I can't believe she'd dare say something so stupid. You don't mess with people like this. You never know what a person is willing to do to stay in good standings with Fishgold and the other Institute leaders. But Taryn doesn't seem to notice that her flippant comments could be counted as treason.

My gaze flip-flops from one guy to the other, gauging whether they are offended by her statement. Neither seems upset, so I think we've managed to avoid an issue.

"This is where we work," Cam says.

"And what exactly do you do?" I ask.

Saul grabs our dinner from the front seat and leads us to a little tree-covered area behind the building. Past the fence that surrounds the grounds are the Outer Lands. So close. "We're in military training."

"Not just *any* military training," Taryn adds, sidling up next to me. "Tier two military training."

Crap. I'm with the wrong guy. Tier two military training is for those in charge of the rebels. Specifically, capturing and torturing the rebels. Though, if you ask The Institute superiors, no torturing takes place. Ever. They say we're too civilized to torture someone, but their public displays of power certainly prove otherwise. If they're willing to cut the skin off someone's neck in public and not call it torture, I can't imagine what they're willing to do in secret.

Taryn's all over it as the guys lead us to a dry spot under the trees and pass out our food. "Wow, that must be fascinating."

Saul puffs out his chest. "Yeah."

"Don't let his sweet, good boy side fool you," Cam says. "Saul's at the top of the class. He's badass when it comes to new techniques."

Saul slaps Cam on the back of the head. "Shut up, punk. I have a girl here." He nods toward me, and Cam laughs.

"Aww, trying to hold back to impress the pretty one, huh?" Cam takes a seat next to Taryn, and the two are quickly involved in a private conversation. Saul sips his drink and looks into the distance, trying to ignore the awkward silence between us.

I figure I'll try to make small talk with Saul about his training. I'm sure he won't go into details. He doesn't seem like the kind of guy to brag about it. "So, what's your training like?"

He turns his head sideways to look at me before leaning back on his elbow. "I dunno. Normal, I guess. Mostly, I get to boss around the Tier fives. Drills and stuff. You've probably seen me and Cam on the front lawn of The Institute. We're the ones responsible for whipping those peons into shape."

"Ah. That's why you looked familiar." His smile softens his face, and I find myself smiling back. "So, is it true what Taryn and Cam said?"

"About me being the top of my class? Yeah."

"About you creating new techniques."

"Yeah. I guess."

"What sort of stuff do you do?" I pop the last bite of my sandwich into my mouth. "I mean, what kind of techniques?"

"Stuff to get people to talk."

I don't say anything, wondering if he'll tell me. I shouldn't want to know, but my curiosity wins.

A small grin plays across his lips. "Okay, so you know that guy they brought on stage this summer at the Parade of Values?"

I nod.

"Well, they brought him back here." He points to the building a few yards from where we sit. "Told us each to come up with a viable punishment that might get him to talk about the whereabouts of other NBRs. The Natural Born Rebels. Like a test. Best idea wins, you know. And, well, mine was chosen."

Now I can't help myself. I have to know what this guy is capable of. "So what did you suggest?"

"Fishgold actually gave me the idea when he scalped the guy in front of everyone. I suggested they take off all his skin that way. Little bits at a time. Then when it was gone, they could cut down further."

I try my hardest to hold my face in such a way that it doesn't reveal how horrified I am. It didn't equate. This calm-mannered guy who opened doors for me couldn't have possibly suggested something so horrific. And he doesn't look the least bit remorseful. Perhaps he sees my discomfort because he says, "Sorry. I shouldn't talk about it. It's supposed to be confidential. We all know The Institute doesn't harm people." He winks at me.

And we all know soldiers are *so good* at keeping their duties confidential.

"Enough about me." He waves his hand through the air, brushing the idea away. "Want a drink?" Pulling a flask from his back pocket, he unscrews the cap and smells the harsh liquid.

I smile. "I thought soldiers didn't drink?"

He brings it to his lips and takes a swig. "Soldiers aren't as keen on following the rules as you may think." He hands the bottle to me, and I drink. "And we're pretty trusting, too because we have ways of keeping people quiet."

I shudder.

"But," he continues, "any friend of Taryn's is trustworthy, right?"

I take another long draw on the burning alcohol to force up the courage to look at him. "Of course."

After that conversation, the night can't end soon enough, but we still have to wait out Taryn and Cam's make out session, so we take a walk to give them a little privacy. Saul asks details about my training as a creation specialist, but I don't have answers for many of the questions he asks.

After telling him that, "No, I hadn't yet performed a disposal," and, "Yes, I'd seen a live birth," we make it back to where Taryn and Cam are sitting. Taryn buttons up her shirt and pats down her mussed hair.

"We should head back," she says.

I agree, anxious to end this poor excuse for a date. Taryn would hear about this later.

***

Back in my bedroom, I flop down on my bed in an angry huff. "Seriously, girl, you are never allowed to set me up with someone again. I don't care how hot he is!"

"What? Was he a bad kisser or something?" she asked, pulling a comb through her strawberry locks.

"I don't know. Never got that far. He was too busy telling me about various ways to torture people."

"I know! Isn't it cool?"

I give her a look. "Seriously? What's wrong with you?"

"Oh, come on. They don't do that. He was just trying to impress you."

"Impressing me would mean bringing me flowers. Or helping my kid brother with a science project, *not* talking about war techniques."

"You don't even have a brother."

I shake my head and roll my eyes. "That's not the point." I lay down on my bed to stretch my legs.

Strapping her hair into a ponytail with a rubber band, Taryn crosses the room and sits next to me. "It's that Micah kid from the labs, isn't it?"

"What? No. I barely know him."

"You don't have to know someone to want to get naked with him."

"Taryn, not everyone has sex on the brain twenty-four hours a day."

"I don't see why not." She smiles and slides under the covers. "By the way, I'm sleeping here for the night. I told my parents before I left."

ELEVEN

TAKING OUT THE GARBAGE

W RITTEN ON THE BOARD at the front of class are two words: Disposal Techniques. Our topic for the day. Just what I need after my failed date last night. A heavy topic for study. It's simple. We breed the next generation, but sometimes during the breeding process, something goes wrong. In those cases, it's necessary to get rid of the developing fetus as soon as possible. Who would want invalids or deformed people living in our society? No one, of course. Only strong, intelligent, capable humans make up our community. No mistakes. We'll continue on our way to creating the medically perfect human being. Six feet for men and five-feet-eight inches for women. Everyone will have brown hair and brown eyes. So far, there's a little discrepancy when it comes to intelligence, but the MIH provide intellectual and physical enhancements every few years. The only thing the community allows us is our personalities. This way, they can't direct our career choices and spousal choices when the time comes. Maybe one day these will be selected for us as well.

The seat next to Taryn seems foreign. It's been a while since we've sat in the classroom. We've been too busy in the lab studying the stages of development. I slip into the chair and set my compact on the desk, pressing the button that makes it whir to life.

"Hey, chick!" Taryn's enthusiastic voice greets me. "Ready for this?" Her eyes glance at the whiteboard in front, and she gives me the double eyebrow raise.

I shrug. "I guess." It's the dismal part of this job, but we have to take the good with the bad, right?

"Seems kinda gross, but it's cool that we're the ones who have lives in our hands. Can you feel the power?" She laughs.

Before I can respond, the professor enters the room, turns off the lights and pulls in a two-tiered cart stacked with oversized Petri dishes behind him. "Sorry about the lack of light, students," he begins. "But instead of bringing you all to the lab for this first procedure, I brought the lab to you. Later on, when we learn the more advanced disposal techniques, we'll spend our time in the lab, but for the beginning of class today, this set-up is more practical."

No one says anything. We all watch as Professor Limbert stacks the dishes on his desk, placing one under the projector. This way, we can all see the proper ways to destroy the zygote as it's magnified on the screen.

"These zygotes have been marked for disposal." He reaches up and scratches his beard before looking around the class. It's a habit I've seen a hundred times in the classes I've had with Professor Limbert. I should be used to it now, but something about the way he winds his fingers through his own facial hair makes me cringe. Like he's scratching for bugs or something. Nothing like the way I've seen Micah make the same movement. For him, it's sexy. With the professor, I'm repulsed.

I glance at Taryn next to me who is scratching her own chin in response. It's like an unconscious reaction. She meets my gaze, and I smile at her before looking back toward the front of the room.

Professor Limbert flicks on the projector and sets one of the containers under the scope. Instantly, it comes into view on the big screen. Then he looks up at the class through the dim light. "Can anyone tell me why this one has been labeled for disposal?"

All eyes focus on the screen, some squinting to see better as if squinting will tell them the answer faster. The professor centers a cluster of cells so it's in the middle of the screen. Immediately, I spot a few that are warped. This could indicate diseases like sickle cell anemia or cancer.

It doesn't necessarily mean the baby will get those diseases, but there's a high probability they may develop into something in the future. It's better to destroy it now. That way, any hereditary diseases can be eradicated. A long time ago, there used to be more diseases like this. Diseases stemming from environmental factors. Now, our MIHs detect any disruptions in our bodies before they grow to a level of concern. These sort of sicknesses are taken care of at an early stage. Before birth early.

"Katherine Dennard?"

I look up.

"Can you tell us why this zygote was marked for disposal?" He's testing me to see if I've studied the material.

"Some of the cells are warped," I say. "It's more likely the baby will develop diseases like cancer in the future. By disposing of it now, we can prevent another strain of disease and hopefully rid our community of such devastation."

The professor breaks into a smile. Probably didn't expect me to answer proficiently. "Very good, Ms. Dennard. Since you answered correctly, you can assist me in disposing of this zygote."

I step out of my desk and move to the front of the room next to Professor Limbert, my hands growing clammier with every step. It's hard to see the faces of my classmates with the lights off, but when I turn my head to glance out the window, there is movement. Micah, standing with his face furrowed, is peering through the smudged glass. How has no one else seen him?

"It's pretty simple in these beginning stages," Professor Limbert says. "A few drops of Sodium Chloride will do the trick. It will stop all functions and render the cells incapable of dividing."

Why can't he just say it'll kill the cells? The professor always has to make things sound big and important. He hands me the dropper and motions to add some of the solution to the Petri dish.

I hold the dropper above the cells in the dish and squeeze lightly. It splashes when it hits the glass case. Turning, I watch the screen behind me to see the cells slow down and finally stop all movement. Strange how something so simple can end what would have been a life. It's better this way. It's just a mass of tissue, so there's no harm to anyone.

So much better to do it now than to wait until later. Imagine the pain a person might have to endure if he or she had to live with those diseases. It's ludicrous.

I set down the dropper and step away from the table, intending to return to my seat, but Professor Limbert stops me. "Miss Dennard, stay here a moment. I'll allow you to assist on one more procedure."

Without a word, I step forward again.

This time he reaches under the cart and pulls out a larger container, revealing a wiggling creature inside. It's only about an inch or so long, but there are arm buds and bulging dark spots that will become eyes. At the base of the container is written Ten Weeks. He places it on the viewing table and hands me a metal instrument.

"This one has been identified for disposal because after having been genetically screened, it tested positive for an abnormality on chromosome twenty-one, which indicates assured mental retardation." He hands me a pair of forceps, which feel like icy blades in my hand. "This is an embryo that would not be allowed to continue under any circumstances. In some cases, we wait to see how the developing embryo grows to see if it is solely a matter of birth weight or another minor issue that may resolve itself, but with a chromosomal defect, this is a definite disposal."

I'm trying to listen to his lecture, but the instrument in my hand feels heavier than I remember.

"The most common technique at this stage is to crush the skull and then dismember the rest." His voice is placid like he's said this a thousand times with no emotion.

Professor Limbert turns to me. "Hold the forceps around the skull."

I widen the edges so they fit around the head of the tiny fetus.

"Just a little bit of pressure will do the trick."

I barely have to close my hand to do the job. A lump catches in my throat, and I hear a few quick inhalations from my fellow classmates, who apparently find this procedure as repulsive as I do. Or maybe they're fascinated by the idea. If one is to become a Creation Unit Specialist, this comes with the territory. I suck in a breath and hold it a second to gain the composure I lost when the tiny creature ceased its movements under my slight hand pressure. It's not like it's a big deal, I convince myself. At this point, it's still a lump of tissue. If I'm ever going to be a Creation Specialist, I can't get emotional about every zygote and embryo I have to destroy.

The professor hands me another instrument, and I finish the job according to his instructions. I know I'm just doing what will be my profession, but something about it seems wrong. *Suck it up, Kate. You're pathetic if you can't do this little procedure.*

When I'm done, I set the instruments down and wait for permission to return to my seat, slightly sickened by what I've just done. The professor grants it, and as I turn to walk down the aisle, I glance toward the window to see if Micah is still there.

Clearly, no one else has noticed our fearless lab leader loitering on the grass outside the classroom. He's been there the whole time. Watching me. Micah's wide eyes stare deep into mine. Before he shakes his head and turns away, I see his jaw clench, hardening his stone features into granite.

For the first time in my life, I want to have the ability to read someone's mind. At this moment, I can't concentrate on what Professor Limbert is saying. Instead, I'm attempting to decipher the look on Micah's face as he walked away. Makes me wonder if I did something wrong. If so, wouldn't the teacher have said something? Ugh. He's so difficult to read. One day, we're nearly kissing and the next, he seems indignant. I need to stop caring what Micah is doing or thinking.

In the hushed bustle of the classroom, I return to my seat, my mind flicking between the images of the destroyed embryo and Micah's face through the window. Even when Professor Limbert hands out Petri dishes and syringes to the rest of the class for practice, I barely hear more than muffled grunts. I just sit staring at the front of the room, wondering what I'd just experienced. Because it was more than mere disposal techniques.

TWELVE

COMFORT FROM THE OLD AND SENILE

Code of Conduct and Ethics: The Institute—Sector 4, USA
Section 1 Article 4.1: Honor the elders in our community.

A s soon as class lets out, I text my mother.
Goin' 2 Grans.
Somehow Gran always has a way of putting things into perspective, so I figure a chat with her might help me sort out the millions of thoughts floating through my head.

My phone beeps. It's Mom. B home by dinner.

Sure, no problem. I can't afford to miss another dinner. If so, I'll rack up a demerit on my record and will be escorted wherever I go by a member of The Institute's police force. I think I'll avoid that.

I'm trying to text back when a tall, lanky body steps into my path, practically running into me. I'm about to mumble something snide until I look up and see Micah. This bumping into each other is becoming a habit.

"Oh, sorry," I say as I attempt to step around him.

He sidesteps, but quickly falls in line with me. I'm still looking at my phone, trying to ignore him through the muddle of my brain. I mean, sure I like him and all, but after today, I need some alone time. Though

I am curious to know why he milled around outside the class today like a Peeping Tom.

We're quiet for another few steps. Then he sighs lightly and runs his hand through his hair. It flops back into the same place on his forehead when he releases it. His voice sounds tentative, and he sticks out his neck and whispers a little. "You okay after that class?"

"Yeah, I'm fine. Why wouldn't I be?" I curl my shoulders around myself in a miserable attempt to hide the truth, the truth I want to ask Gran about.

His hand hovers behind my back as if he's not quite sure if he should touch me or not. "No reason," he says. His hair falls in his eyes again.

Maybe you should just cut your hair, I think. But then I wouldn't be able to admire his hand-in-hair habit or that little neck flick that makes his chiseled jaw stick out. It's a nice distraction from my worries.

Micah's feet fall into step alongside mine. "I know a first disposal can be a little rough. Seen it happen hundreds of times." His eyes glisten in the light, but he blinks the glaze away. "I mean, I know it's just tissue," he adds as an afterthought, "but it still can have an effect on certain types of people."

"Really, Micah, I'm fine. Thanks for your concern, but you don't have to worry about me. I'm not that *type* of person." It sounds authentic even if it is a fib. The sweaty palms and queasy stomach I've been fighting since class prove to me he's probably right. I can't say I feel the disposal was wrong, just strange. Foreign. New.

"Can I walk you to where you're going?"

So much for shrugging him off. I can see I'm not going to win this one, so I give in. "Yeah, that'd be nice." Maybe alone time isn't what I needed anyway. Wasn't I headed to visit Gran in the first place? Not like I'd be alone there, anyway. And I have to admit, his presence calms my nerves.

We're halfway across the grass before he asks, "So, where are you going?"

I snicker. "Sorry, um, I'm headed to visit my gran."

"And you don't mind the company?"

"No, in fact, Gran loves meeting new people." A chance to talk about something else is nice. "It'll give her something to gossip about for days. She's one of the last remaining Wombers, you know."

"Really? A Natural born?"

"Yeah. She's my great-grandmother, and I have to warn you. She's a little senile. She'll probably say some crazy stuff." The lie slips easily past my lips. It's become second nature. "Some days are better than others. She could be non-communicative or she could be chatting to Van Gogh."

"Van Gogh?"

"She has a print in her room of *Starry Night*. She talks to it. Tells rambling stories about the old days, at least until someone comes to give her extra meds she doesn't need. They think drugging her up till she can barely function is the best option." Staring at my feet suddenly seems like the right thing to do. Adding that bit about the meds wasn't smart. Micah could assume I'm against medicating my gran, which would mean I'm against the policy of The Institute. I have to be more careful.

We're quiet as we walk the rest of the way there. Passing the soldiers in their drill formations with Saul at the front makes my silence even louder. And when I see him and Micah make eye contact as we pass, I want to curl up into a ball and roll away. But thankfully, nothing happens and no one says anything.

***

A few minutes later, we're standing outside Gran's room. Leaning on the door, I poke my head inside. "Gran, it's me, Kate."

She's sitting in her bed covered with a thin blanket. "Katie-Did!" she squeals.

Normally, my visit would allow her time to be herself if I could get her out of her assigned room, but I sharply shake my head to let her know that's not the case today. Today, she has to keep up her senile act.

"I brought a visitor."

A look of disappointment flashes across her cheeks, but she understands. Our visits are becoming fewer and fewer thanks to the increased surveillance at The Institute. The only place we can talk now is by the river. Since the lawns crawl with soldiers, a simple walk over the grounds is too dangerous for a normal chat anymore.

When I was younger, I used to visit at least three days a week. We'd stroll around the campus or sit by the river, and Gran would tell me stories about her childhood. A time when nobody had to watch their backs. Some days she'd tell me things she'd overheard that morning. "They're disposing a larger batch of embryos today, Katie-Did," she had said. "One doc said they'll just have to randomly choose since so many were healthy. To think that someone's future is in the hands of one doctor's opinion. Maybe when you're a Creation Engineer, you can stop all that nonsense." Another time she told me about the meds. "You know Mitzy Hart, the Womber from down the hall?" she asked me that day. "She overheard something the nurses were saying and tried to tell her son about it when he came to visit. The next day she was so drugged up, she couldn't even speak. They've kept her like that ever since. I know; I was visiting her when it happened." It had to be true. Ms. Hart never uttered a word and lived in a medicated haze until she was discharged a year later.

After that incident, we began to see changes. More patrol officers in the hallways. Surveillance cameras in all the rooms. Our talks became fewer, and we had to be more creative with our communication. It was then Gran started pulling the dementia bit. She thought she might be able to observe better if they didn't think she could understand. It took years to perfect the act and to get to the point where the doctors recognized the signs. I knew better then, and I know better now. So when she goes into one of her rants, I listen carefully, sure she's giving me information on something she's overheard. I'm usually right.

Moments later, Micah pulls a chair around for me to sit, and we nestle in on opposite sides of the bed. A glance around the room reveals bare walls. They've even taken down her painting, the sole bright spot in this dismal place. I make the introductions. "Gran, this is Micah. He's my lab assistant at school." I motion with my hand. Her head sways in his direction, and her eyes stare emptily at his face. "Micah, Gran. One of the last surviving Wombers."

Reaching out his hand, Micah offers his greeting. She places her wrinkled hand in his, and he lightly kisses it. "Nice to meet you, Mrs. Dennard."

I must be imagining things, but for a second, I swear Gran's eyes sparkle at him.

"A true gentleman treats a woman with respect. 'Looking at the stars always makes me dream.' Until the stars are gone," she says. "I want my stars back." The pendant around her neck glints against the florescent lighting, a small turtle with a jade shell. She caresses it with her fingertips as she talks. "I want the stars. I need to see the stars. They took them. Said they were broken. They do *not* like broken stars!"

Micah leans halfway over the bed, looking extremely uncomfortable. "What's she talking about?"

"Not sure," I lie. The Van Gogh is missing, and she knows it. It's one of the few things she actually owns. That and her pendant. Everything else was stripped from her possession when she came to live here. I have to get it back for her. Or, at least, find one like it. "I'll take you to see the stars sometime soon, Gran. I promise."

Micah has eased back into his seat and looks slightly more comfortable. "Mrs. Dennard, when I was a kid, my dad used to take me outside to look at the stars. Have you ever seen the pictures in the stars?"

Her eyes grow wide, and she examines his face. "Words. In the stars. I read words in the stars."

"No, not words. Pictures. Like the great bear or Orion, the hunter. It's like a connect-the-dots."

"Words. I read words in the stars." Gran's growing increasingly frantic as she looks back and forth from Micah to me. "I need my stars."

I lay my hand on her arm. "It's okay, Gran. I'll get your stars. Micah was just telling you stories." My touch calms her. She lays her head back on the pillow and closes her eyes for a minute. When she opens them, she looks at Micah again. This time, she sounds entirely lucid.

"Who are you?"

With a smile he says, "I'm Kate's friend."

She rolls her head toward me. "He's handsome. A handsome boy. A handsome boy for my Katie-Did." Her shaky hands pull Micah's hand toward mine where she places his on top of mine over her lap. "There, that's better."

The look on Micah's face is a mix of embarrassment and contentment. I smile and pull my hand out from under his, but Gran sees the motion and replaces my hand on top of his before turning to him. "You take care of my Katie-Did, you hear? A strong, handsome boy like you can take care of her."

He nods and covers her hand with his free one. "I will, Ms. Dennard. I promise." Then he looks at me and shrugs.

"Maybe we should get going," I suggest. "She's not doing well today."

"Sure. No problem." Micah steps into the hallway as I take a moment to tuck the blankets around Gran's legs again.

"We have to go, Gran. I'll come back soon, okay?" Unexpectedly, Gran's hand snakes out from under the blanket and grabs my wrist.

"Kate, things are going to be right as rain," she whispers. "He's unmarked. Like me." She puts something cold and hard in my hand and closes my fingers around it. Opening my hand, I see the necklace that usually hangs around her neck.

"Gran, I can't take this." But she closes my fingers around it once more.

"Go," she says.

I don't argue because right then a nurse comes in to check on her. I slip the necklace over my head and tuck it in my shirt. It's not till I get to where Micah is standing that I remember what she said about him. But I know it's impossible. An ID tattoo isn't exactly something you can hide.

Perhaps Gran really is going senile because she obviously doesn't know what she's talking about. Must be she didn't see his mark. Micah's back is turned, and though his hair curls over his neck, the black barcode is clearly imprinted at the base of his skull. Obviously, she's wrong.

Our feet hit the grass, and we walk without a sound for a moment. Then I let out an awkward snicker. "You'll never guess what my gran said to me just as we were leaving."

"What's that?"

"It's so absurd, you'll laugh."

He smiles. "What is it?"

"She told me you were unmarked. Isn't that crazy?"

His laugh is slow and uneasy. Then he raises his dark eyebrows at me, and I nearly forget what we're talking about for a second. All the colors of the earth blur by in a muddled mix, and all I see is his face. "Must be she didn't see my tattoo," he says. "Guess that means I need a haircut." He grins and runs his long fingers through the back of his hair, grabbing a handful of messy curls, lifting them high enough for me to get a good look before scratching the back of his head. It's the same as the rest of ours. About an inch and a half long with lines varying in width. His number is inked underneath. 1105103.

Man, I wish I could run my fingers through those curls. "Heh, yeah, I guess not." I shake my head. This whole conversation is awkward, and I wish I hadn't brought it up. No need to make anyone uncomfortable. Not to mention it's another thing I should've kept to myself. What is it about Micah that makes my brain want to reveal secrets I've kept from everyone I know? I change the subject before I get myself into any more trouble. "So, where're you headed now?"

"Home, then back to the lab for the evening class. I have some research to do later, too. You?"

"Home for dinner. Mom was specific about being home tonight. She must have something planned." I leave out the part about any possible demerits.

"Well, in that case," Micah says, "I'll leave you here."

We're standing at a break in pavement where the sidewalk splits into two paths. "Oh, right. Have a good night, then."

"You, too." He takes off down the path, and I'm ashamed to admit, I watch him until he disappears behind a patch of trees before turning to walk home.

With each step, I find myself chanting his number in my head. *1105103. 1105103. 1105103.* There's something strange about that number. Something not quite right. By the time I open the door to the smells of my mother setting the evening meal on the table, I still haven't figured it out.

THIRTEEN

APOLOGIES WITH GIFTS

Code of Conduct and Ethics: The Institute—Sector 4, USA
Section 2 Article 7.3: Respect one another's property. Crimes such as
theft, defamation, or vandalism will lead to severe justice with the
possibility of jail time.

URING THE NEXT LAB, Micah whispers he has something for
me.
"What is it?"
"A surprise," he says, "But I promise you'll love it."
Right. Because he already knows me well enough to buy me gifts. I
doubt it. *Positive thinking today, Kate.*

When there's a break in the lab procedure, we head to the back room
and sit while the tests finish running. Some of the other students, including Taryn and her partner, lounge on couches to wait out the thirty
minutes we have for the chemicals to set.

I'm just about to sit next to her when Micah grabs my elbow and
says, "Hang on. I have to show you something."

I give him a fake annoyed look even though I secretly want to jump
into his arms. "Right now?"

He raises his dark eyebrows as if to say, "Um, yes, remember I have
something for you."

"Oh, right." I turn to Taryn. "Be right back."

She cocks her head, confused.

"Tell you later," I mouth silently.

"You better," she mouths back.

Micah ushers me into a tiny storage room and shuts the door behind us. Turning to me, he puts his finger to his lips. With an extension pole, he slowly pushes the camera just inside the door so the lens is pointing toward the far wall. Propping the pole against the doorway, he turns to me and smiles. "If we stay near the door, they won't see us. The cameras in these storage rooms are older. They don't record sound."

I smile and finger the necklace Gran gave me that hangs around my neck.

"What?"

"Do you realize what people are going to think when we come out of here? Okay, not all people. Just Taryn."

A mischievous smirk pulls back across his face. "I guess we better make sure your hair is all nice and neat when we leave then, shouldn't we?"

Oh dear, that's not what I expect him to say, and I immediately feel the red rush of heat spread across my cheeks. The wink he adds sends the heat down over my arms and legs, but I manage a subtle smile and quickly change the subject. "So what's this big surprise?"

"First, I need to make sure you're okay with bending the rules a little."

That's an odd question. "What do you mean, 'bending the rules'?"

He shakes his head. "Nothing major. Nothing that'll get us in trouble if you don't say anything, which I'm thinking you won't. But if you'd rather not chance it, just say so, and I'll forget all about it."

Okay, way too confusing. "Just tell me. I'm not going to say anything to get you in trouble unless you're a total psycho freak who's brought a gun in here to try to kill me."

Micah smiles and reaches into the pocket of his bag. I take one step back, just in case. But when I see what he's holding, I jump toward him and toss my arms around his neck before I realize how inappropriate this is. *Code of Conduct and Ethics: The Institute—Sector 4, USA Section 5*

Article 5.13: Public displays of affection are strictly prohibited. Infractions of this rule will be subject to a personal escort and community service.

I awkwardly pull away, relaxing when I see the grin on Micah's face. His fingertips linger on my hip.

I take the slightly squished pumpkin scone from Meg's Café out of his hands and bring it to my nose to smell. "Oh my goodness! How did you get this? It's fresh! Why did you …? I'm confused." I stumble over my words.

His grin grows wider, obviously content with my overreaction. "Let's just say I have connections. I wanted to make up for the awkwardness the other night by the river. Thought maybe a little gift might earn me some bonus points."

"You totally get bonus points. And a gold star."

"What do I get when I get five gold stars?" Brushing the crumbs off his hands, he continues, "I know you probably had a scone this morning, but it won't hurt to have an extra, now and then, without recording it into the database. The Institute doesn't have to know everything."

His face holds something mysterious. Like he's said more in that statement than he intended.

"Agreed." I bite into the soft, spicy dough. It tastes dangerous as it melts in my mouth. I've always wanted to do this. Eat extra without recording it, but until now, there's been no way to acquire extras. The pre-portioned meals and anything purchased at a restaurant or café makes it impossible to do this. Makes me wonder why we have to record at all, but I suppose the tracking system is just another way to make sure the people are doing what they're supposed to be doing. All I know is that if we miss a day or two, we receive a warning notice on our compacts. If we miss more, our food portions will be diminished and our treat allowance will be revoked. So it's wisest to suck up the inconvenience of it and give The Institute what it wants.

"Make sure you hide it, or others will notice. Better to let them think we were in here doing something scandalous." Raking both hands through his hair, he makes it stick up in all directions and untucks his shirt. "Messy enough to start some good rumors?"

I laugh. "Definitely!" But when he reaches for the door, I pull him back, giggling. "Micah! You can't go out there like that!" He laughs as I wrap the half-eaten scone in a napkin. I set it aside and do what I've been dying to do since I first saw him. I run my fingers through his dark hair, taming it back into place. It's silky, and the waves wrap around my fingers as I tuck them behind his ears. My fingers slide down his jaw, tracing the scratchy stubble along his chin and stay there.

His eyes turn turbulent as his gaze flits across my face. Without warning, his calloused palms cradle my cheeks, and before I can think to pull back, his lips are on mine. Soft and hungry.

The kiss doesn't last long, but it's followed by more that linger on my tingling lips. They take my breath away. I've never been kissed like that before. A small peck on a first date I had to report to the database because my mother nagged me about every intimate detail, but nothing like this. I want to hide this kiss. Not report it to anyone, much less to The Institute's database. I want this kiss to be just for me and Micah—a secret we share.

Finally, he releases me from his grasp and steps back. "Sorry, I shouldn't have done that." He presses his eyes shut and runs a thumb and forefinger across his eyebrows, relieving the stress that's gathered there. "This isn't why I brought you the treat."

"No. It's fine," I say, as the hot flush returns to my face. I look at my feet. He opens his eyes and meets my gaze. "Really."

"Apparently, there's something about you I can't stay away from." His shoulders relax, and his lips pull back over his teeth. For a second, I think he's going to kiss me again, which would be okay with me, but he doesn't. "I'm sorry."

"Really, Micah, it's okay. Better than okay."

"I'm glad." He glances at his watch. "We should probably join the others before they start to wonder what we're doing."

"You're right," I smooth my hair into place.

How did I go from thinking he might be an Institute spy to making out in the storeroom in a matter of four days? I probably should still be careful, but any guy who manages to get his hands on illegal scones for me and kisses me like that is on my *Oh my … Yes!* list. And I won't say a word to anyone.

With the remnants of the scone tucked safely into Micah's bag—I left mine in the classroom—we exit. I'm met by Taryn's questioning grin. Micah busies himself with some administrative work as he stands near the door. Sitting down next to Taryn, I lean over and whisper. "He showed me some new instruments we're going to use in the next few labs." It's a lame lie, but with my mind spinning and my lips still tingling from his kiss, it's the best I can come up with.

"I'm sure," Taryn says, clearly doubting my explanation. She raises her eyebrows at me, and I return her look with a shy smile. "That's what I thought!"

Dang! "Don't say anything, okay, T?"

"I promise, I won't say a word, as long as you give details."

"Not much to tell other than he's the best kisser I've ever known."

She beams and pats my leg. "About freakin' time."

"Taryn, we've gone out once, and it didn't go well. A bit awkward, actually."

"That's never stopped me. I don't even have to date a guy to make out with him." It's true, and I know Taryn won't say a word. She's done much more than kissing without reporting it. I still can't believe she's never been caught.

A few minutes later, Micah announces to the group, "Time to head back to the lab, people. The chemicals should've set by now." He leads the way, with me in tow followed by the rest of my classmates. It's then that my phone rings. Micah glances at me with a questioning look. I hold up my finger to indicate I'll be a minute and step to the back of the group.

"Hello?"

"Hello, Kate?"

I don't recognize the voice. "Yes, who is this?"

"It's Saul. Remember, we went out with your friend Taryn the other night."

Right. Mr. Freaky Torture guy. Why is he calling me? "Um, Hi. How did you get this number?" I know I didn't give it to him. Then I get nervous.

"Soldiers have access to personal accounts. I looked it up."

Creepy.

I need to bring this conversation to a close. Actually, I need to bring this whole relationship to a close. Make it clear I don't want to see him again. "Oh. I see." I'm trying to sound cheerful. "Look I have to get going. I'm in the middle of a lab."

"Sorry about that. I just wanted to apologize for the other night. I didn't mean to scare you off."

Great. He's apologizing. Now how do I let him down? "It's okay. It was … nice to hang out." It's the only thing I can think of.

"Will you let me make it up to you?"

Umm, pass …

"Saul … It's not a great time for me right now. I'm swamped with my studies, and I'm in the lab all the time."

His voice loses its luster when he says, "In that case, I won't call again."

"Saul … I'm s—" But it's too late. He's already hung up.

When I reach the lab, everyone's already at their stations working. I slip my coat on and find Micah standing over a microscope. He glances up. "You okay? You look upset."

"I'm fine."

"Who was on the phone?"

"No one. Wrong number."

His eyes meet mine, and I know he knows I'm lying. But thankfully, he doesn't push it. "Take a look at this," he says. And I do. Because I'll do anything to rid Saul from my mind.

FOURTEEN

···································

CAUGHT

Code of Conduct and Ethics: The Institute—Sector 4, USA
Section 3 Article 2.8: ID badges shall be carried at all times.

"YOU UP FOR A walk later?"

Since our kiss, I've barely seen Micah other than in class, so when he offers a walk during lunch on Thursday, I jump at the chance.

"I'll meet you outside the Education Department doors at noon," he says.

"Sure."

Noon rolls around, and he's waiting for me on the front steps, leaning against the stone wall lining the sidewalk. His hands are shoved deep into his pockets, and he's missing his usual attire: a lab coat. With the top few buttons of his shirt undone and his dark, wavy hair curling around the base of his neck, I want to kiss him. But I don't. Too many people would see.

He smiles and nods his head toward the walkway. "Ready?"

"Where're we going?"

"Nowhere in particular. Just thought you'd enjoy the outdoors for a little while."

We stroll toward the tree line along the far side of The Institute's borders and travel up the sidewalk near where I take Gran on our special walks. Since Micah and I have been there once before, I wonder if we're headed there again. But instead of leading me to the clearing, Micah enters the line of trees a little farther down.

"Are you taking me to the Outer Lands?" I whisper. Excitement bubbles in my gut.

Micah smiles. "Not quite, but you'll be able to see it from where we walk."

He's right. As we hike along the riverbank barely inside the trees, I can see the fencing in the distance. It's as close as we can get to the Outer Lands without crossing boundaries. A tease. But being here in the forest with Micah excites me enough. I don't need the rush of rebellion just now. This is my opportunity to get to know him more intimately. Well, not *that* intimately.

A tree branch bends toward us in the wind, and Micah reaches up to snap off a branch. He twists the leaves off as we walk farther. "So, tell me why you chose the Creation Department? Aren't plants your thing?"

"Plants? Um. No. Definitely not." The sound of crowds rushing down the sidewalk just inside the tree-lined border distracts me. "I think I wanted something different from what my parents do. My mom's a criminal interpreter. Working with criminals doesn't interest me in the least. And my Dad works at the Data Collection Agency. That seemed a little mundane to do the rest of my life, so I sought out biology. I was pretty good at it, so here I am."

"Do you love it?"

"Of course. Why?"

"Because even if The Institute chooses what we do, we should be able to love it," he states matter-of-factly. "How sad if we were stuck in a job we hated, with no way out, you know?"

"But The Institute doesn't make mistakes, remember?"

He drops the twig and takes my hand in his. "Yeah, I know." There's a distant look in his eyes, but it fades when he cradles my face, pulling it closer to his for a kiss.

When I pull back, I see movement over Micah's shoulder. Through the break in the trees, I recognize where we are. The building where Saul works. And leaning against the door is Saul, staring right at us.

I drop Micah's hand, and we cross out of the trees and into the sunlight, walking straight toward Saul. I would have liked to have crawled back into the brush of the forest, but addressing the issue might be the best way to handle this predicament.

"Saul?"

He's not impressed with my attempt to make conversation. Maybe it's because I blew him off on the phone not long ago. Sorry, but talking about how to put people in pain is not my idea of a love connection. Apparently, it is for Saul.

"IDs, please."

Crap! There will be no talking ourselves out of this one. Micah draws his wallet out of his pocket and hands it over while I dig for mine. "We were just enjoying the warm air on our lunch break, Mr. ...?" Micah says.

"Goodman."

"Mr. Goodman. Spending all day in the Disposal Center makes the eyes go buggy after a while."

"Disposal Center?" Saul asks.

I jump in. "Yes, Micah is in charge of teaching proper disposal techniques to residents like me."

Saul flips my ID over in his hands without even looking at it. He's too busy examining me and Micah. Probably determining if we're worth the hassle of all the paperwork he'd have to fill out in order to report us. His eyes shift from me to Micah. "Stick to the sidewalks next time."

"Absolutely, sir," Micah replies.

We take our IDs and rush across the fading grass around the building.

"That was close," I say when I know we're out of hearing range. Why on earth would Saul let us go? Especially after I denied him a second date. He's got to be irate with me, so there's no reason to be nice and let me off the hook. It doesn't make any sense.

"Too close." Micah slows our pace as we near the education building. "So, you know that guy?"

My eyes roll back into my head. Like Micah didn't already know. He saw me leave the diner with Saul that night. "Had a date once."

This piques Micah's interest, and he stops in his tracks and turns, waiting for me to continue as if he hadn't seen us that night. "Really? Now that is interesting."

I grab his wrist and give it a tug to keep him walking. "You don't have to play dumb. I know you saw us. But don't worry, it didn't go well."

He concedes with a nod and lets his hand slide into mine, lacing our fingers together as we walk. "Like our first date?"

The sensation warms me, but I try my hardest not to look at our intertwined fingers. For now, I'll revel in his touch.

"Worse. Much worse! Believe me; you don't want to hear about it, and I don't want to tell."

We're almost to the front steps of the Education Department. "Thanks though," I say.

"For what?"

"Saving my butt back there with Saul. If you hadn't mentioned the disposal unit, I'm sure he would've written us up." I avoid his eyes. "Saul doesn't like me much anymore. We didn't get off to a great start."

"Sometimes knowing what they want to hear is half the battle." Micah grabs the door. "After you," he says, stepping aside.

FIFTEEN

....

SECRETS

Each passing week brings with it more work. Between Professor Limbert and Professor Donovan, who've taken to asking me to assist them on just about any menial task, I've been swamped. So by the time I get out of labs, it's dark again. It doesn't help that the days are growing shorter and shorter. It's not terribly cold yet. No snow or anything, but the crispness of autumn is in the night air. How did the summer pass so quickly? Swinging my coat over my shoulders, I button it tight and wrap the grass-colored scarf several times around my neck. Gran made it for me when her hands could still hold the yarn steady. The wrap is tattered and some strings are tied together by my amateur hands, but it still holds its original beauty.

Apparently, my bundled look isn't a clue to Professor Limbert that I want to head home.

"Katherine," he calls as I'm walking out the door. "Could you file these papers for me before you leave tonight? They're the fetuses marked for disposal."

Sigh. Here we go again.

"I've been called on an emergency and need to leave now. These need to be in by the end of the night."

I glance around the lab; Stewart Johns is hovering over a Petri dish. There's no way Professor Limbert would ask him. He'd screw up the filing system for sure. I'm sure he can't afford another demerit for disorganization. Other than him, the room is empty.

Sigh again.

"Sure, Professor. No problem." *Code of Conduct and Ethics: The Institute—Sector 4, USA Section 3 Article 4.2: An upstanding member of our community always volunteers for any task*—or in my case, gets volunteered.

He hands me a stack of files and zips his briefcase while rushing out the door. "Thanks, Katherine. I knew I could count on you."

Of course, it's not just two or three files. No. He's given me at least fifty. Great. I'll be here for another hour. With a humph, I trudge down the hallway to the records room, yanking the scarf off my neck with one hand as I go. *Code of Conduct and Ethics: The Institute—Sector 4, USA Section 3 Article 1.9: All work should be completed with a joyful, healthy attitude. Nonadherence to this ethic will result in weekly counseling.* Screw the Code of Conduct. There's no one around to notice my grousing anyway, so I head down to the filing room grumbling under my breath.

The hallways are quiet tonight; though by nine o'clock, this part of The Institute is usually calm, all the students having already gone home to download and memorize the next day's notes. Perhaps there'll be a few stragglers finishing up a lab, but as I walk past a few doors, no one is in sight.

The records room is just down the hallway from the lab, and as I lean my weight into the door, I notice the lab door is ajar. No lights are on, so I ignore it. I'll make sure to close the door when I leave, but right now, I want to get these files put away as fast as possible.

Slapping the pile of manila folders on the counter, I whip off my coat. The less cumbersome I feel, the faster I'll work. The faster I work, the sooner I can get home and fall into bed.

"Numerical order first," I whisper to myself, but in the silence of the room, it sounds like a scream. Once I have them in order, I start filing. Having to document files takes longer than I anticipate. I have to record the fetus's number and the number of the potential parents on a separate chart before I place the file in the cabinet. Ugh. What a pain. But after a few files, I start to get into the groove and move a little faster. Professor Limbert gave me an access code to the fetal database, so I don't have to do everything by hand, which is good. It saves time.

I'm nearly to the end of the pile with an hour and fifteen minutes under my belt—so much for a decent night's sleep—when I spot something out of place.

I'm writing the numbers on the chart without thinking. Fetus: 1298732. Mother: 1205901. Father: 1200743, and I'm about to squeeze the file into the cabinet when I stop short.

Not believing, I check the numbers again. Mother: 1205901. Father: 1200743.

No.

It can't be.

Wrestling my ID card out of my bag, I triple check.

It's not possible. An unauthorized creation.

It's my ID number. I have a baby.

One marked for disposal.

. . . .

SIXTEEN

A GOVERNMENT COVER-UP

Code of Conduct and Ethics: The Institute—Sector 4, USA
Section 2 Article 3.5: Honesty is always best. Whether young or old, a
demonstration of truth is expected.

N A DAZE, I file the last few papers for Professor Limbert. The feeling of dread is so overpowering, my only thought is how quickly I can get out of here and end this living nightmare.

A baby.

My baby.

I shake the thought out of my head for a millisecond, but it sneaks back in, crushing all rational thought. I go through the motions of locking up in a zombified haze.

Closing the drawer, I press the lock on the top of the cabinet, safely shutting away the secret forever. Gone. I can put it out of my mind, walk out of this room, and forget I ever saw it.

I suck in a deep breath, attempting to stop the shaking that's taken over my limbs, but it doesn't work, and soon, I find myself on the floor, hugging my knees.

How is this possible? I never authorized my eggs to be used. I certainly didn't apply for a child; even if I wanted to, there's a minimum age for motherhood, and it's not seventeen. It must be a mistake. A huge mistake. The problem is that The Institute doesn't make mistakes, much less big ones. But there has to be some explanation. Like a student wrote down the wrong number. More than anything, I hope this is the answer.

An inkling of peace washes over me knowing this particular fetus has been marked for disposal. In any case, I won't be a mother. But The Institute will try again, I'm sure. They always do, until they're successful. It's the way of things around here. But what does that mean for me? Are they going to start creating children and assigning them to the parents before they're even wanted? Heck, I'm not even married. Who would raise the child? Me or the father?

I stop at the thought. Who is the father? I didn't recognize the ID number, but then again, I didn't look closely.

What am I going to do? How is this possible? Questions race through my mind in a rollercoaster of emotions, and fear sweeps over my body like the wind. Then it all comes to a screeching halt. I suck it up, wipe my face of the tears that rolled onto my cheeks, and stand up. I hold the wall until I'm sure I can walk without passing out. The shock is still flowing through my veins, and I'm afraid I'll fall over if I can't get a hold of myself.

The records room sits in the back of the lab, which means I'll have to walk through the third trimester room, seeing all the fetuses lined up. Each one with its tiny face and fingers. So perfect. Taking a cleansing breath, I push through the door, keeping my eyes on the exit at the far end leading to the second trimester room.

I rush through so I don't have to look at the growing babies because the thought makes me wonder what this child of mine would look like. But when I reach the door on the far side leading to the last room, I pause. He's in there. Or she. In one of those growing chambers.

It's no big deal. I tell myself. *The child will be disposed of. I filed the paperwork myself. It's not like I have a connection to it. So it shouldn't be difficult to walk through the room it's in.*

The *Code of Conduct and Ethics for The Institute—Sector 4, USA Section 4, Article 7.8: Familial obligations are the backbone of our community.*

Quality time with family members creates a safe, loving environment necessary for raising children.

What about raising the children who were never meant to be? Do I have obligations now?

Buying another minute to collect myself, I take a deep breath and work on the whole coat-buttoning, scarf-tying ritual, which serves to calm my spirit again. But while I'm standing in front of the last lab door, fighting with a stubborn button, I hear a noise. The door's propped open with a pencil.

A dim pink glow filters through the window. It's not bright enough to be from the room itself. As I peer closer, it moves, flickering through the darkness.

Someone's in there.

I look through the glass pane of the second door and into the darkness. It takes my eyes a moment to adjust, but soon, I see the source of the stream of light. It's a flashlight held in the mouth of a hunched figure. The light coming from the end is filtered red, hence the pink glow I observed. He's standing along the far wall where the Petri dishes are stored. The door to the storage unit is open. He doesn't appear to sense me watching him, so I inch the door open to get a better look at the intruder. Suddenly, my foot connects with something and sends it skidding across the floor. The pencil.

The figure shoves something in his pocket and turns to face me. He's about to make a break for it past me when I see his face.

"Micah?"

"Kate?"

His stance instantly relaxes and turns casual, and his gait morphs into a saunter as he crosses toward me like there's nothing weird about this situation at all. Doesn't everyone sneak around the lab with filtered flashlights after dark? It's perfectly normal.

"What're you doing here?" I ask.

"Me?"

I look around at the lack of bodies in the room before I say. "No, all the other guys with flashlights in here. Yeah, you."

"I forgot my keys earlier. Got all the way home before I realized it." He pulls them out of his pocket and jangles them in front of my face.

I purse my lips and raise my eyebrows. "And you needed a red, filtered flashlight to look for them?"

He smiles slightly. "No need to turn on the lights or filtration system. I was only going to be a minute. He looks at me and smiles wider. "But I think I'll stick around now that you're here."

"Right, because everyone I know carries filtered flashlights in their pockets for just such an occasion."

"Hey," he mutters, "when you're the lab assistant, you'll learn all sorts of tricks like this." He changes the subject. "What about you? Why are you here?"

"Me?" The way I say it makes me sound like *I* have something to hide. I didn't. Not until I came here and discovered I have a child. Even though I've done nothing wrong, I find myself wanting to cover up the secret. "Filing." I pat my bag holding my compact. "For Limbert."

Micah makes a sound of understanding, and his eyes flick around the room like he's looking for something. Or someone. He shoves his keys deep into his pocket. "I was just heading out."

"Don't let me stop you from leaving," I say.

Micah turns back and holds the door open like a gentleman. I step through and walk into the hallway. I don't feel like being pampered with doors held open for me at this particular moment. I just want to get home and try to figure out this whole fiasco. Being tired and cranky doesn't wear well on me.

"Can I walk you home?"

His face shines an eerie red in the glow of the exit sign above our heads. I'm about to say no, but he's got this innocent look on his face, and maybe being with another human being, even for a few moments, might help clear my head. Before I can catch myself, I hear my own voice as we step into the hallway. "Sure, that'd be great."

The heavy door clanks shut behind us, burying my secrets behind its thick metal.

It's dark, so when Micah says, "It looks like something's bothering you," I wonder how he can even see it. Am I that transparent?

"Do you ever wonder if we have any control over our lives at all?"

"What do you mean?"

"I guess I feel like things are happening around me, and I can't control them."

"Actually, I'm pretty sure we make our own choices."

"But what if we don't?" The clomp of our footsteps along the pavement taps a rhythmic pattern that comforts my chaotic mind. "Think about it. Fishgold and the other leaders make decisions for the entire community all the time. They can choose what they want, and we all have to live with it. Not that that's a bad thing. I'm sure they make good decisions for the success and health of us all. But what if they don't tell us all the things they do to keep our community safe? Whatever they do, we are forced to deal with the consequences."

His hands still in his pockets, he leans a little closer but doesn't reach out. "Sounds like you've been doing a lot of thinking lately. What's got your mind churning?"

I tighten my coat against the chilly night air and look at the stars above me. "Nothing. I guess I'm just struck by the idea that one decision someone else makes influences all the choices I have to make."

"But," he says, "no matter what comes our way, good or bad, we have the power to choose how we respond. No one can make those choices for us."

"Unless they use torture." I glance at him wide-eyed, knowing my mistake. "I mean, I know that sort of thing doesn't happen around here, but theoretically speaking." I wish I could get ahold of my tongue around Micah. The way he is around me … so comfortable … so easy … I want to tell him every secret I've ever known.

Silence slips between us, and I swear I can hear my heartbeat in my ears.

Then he says, "The hardest part is staying true to who you are no matter what other people do. Even under duress, the choices we make are ultimately ours."

With my house just around the corner, we stop to part ways.

"Whatever you're thinking about, Kate, I'm sure you'll make the right choice."

I shove my hands deep into my coat pockets. "What makes you so sure about that?"

"Gut feeling."

It takes a minute before I'm able to look at him, and when I do, there's a slight crinkling around his eyes. "You're a strong woman, Kate. One I'm privileged to know." He bends low to kiss my cheek. "Now, you better go before the patrols catch us lingering here too long."

Only a few steps away, I turn around. He's still standing there. The way he watches me reminds me of how my dad makes sure my mom is safely inside a building when he drops her off. Protective.

"Micah?"

"Hmm?"

"Thanks."

"I'll see you tomorrow, Kate."

***

By 9:15 when I finally trudge through the door to my house, my mother has dinner picked up and the kitchen cleaned. Not that it takes that long to throw away the containers our dinner comes in.

"Hey, Mom." I set my bag on the chair by the front door. She gives me the look, the one that says, *If you leave that bag there, I'll destroy you.* "I'll take care of it after I eat. Promise." This is how Mom and I are. Her facial expressions say so much more than her words, so half the time she negates her need to speak with one well-placed look.

Flopping onto a seat at the counter, I practically melt into it, watching as my mother bustles around, pulling a tray covered with aluminum foil from the refrigerator. She peels back the foil and folds it neatly into a square before tossing it into the garbage. Then she places the plate into the microwave. While it's heating, she takes out a fork, a spoon, and a glass, setting them in front of me, fork on my right side, spoon on my left. Anything else would not be acceptable. This is my mother, for whom the world is black and white. Right and wrong. There are no shades of gray.

Probably why Mom, whose glaring looks and ability to interpret others' expressions, works in the Justice Department as a Criminal Interpreter.

What this boils down to is that I can't keep anything from my mother. She's like a dog sniffing out lies and truth stretching, which is why, when she asks me what's bothering me, I can't just say, "I'm tired." She's trained to see otherwise, to read beneath the surface of the words.

"I found something interesting at the lab today."

"Oh?" She puts the plate in front of me and leans against the counter, wiping her hands on a towel.

"I don't want to talk about it." She knows something's up, but there's no way I can tell her what I discovered tonight.

"Everything okay?"

No. Definitely not. "Yeah. No big deal."

"Kate. Why don't you tell me what's on your mind? It'll make you feel better."

I should have known she'd persist. She doesn't give up easily. So I fib to get her off my back. "Just a challenge at the labs, Mom. I'm trying to figure out this procedure in my head."

She refuses to let it go. "Kate. Just tell me. Maybe I can help."

The tone.

She's as good at that as she is at *the look.* If she doesn't sap all your secrets with one, she'll use the other. An absolute master.

Normally, I'd tell her. But until I figure this out for myself, I'm not breathing a word to her. "Where's Dad?"

The sigh. Usually, when *the look* and *the tone* don't work, the sigh does it. It's her last effort to figure out what's going on with me, but I hold steady, not breaking our stare down.

"Upstairs in the den."

Without another word, I grab my plate and fork and head toward the stairs. Maybe my dad will know what to do. I hear another sigh behind me.

Through the crack in the door, I see my dad hunched over some paperwork. He doesn't hear me as I enter. "Dad?"

"Wha—?" He jumps and papers scatter across his desk. Quickly, he gathers them together and tucks them into a manila folder, sticking it at the bottom of the pile that sits on the corner of his desk. "Oh! Kate. I thought you were your mother." Seeing it's me, he relaxes into the chair and puts his feet up as if he wasn't trying to hide anything just then. "What's up?"

I sit on the edge of his desk and finger through the pile of files. His face flashes nervousness for a second, but he quickly pulls himself together and looks at me. He's hiding something, but one quick glance at my face and he knows I've got something going on too. Cocking his head, he pulls his feet off the desk and leans forward toward me, whispering.

"What'd you find out?"

Dad and I have this thing going. We're "two peas in a pod," Gran used to say. I swear we share more with each other than he and Mom do. So he knows when I've stumbled upon something I shouldn't have. Just like I know he'll tell me what's in that folder he was trying to hide.

"Saw something at the lab tonight." Dad doesn't say anything. Instead, he waits for me to continue. "In the Creation Unit." Why is this so hard? I've told him things I've found before, and he always knows what to do about it, but for some reason, I can't bring myself to say the words.

"It's something big, isn't it?" he asks, pulling on his beard. I nod. "Go on."

I drum my fingers on the pile of folders. "I was filing papers for infantile disposals. Some stupid job Professor Limbert gave me just as I was going to leave. I was almost done when I came across something." I can't bear to actually look at him. It's not like I've done anything wrong, but this shouldn't be the way I tell him he was almost going to be a grandpa. I haven't processed the idea myself, so telling someone else is all the more difficult. But this is my dad.

Just then, my mother pops her head in the door. Both of us jump, and Dad fidgets with his compact, closing something so she can't see. "You coming to bed, honey?"

"Yeah, in a few," Dad says. "You go ahead. I'll be there in a minute."

She looks from Dad to me and back again and walks off shaking her head. It must seem like we have a secret club or something, but she wouldn't understand. If she were to stumble on something like this, she'd report it to the authorities immediately. But Dad and I have to figure it out first. See if it's worth the hassle of letting the proper authorities know. Some things are better left unsaid.

Once Mom is out of hearing, Dad turns back to me. "Katie-Did, what on earth did you find?" The way he looks at me with concern on his face makes the caramel color of his eyes seem to melt.

Glancing toward the hallway, I'm convinced Mom isn't listening. "I had to record the ID numbers. When I wrote down the number—" I can't do this. I can't tell my dad. My hands are shaking, so I hold them together in my lap.

"—It was yours."

When I look up, the sympathy in Dad's face is palpable. How does he know? He answers my silent question. "I work in Data Collections, remember? I noticed your number." His hand taps my leg, telling me to move as he grabs the pile of folders next to where I'm still perched on his desk. "When I saw it, I didn't know if you knew or not," he says, taking the folder off the bottom of the pile and handing it to me. Inside is a print of what I registered earlier that night. On top is a note in my dad's handwriting. *Unauthorized* is all it says. "I don't think I was supposed to find out either. I would know you didn't authorize this, and it would raise a red flag if I saw it." He shakes his head. "There has to be some sort of mistake."

"But The Institute doesn't make mistakes."

Taking the folder from my hands, he says matter-of-factly, "Then someone meant for us to see this."

It's all too overwhelming, and as hard as I try, I can't hold back the torrent of tears that floods my eyes and pours onto my cheeks.

SEVENTEEN

THE MEETING

School the next day is almost unbearable. And, of course, it's not a classroom day. We're in the labs … again. Pretty much every day now. So by this time, it shouldn't be a big deal, but today, as I pass the innumerable pods lining the room, I examine every fetus, wondering if it's him. Or her. One of these babies belongs to me.

Is it this difficult for the adults who work in the creation lab? The ones who've applied for children. Once they submit the application, do they have access to which one is theirs? Maybe that information is kept confidential. I would assume so, but if it were me, I'd want to know which one was mine. I'd find a way to know. I guess, I never thought about how that might work in the future when I am married and applying to have my own children created. Probably because it was supposed to be so far in the future. I shouldn't have to even consider which one of these children might be mine because I'm not supposed to have a child. I'm not supposed to know who feeds the baby or who tests its blood. I'm not supposed to be able to watch it grow because I'm not supposed to know I have one.

But I do.

Today's job is to mix and administer food to the fetuses, and I'm paired with Devin. He could be a decent guy, I suppose if he weren't so touchy-feely. By the end of today, I know I'll need a shower just to get the feeling of violation off my skin. It's his attempt at flirting, and he tries to be subtle about it, but his subtlety feels like a rhinoceros lumbering through the lab.

First it's his arm brushing mine as he reaches for the equipment. "Kate, can you hand me that?"

If he wanted me to hand it to him, why did he reach over me? I'm so not in the mood to deal with Devin today. It takes a special kind of moxie to handle him, and I don't have it in me this morning. Instead, I have one thing on my mind. One goal to accomplish: finding my baby.

I glance around the room in the second trimester Utero and see the ten lab pairs hovering around the pods. Taryn is on the far wall with a girl I've never worked with. We're responsible for all of the fetuses in here today. Over one hundred. And all of the capsules need to be re-loaded with nutrients before we can go home. But even when that job is completed, I won't leave until I find the one I'm looking for. The child who carries my DNA.

Handing Devin the powder he asked for, I watch as he measures it and mixes it in a Petri dish with a few milliliters of blood. It'll be injected into the synthetic placenta resting on the bottom of the pod.

Devin lightly touches my hand. "I need the syringe."

I'd roll my eyes at him, but he has no idea he's repulsing me right now. It must be sad to be so clueless about women. I slap the syringe into his hand and watch silently as he sucks up the enhanced blood sample with the syringe and tops it off with a squirt and a flick of his finger. The gesture sends droplets of blood onto my lab coat.

"Devin! Watch what you're doing!"

"Sorry." His hand reaches forward to brush the drops off my coat, but I slap it away before he can touch my chest. He seriously has no clue.

"I'm gonna go get this cleaned up." It's not necessary; it's just a few drops, but I jump at the excuse to have a moment away from him. "I'm sure you can handle the injection on your own."

"Sure," he says. He's already searching for the tube attached to the pod that leads to the placenta. He'll inject it and mix up another batch before I return.

By the time I get back, he's finished another two pods and is moving to the third. With everyone working, we should have this room finished in another hour. Normally, this is mindless work. Measure. Mix. Administer. Move to the next one. But today, every time we start the process over, I find myself examining the baby in front of us.

Is this the one? Could this be her? But then I scan the barcode, bringing up the child's ID number, and it doesn't match the one I burned into my memory. 1-2-9-8-7-3-2. So we complete the procedure and move on, trading off every few capsules to share the workload.

Devin settles himself on a stool in front of our newest fetus and scans the ID number as he reads it aloud.

"What did you say?"

"1-2-9-8-7-3-2. Why?" he asks.

Then it shows up on the screen of my compact, too. 1-2-9-8-7-3-2. All I can do is stare at the screen. Devin says something, but it doesn't register. Then he grabs my shoulder and shakes it. "Kate!"

I finally break my daze. "What?"

"Are you okay?"

Shaking my head, I focus on entering the number into my compact for records. "Yeah. Fine." But as soon as my fingers are done pressing the keys and I'm able to look at the child in the capsule, I know I'm not fine. Because here in front of me, floating in a mass of liquid, is my son.

He's perfect. Ten tiny toes, barely starting to form. Eyes, nose, ears, hair. He's got hair. Lots of it. And his little hand reaches up to his lips so he can suck on his thumb. I'm overwhelmed with the emotion that floods my mind. It's weird; when I found out about him only days ago, I was horrified, even glad that he would be disposed of. But now, here, looking at something that's a part of me, I can't imagine ridding the world of this perfect little creature. So tiny and innocent. So full of life as he moves around in the confined space. It's instant love.

I reach out to touch the flexible plastic dividing us. It's warm, and the gentle hum of the motors keeping him alive blends into the background. It's only us at that moment. Mother and son. The rest of the world has disappeared. Until Devin breaks my bubble again.

This time he's laid his hand on the small of my back while he leans down to whisper in my ear. "Time to move on to the next one."

"Right. Sure." I pull my eyes from my child, pick up my compact, and slide down the table to the next pod. I finish my job, but every few moments when Devin isn't looking at me, I cast a brief look at container seven. Anything to have just one more glimpse at my son.

EIGHTEEN

THE FINE LINE BETWEEN LOVE AND HATE

Code of Conduct and Ethics: The Institute—Sector 4, USA
Section 8 Article 7.21: It is forbidden to spend time in the Outer Lands.
They are uninhabited and dangerous. Keep to the roads and walkways for
your own safety.

O N A SATURDAY IN late fall, Micah and I manage to find some
free time to spend together. Before my mother can make plans
for me, I inform her Micah and I have scheduled a picnic. She
smiles, pleased with my choice of a potential boyfriend with prestige
and nods in silent agreement. I don't even have to mention it to Dad.
He knows by the time I see him Friday night. Mom must have told
him. He just tells me to have a good time.

If my parents knew the whole truth, they'd never let me go. If they
knew how much time Micah and I have spent with each other before
this, they'd have simultaneous heart attacks if that were even possible
with their microchip implants. As it is, keeping the true nature of our
relationship secret is enough to send them over the edge.

It's not necessary for them to know we're going into the Outer
Lands to be alone.

We do pack a dinner to keep the suspicions to a minimum. No need
to have my mother discover the basket still sitting in the hallway of our

house while I'm out "picnicking" without it. She'd probably search the park grounds, only to discover we aren't there. I'd hate to make her worry without reason. Dad would overlook it; try to calm her down, even. He'd probably tell her to give me some space. Let me grow up without her over my shoulder. Then again, Dad knows I already know more than the average teenager. He knows I've come to understand the real ways of our community better than most. It's partially why we're so close; he tells me the truth no matter how hard it might be.

I open the door to the stone-faced Micah. "Hey. Everything all right?"

His eyes brighten a little. "Yeah, sorry. Distracted a bit."

Here I was hoping this would be romantic, but if his mind is elsewhere, my ideas of really connecting might be tossed out with yesterday's lunch.

"You sure?"

"Yeah. Sorry. Just have some stuff on my mind. Waiting for something at work."

"Wanna talk about it?"

"Not really."

Driving to a clearing near the border, we leave the truck near a picnic area cluttered with couples enjoying the evening air. "We'll walk from here," Micah says as he helps me from his truck. We head toward the far end of a grassy area where a trodden path leads into the woods. "There's a break in the fencing about a mile in. We can cross over there. Patrolling in this area is limited, so I don't think we'll have any trouble."

"Is this why you're distracted? Worried about the patrols?"

He rubs his arm and glances over his shoulder. "Um, yeah. Let's get going before we see any."

When we reach the place he's talking about, I'm surprised to see an intact chain-link fence, but Micah reaches for a particular section of fencing and pulls it back with ease. The hole is small, but we're both able to squeeze through with only a scratch. He kneels down and reattaches the fencing so no one will even notice a disturbance. "Ready?"

I nod, and we trek another mile or so into the Outer Lands before finding a small clearing.

"This looks okay, doesn't it?"

We spread the blanket on the ground and sit. "Yeah, this is great. I've never been out here before."

Micah twists his neck to look at me. "You mean, out here," he points to the ground, "or to the Outer Lands at all?"

I feel my shoulders shrug in embarrassment. "To the Outer Lands at all."

He runs his hand halfway through his hair, stopping at the top of his head. "I wouldn't have brought you out here if I'd known that, Kate. I don't want to make you feel uncomfortable, much less get you in trouble."

"We aren't going to get caught, right? So it's no big deal. Besides, it's like a rite of passage to break the rules of The Institute at least once, right?"

He smiles and starts to ease up. "I'd say so." Chomping into a sandwich, he asks, "So, you're okay with this?"

"Sure."

After eating, we relax on the blanket Micah's brought, me playing with my necklace and him on his side, head propped on his hand.

The way Micah looks at me makes it hard to breathe. I'm drawn into the strength of his arms as they flex with every twist of his forearm.

"Sorry, I've been distracted," he says.

"Did something happen?"

"No. It's fine. I was hoping for some news from work and didn't hear, that's all. I'll have to figure things out on my own."

"I'm sure you'll do fine."

The corner of his mouth twitches. At first I think he's going to smile, but it doesn't make it that far before he bites his lip and shakes his head.

"Come 'ere," he says, tugging at my sleeve.

I scoot over, leaning against him. My legs are stretched out in front of me, and I lean back on my hands, creating a tee-pee over his hips. It's nice to be like this. Relaxed. No worries. Comfortable.

"This is beautiful, don't you think?" I look through the canopy of trees above us to the fading sunlight. The setting sun rests in the center of the break in the trees above us, shining a spotlight where we lay.

"Mmm Hmm." He twirls a lock of my hair around his finger, and I glance to see him. He's not looking at the sky. I'm caught in his vision as his eyes flicker over my face.

He shifts his position to sit behind me, and I find myself wrapped in his arms. Leaning back into his chest, I can feel the stubble on his chin through my hair and his breath on my ear. For the first time in a long time, I feel safe in the confines of his arms.

He runs both of his hands down my arms and encircles my wrists with his fingers. I'm struck by the contrast. His massive, strong hands. My small delicate wrists. Yet somehow, they fit together. When he traces a trail along my sleeve with the tips of his fingers, even though he's not touching my skin, goose bumps rise on my flesh. My heart races, and I swear he'll be able to hear my heartbeat if I can't calm myself.

"Kate," Micah breathes into my ear.

"Hmm?" I reply, not paying much attention to his words. I want the world to disappear and let me live in this moment forever. Micah's arms around me, warming me from the cool night air. He's the safe spot in my unsure world.

His voice is a muddle in my head. Whatever he needs to say can't possibly be as important as staying in his embrace. Maybe if I ignore him, he'll not break my fantasy bubble and let me savor just being *us* for a few more minutes.

As if he reads my mind, his fingers lace between mine and pull my hands out to the side, then back and up around his neck. I melt into him.

"I ... I'm ..." A forceful breath escapes through his nose.

Stumbling over his words isn't like him, and when I twist around to see his face, it's conflicted, eyes squeezed shut.

"What is it?" I ask.

"I'm sorry."

That makes me stop. "Why are you apologizing, Micah?"

Suddenly, it's hard to breathe, and I feel trapped. He pulls me in and presses his lips lightly against mine. I'm lost in the scent of the air surrounding him, like cedar and soap. His hands linger on my neck before sliding down my arms where he clasps his hands tightly around my wrists again. Too tight.

Panic sets in, but I rein it in, trying to keep a rational head. Moving a little, I try to wriggle away, but his grip is stronger than I anticipate, and I'm held steady. "Tell me why you're sorry, Micah!"

Pulling against him does nothing. His hold on me is like a vice.

"I'm sorry for this."

Before I can writhe out from his grasp, he moves both my hands into one of his, pulls something out of his pocket and slaps it over my wrists.

Zip ties.

NINETEEN

KEEP YOUR FRIENDS CLOSE AND YOUR ENEMIES CLOSER—UNLESS THEY'RE TRYING TO ABDUCT YOU

THE LOOK IN HIS eyes is blazing, flashing between regret and duty. I kick with all my might and manage to twist out from under him and scramble out of his embrace. One of the ties cuts into the flesh on my wrist, but the other is loose. Micah didn't have time to tighten it before I got away. I slip my hand out of the tie. Grabbing a large rock from the ground with one hand, I hold it in front of me. I clench the stone tightly in my fist, squeezing until I feel the edges digging into the flesh of my palm.

Micah doesn't even attempt to pursue me. And he won't look at me either. Instead, grabbing his shirt from the ground, he stands up and slowly slides it over his head. Then his hands slump to his sides, and he looks at his feet before raising his gaze to meet mine. The fire inside me is burning now, and it's spreading fast as the adrenaline rushes through my veins. Already, I've glanced around and seen the stomped-down pathway that will lead me back to the road.

But it won't matter.

Micah can outrun me in three strides of his long legs if he wants to. And his strong arms can pin me to the ground or snap my neck in an instant. There is no escape. Not from him.

I'm trapped.

There's a look on his face I can't interpret, but no matter what it means, his eyes reveal everything. Well, not everything. Not why he's been playing this little, *I like you and will pretend to date you* game. For a second, I think those gray eyes seem to glow a sad silver in the light that's crept through the trees. He says it clearly this time. Unwavering. "I was sent here to abduct you."

That's all I need to hear. No explanation necessary. Without hesitation, I throw the rock in my hand as hard as I can. It's a straight shot, and it catches him alongside the head before he can react. He topples over, stumbling to gain his footing.

I don't stay to watch him agonize, even though I want to. Part of me can't believe what he's said is true. Not after he saved my butt that day with Saul. Not after he risked a demerit to get me a scone. Not after the little origami butterfly he gave me. This isn't like him. But I can't stand here and philosophize about what may have been. There's no time to waste. Instead, I run.

Fast.

I'm barely to the footpath when I hear him yell.

"Kate! Wait! You don't understand."

Oh, yes I do. He's going to abduct me, take me wherever to do who knows what. I have to get away from here, but I know he'll catch up with me any second. Maybe I can find a place to hide. It's a long shot, but it just might work.

Everything we've done together, every nice thing he ever said to me, all lies. How could I have possibly trusted him? I should have known better. *Keep your eyes open and trust no one.* Isn't that what Gran had told me so many times? Why did I choose today to ignore her warnings? Probably because she seemed to trust him.

Why him? Why did it have to be Micah?

The tears stream down my face as I dodge the branches that scratch at my arms. It's like all those nights I ran through the park, convinced someone was following me. Now I know. It's Micah who's chasing me now. And it was him chasing me then.

Up ahead, I spot some low brush thick enough it just might conceal me. I hope.

"Kate, don't run, please."

Yeah right. Don't run from the man who's just admitted he was going to abduct me? That's a brilliant plan. I think I'll pass. I'm kicking myself for all the things I told him, for the times we spent together. All lies.

I don't look back, but by the sounds behind me, he's struggling to keep up, probably staggering through the limb-covered ground.

I reach the brush and slide underneath the thorny undergrowth. It scratches at my face and hands as I creep nearer to the center, kicking back the twigs to cover my feet. Pine needles dig into my still-exposed stomach. Patches of this plant cover the forest ground all around. He won't know where to look. From between the leaves, I see him rounding a far tree.

He stops in a clearing to catch his breath. "Kate! Please! Listen to me. I know you're hiding somewhere. You can't outrun me."

Exactly the reason I won't listen to your sad little story.

"Come out, Kate. We need to talk about this." He rubs the stubble on his cheeks, fingers the gash on his forehead, and lets out an exasperated sigh.

He's frustrated. And angry.

"I'm not going to hurt you, Kate. Please. Come talk to me."

He spins around and peers into the distance. When I don't respond, he kicks the ground. "Fine! I'll tell you now. Yes, I was sent to abduct you. But I'm not going to. You want to know why?"

He turns slowly in a circle with his arms out as if waiting for my reply while talking to the trees. "Because I'm in love with you."

I gasp.

"Do you hear me, Kate? I love you. I recently sent word to my superiors to come up with a different plan because I didn't want to go through with this one, but there was nothing. Radio silence. So I had to do what they wanted. Except now, I refuse. I'll defy orders. They can punish me if they need to, but I can't do what they want. I won't. Even if it means sacrificing others in the process, they'll have to find another way."

By this time my breathing has slowed; my heart, on the other hand, still races as I listen to his words. Can I trust him? What if this is just a trap? Use a love confessional to get me to come out of hiding and nab me then.

But the way he stands there in the clearing, speaking to the trees as if they can answer; and the slight waver in his voice, like he's choking up on the words he's trying to say; maybe he is telling the truth.

"Look, I know you probably don't believe me. You probably think this is a trap."

Yep, pretty much.

His back is to me now. He's searching the brush surrounding the clearing looking for me. He knows I'm near. "To prove it to you, I'm going to tell you something about me. Something no one else in our society knows."

No one else in our society? What does that mean? I move the branches to the side a little so I can see his face more clearly as he circles around toward where I'm hiding.

"I'm a Womber."

The words hit me like a sucker punch to the gut, and I let go of the thorn covered twigs I'd just peeled back. They smack my face as they fling back, scratching a deep gouge down my cheek. "Oww!" I gasp, raising my fingers to the wound. It's sticky and hot, and as I pull my hand away, I see the blood on my fingertips.

Micah whips his head around toward the sound. "Kate, is that you? Did you hear what I said? I'm a Womber, a Natural Born."

"I know what a Womber is," I say, still hidden in the underbrush.

He steps toward my voice. "Of course you do. Your great-grandmother—"

"Don't come any closer," I say. "I still don't trust you."

I've wrestled out of the brush, grab another large rock as my only protection, and am standing a few yards from Micah. He's tattered and scratched, and the lump on his head from where I whacked him with that rock is swollen and dripping blood onto his shirt. This is not how

I envisioned our time together. It was supposed to end differently, with me in his arms listening to his heartbeat.

"But I just told you I'm a Natural Born."

"That doesn't mean anything. You also told me you were sent to capture me, so your word doesn't really mean much right now. Besides, there are other Natural Borns."

"Think about it, Kate. The only other Natural Borns are your great-grandmother's age, and soon they'll all be gone. None like me. And none that have infiltrated the society in order to filter information to our underground network." He lifts his hand to his head, which is still bleeding and pulls it away, examining the blood on his fingers, like this sort of thing happens every day. "I'm telling you secrets that could get me killed, Kate. You've got to believe me."

Okay, so what he says about the only Wombers being old is true, but that doesn't mean he's telling the truth. He could be making the whole thing up. This could still be a trap.

He tries to explain further. "My superiors are constantly looking for ways to infiltrate The Institute. Sometimes that means replacing one of theirs with one of ours. You were chosen to be replaced. I was the one who was supposed to get you out of the way so the other could take your place."

"So, what? You take me hostage then kill me?"

"No. No, we don't do that. Killing would make us just as bad as The Institute."

"We? Who's we?"

He doesn't respond.

"So what was the plan then?"

"Prison."

"Not sure rotting in a prison is any better than being dead."

Despite the tension, a tiny smile appears on his lips before disappearing into the pain radiating from his head. "I refused to do it, you know. Told them there had to be another way. No need to get rid of someone just to bring one of ours in. But you know as well as I that no one moves to Sector 4 without insane levels of security checks. My superiors insisted I go through with ... things. We can't always wait for the right opportunity. Sometimes we have to create it ourselves. Counting on the sympathizers isn't enough anymore. I told them we had to find another way, but they didn't respond. Didn't get my message, so I had to go through with it. I thought I could bring you there and then convince them to let you go."

"What happened to, 'you always have a choice no matter what other people do?'"

His head drops, and he kicks at the ground. "I know. I'm sorry. I screwed up."

Screwed up doesn't even begin to cover it.

"Why me? Why do they want me? I'm just a student."

He tries to take another step closer, but my raised hand still clenching the rock stops him. "Because you're on your way up. We've been watching you for a while. It won't be long before you're a Creation Specialist, and we wanted to get to you before it was too late. We need someone in the creation department. With your mother as a Criminal Interpreter, we couldn't take our chances to convince you to become a sympathizer. There wasn't any other way."

They've been watching me. Following me. It's all falling into place now. Ugh, how stupid I've been.

"So, what? You have a look-a-like of me somewhere or something?"

"Something like that."

I don't believe him. And I don't understand all of this, but maybe there's a chance he's telling the truth. "Fine, if you're really who you say you are, then you're going to let me go without following me. I'm going to run out of here, and you are going to stay put."

He's lost a lot of blood, and his shirt is soaked with crimson. He looks directly at me and says, "Fine, go. I won't follow." He wobbles toward a tree and puts his hand out to steady himself. "Go quickly."

He's letting me go without a fight. I dash away, but after a few steps, the curiosity in me wins out, and I glance over my shoulder to see if he's keeping his word.

That's when I see him collapse.

TWENTY

LOVE THINE ENEMIES

A THOUGHT FLASHES THROUGH my mind. *I could leave him here, and no one would know.* But that nagging feeling that maybe he actually cared what happened to me won't let me do it. "Micah! Micah." I drop the rock and run to his side. When I reach him, his face is pale. He's lost so much blood. It's everywhere. On his shirt, matting his hair to his face, covering the ground. Head wounds bleed like hell. I wipe it away from his eyes and pull him into my lap. "Micah, can you hear me?"

Ripping two scraps from my shirt, I fold one and press it to his wound. Taking the other, I wrap it around his head tightly and tie it over the bleeding gash.

"I'm so sorry, Micah! Please don't die." His eyes flutter open, and he blinks.

"Come on," I say, pulling him into a half stance. "You have to walk. I can't carry you by myself, and you need help."

He doesn't say anything, but his feet move in an attempt to step. His arm around my neck, he leans over me and the blood from his wound drips onto my cheek.

"We have to get you to a hospital," I say.

A moan escapes his lips, but I can't understand what he says.

"Pocket," he croaks.

"Pocket? You have something in your pocket?"

He nods.

I reach for his pants pocket, but the shift of my body causes him to tumble to the ground. I'm under him.

"Micah. Are you okay?" I slither out from underneath his limp body and cradle his face in my hands. The blood has soaked through my makeshift bandage. His eyes flutter for a moment then close.

"Micah! Micah, wake up! Please. I can't leave you here." I look around, hoping that by some small miracle, someone will be walking this way. But I know better. We came out here specifically because no one ever walks through this area. Now it's all up to me.

I scream at the top of my lungs. The tears flood my cheeks as I attempt to pull myself together. There are too many emotions to sort through, but I push them all down in an attempt to save Micah. I must have hit him harder than I thought to cause this amount of bleeding.

Pocket. There's something in his pocket. I pat his leg. Nothing. Must be in the other one. The one trapped under the weight of his body. I push on his shoulders with all my strength and roll him onto his back. Plunging my hand into his pocket, I pull out something square.

It looks like a miniature speaker. I flip it over a few times and find a tiny button on one side. I push it, not knowing what will happen. Expecting an explosion of some sort, I cringe and toss it into the weeds, just in case.

The tiny thing vibrates and speaks. "Code?" a woman's voice asks.

Not expecting the voice, I scream.

"Code!" The woman's voice is harsh and demanding this time.

Rushing toward where I threw the device, I fumble through the brambles and weeds trying to find it, but it's disappeared in the foliage.

There's a crackling before the woman says, "Micah? Speak the code, or I'll detonate the memory chip in your brain."

Crap. That doesn't sound good.

Scrambling, I brush the leaves away, frantic that Micah could die any minute. I have to find the device.

"Detonation activated in five, four, three …"

My hand brushes something hard, and I clench my fingers around it and hold it to my lips.

"Wait! Don't! I don't know who you are, but I'm with Micah Pennington. We're in the woods outside of River Trail. He's hurt. His head. There's blood everywhere, and he's passed out. Please, I can't get him out of here by myself."

"Who are you?" the voice asks.

"Kate. Katherine. Katherine Dennard."

"Stay with him. We're sending someone to help."

Abductor or not, I can't let him die out here. That's my choice. I pull Micah's head into my lap and wait.

***

"You Kate?"

"Oh!" I jump as two men approach from the side. I didn't hear their footsteps. Silent. Stealth.

"Yes. I'm Kate. Micah's hurt." I'm talking rapidly as the men lift Micah by his arms and legs.

They look like government officials, dressed in the normal khaki pants and blue shirts common to workers of The Institute. But something's off.

"We can see that. How'd it happen?" the larger of the two asks. His eyes are light and his hair dark.

I can't tell them the truth. If they are government workers, both Micah and I will be in a heap of trouble. I suppose we already are for being out here alone, but how am I going to explain this one?

With my free hand, I push the zip tie still dangling from my wrist up under my sleeve.

"We were out here for research lab. He fell and hit his head on a rock," I said, matter-of-factly. It was partially true. His head did connect with a rock. No need to mention I was the one who threw it at him.

"We weren't fast enough with the message." The smaller man with light hair lets out a hearty laugh as they trudge along, balancing Micah's limp body between them. Apparently, he doesn't believe my explanation. I don't see how this situation is even remotely funny.

I trudge beside them across the forest floor until we reach a white truck parked off the trail. It has the forestry logo painted on the side, and there's a fresh coat of paint covering the vehicle. It's an older model. A cast off. If that's the case, then who are these men, and where did they come from? Because this isn't a truck driven by government officials.

The men lift Micah's body into the back. They both climb in the back, situating Micah's now unconscious body so it won't slide over the bed of the truck.

"Where are you taking him?" I ask, almost afraid of what their answer might be.

"Both of you. We're taking both of you."

Here we go again. Didn't I just escape one abductor? … Sort of.

A burning sensation rises in the back of my throat.

Not if I can help it.

································

TWENTY ONE

RIGHT AS RAIN

"**C**OME ON," THE LARGER man says, offering me a hand. Let's see. I can't run because they'd surely catch me. And I can't go with them because—well, because I don't know what will happen, but what choice do I have?

No time to sneak a spare rock into my pocket without him noticing, so I take his hand tentatively, and he yanks me up. His skin is warm and calloused. He seems calm, but I'm not taking any chances. I sit as far from the man as I can without looking suspicious, which in the back of a truck, isn't far enough away.

He pulls two blankets out of a toolbox and places one under Micah's head and the other over his body. He adjusts the band on Micah's wound, which is now seeping blood. Meanwhile, his partner takes to the driver's seat and revs the engine, spitting a trail of rocks as we speed away through the trees.

My body lurches forward as the truck takes off. Mr. Truck Bed Guy crouches next to Micah to make sure he is stabilized.

"Rock, huh?" The man holds onto the edge of the cab and keeps another hand over Micah. Almost protective.

His face is a mixture of concern and amusement, and I can't tell if he's making fun of me or not. It's like he doesn't believe my explanation. Not that he should. It *is* a total lie. But he doesn't know that. And why would he be amused when his friend—if Micah really is his friend—is hurt and bleeding in the back of his truck bed?

Does Micah even know this guy? Is he a Natural Born, too? Well, that is if what Micah told me is true, which I'm still not sure of. The mere thought of it blows my mind.

No. No one would be able to hide here. Not in our society. It's not possible. The Institute is too observant. Sure, there are a lot of kids who know a few hiding spots where they make out with their boyfriends or girlfriends, but that's piddly next to actually conducting a life and job within the community with no one knowing. They wouldn't get away with it. It's one thing to sneak a few scones or talk to a perfectly lucid great grandmother, but quite another to infiltrate an entire community with innumerable spies who may or may not be trying to replace various community members. If The Institute found out—Yikes! Let's just say I'd rather not be around if that's the case.

I brush the thought from my mind.

"Yeah, he fell right onto it. Started bleeding all over. I couldn't do anything to stop it."

The man's eyes crinkle into a tight smile, but he holds it from his lips. "I see."

The driver rounds a corner, and we lunge across the back of the truck. The man loses his grip, and Micah's still-unconscious body slides toward the far side, bumping his already bruised face against the hub. I lose my balance and end up in a pile right next to him.

Oh no. The bandage I wrapped around his head is soaked and sticky with blood and the skin around his eyes is a deep purple bruise.

Don't die. Please don't die.

"We've got to hurry; he's bleeding a lot," I manage to squeak through the tears I'm choking back.

I can't hide the horror on my face.

"Don't worry. He's going to be just fine. Head wounds are always not as bad as they seem. Bleed like a bugger, though." The man bends down and gazes into my eyes like a father reprimanding his little kid. "Those doctors will fix him up right as rain."

I cock one eyebrow and twist my head. Did I just hear him correctly? 'Right as rain'? Only my gran uses those kinds of phrases. My gran and her friends.

The Wombers.

My eyes grow huge, and the shock I feel is sure to show. I search the man's face.

"You're a—"

"We're here," he interrupts, looking over his shoulder to the brick building behind him.

In all the confusion, I didn't notice we'd pulled out of the forest and neared the hospital of The Institute.

He hops over the side of the truck bed, opens the tailgate, and offers me a hand. "Sorry we weren't quicker." The second my feet hit the ground, he merges into the crowd of medical professionals. In seconds, the sidewalk in the alcove is swarming with people in lab coats.

The emergency bay.

They yell out medical terms to the nurses and doctors who scurry to get Micah onto a gurney while I'm left standing in a daze. I scan the crowd, trying to find the man from the truck, but his face has melted into the sea of faces. I have to find him so I can ask him about the piece of paper he left in my hand.

I can't look at it now—not with all these people around—so I tuck it into my pocket for now.

In the distance, I see the older of the men from the forest pull a young doctor aside. He motions to me and whispers something I can't hear. The doctor nods. Then he turns and heads toward me as the nurses work to strap Micah to the bed.

I glance at his name tag. Dr. Drew Rosenberg.

"What happened?" he asks.

I try not to make eye contact. "He hit his head."

"I gathered that. How?" He's curt, and the way his lips press together tells me he's not believing a word I say.

I'm in a daze, watching the chaos around me. Trying to keep my head together enough not to reveal anything I shouldn't.

"Miss?" His voice draws me back to reality. "How?" he repeats pointedly.

I can't tell him the truth. If I do, they'll know something is wrong. I hold one elbow with my hand, feeling the zip tie still on my wrist under my shirt. "Um … rock," I say. "We were doing research near the river. Wasn't looking. Tripped over a tree root and landed head first on a boulder sticking out of the ground." That sounds believable.

"Must've fallen pretty hard to cause such a deep wound," he replies.

"Yeah."

"Miss—"

I turn to him.

He holds out his hand like he's about to touch me, but I shrink into myself. His soft voice practically floats to my ears when he says, "I'm going to make sure Micah's all right." With that, he rushes toward Micah as they wheel him into the Emergency Center.

I don't know what to do. Stay? Go? I want to make sure Micah's okay, that the doctors are doing everything they can to save him, but sticking around might beg more questions. Questions I'm unwilling to answer.

In the distance are the two men who brought us here. They make eye contact with me before slamming the door to the truck and drive away, leaving me. Alone.

I can't quite piece together everything that's just happened. Should I go in and see if Micah's okay? What if he regains consciousness and tells them what I've done? I can't go in there. Besides, the men promised me he'd be okay. Anything I do now will just interfere. Even the doctor said he'd take care of Micah.

That's good. They'll fix him up right as rain.

....

TWENTY TWO

UNDER THE SURFACE

B Y THE TIME I get home, it's late. Way past curfew, which can only mean one thing: my mother will be up waiting for me with a reprimand on her lips. When she sees my blood-covered shirt, she's going to freak.

Creeping in the back door as quietly as I can, I make it to the bathroom and am taking off my shirt before I hear her.

"What happened to you? Why are you home so late? Do you realize I'll have to report you?" The look on her face is a mixture of fear and anger, and I know there's no lying my way out of this one. There never is. Dealing with my mother is a game of telling just enough truth not to lie, and just enough lie to still tell the truth. Her eyelids peel back revealing something close to terror when she sees my blood-stained clothing covering the bathroom floor. "Kate! Are you all right?" She rushes toward me, lightly pressing her fingers around my skin to check for cuts.

I pull away, not wanting her so close to me, afraid she can smell my deception. I wasn't supposed to go to the Outer Lands. "Yeah, Mom, I'm fine. Micah fell and hit his head. We had to take him to the hospital for stitches." See, it's not a lie.

"We?"

Crap! "I ... I mean I took him. He was bleeding pretty badly, and I got it all over me."

She calms down an inkling. "Is he okay?"

"I think so. They're keeping him overnight in the hospital wing at The Institute. I'm going to head over there tomorrow or the next day to see how he is." *Nice save, Kate. No need to mention he was attempting to abduct you in the process.*

"Get cleaned up and head to bed. Be sure to let your father know you're home. He's been worried sick. I'll notify the database about your condition."

"Sure, Mom." I'm glad I kept my story straight. The whole 'partial truth' stuff is getting easier every day. Let's just hope she continues to believe it.

The first thing I do when I have a second of privacy is cut the zip tie still dangling from my wrist and bury it deep in the garbage. After changing into my pajamas, I pick up the clothing covering the bathroom floor and carry it to the laundry room, but one look at the items, and I decide there's no saving any of them, so instead, I shove them in the trash with the zip tie. Taking the garbage out will make my mother happy. *Note to self: Find a new favorite pair of jeans soon.*

Then I remember the paper. Digging through garbage isn't my idea of a fun time, but there has to be something about that paper. The jeans rest on the top of the pile, and I find the paper still tucked into the back pocket where I left it.

Back in my bedroom, I can get some privacy. I flop down on my bed and pull my feet cross-legged to examine the paper. It's folded like the butterfly Micah gave me in the lab that day and like the fish I found on the shelf at the library. This one's a little harder to distinguish. Its folds aren't as crisp, indicating a quick fold.

Looking closer, I turn it over a few times and see that it's a turtle. Okay. There has to be something more. *Why would the guy from the truck give me a folded turtle? Maybe there's something written inside.*

Unfolding it is painstaking because I don't want to rip the paper. Not if there's a message of some sort inside. Finally, after several minutes, I spread the paper flat.

It's blank.

Blank? Really?

The utter exhaustion from an emotional day and frustration from this supposed message threatens to overwhelm me, so I flop back on my bed, ready to give in.

It isn't long before I hear a soft knock on my door.

"Kate? Can I come in?"

"Mmm hmm. It's open."

He crosses my room, sits on the edge of my bed and places his hand on my calf. "Your mother told me what happened. You okay?"

"Yeah. I guess."

Then he gets that look in his eye. "What *really* happened?"

We've had this conversation many times before, and I still can't figure out how my dad knows these things. It's like he's got a sixth sense about situations. "Micah said some stuff, and I freaked. Threw a rock at his head." My father's lips pull back into a subtle 'atta girl' smile, but he controls it while I continue. "Then right before he collapsed he told me something else. Something about the NBRs."

"Which was ...?"

I shake my head and stare at the ceiling. "I don't know, Dad. I don't feel right saying anything until I figure it out for myself first." He pats my leg as if to tell me he understands. "Let's just say there are more Natural Born in our community than Great Gran and her friends."

The soft smile pulls back into a huge grin, revealing the pride that's bursting from within him. "Honey, I could have told you that a long time ago."

Those words pique my interest, and I sit up, ready to inquire more, but Dad gently pushes me back down. "You take a few days to figure things out in your head. Then we'll talk ... *after* you've gotten some rest. Let me leave you with this before I go: there's always more to a person than what they portray on the outside, no matter how hard they control themselves."

"Dad, what do you know about turtles?"

His face scrunches up in question, and he shrugs. "Turtles? Um, they're reptiles with hard shells?"

"Dad, I'm serious. Is there something significant about them?"

"Significant how?"

"I don't know. Like, do they represent something?"

"I don't know what you mean."

"Like in stories, how some animals are symbols of death and stuff."

"What's this about, Kate?" Dad sits on the end of my bed and pats my foot.

"I'm not sure. I just need to find out if there's any sort of message or symbol attached to the turtle."

"I've never read anything about it, but Gran used to have this tiny glass turtle that sat on her shelf. She always said it reminded her of herself because some turtles are supposed to live over a hundred years. She said she was going to live that long despite being a Natural Born and prove The Institute wrong. Then she'd tap the glass shell with her fingernail and say, 'I'll do whatever I can to protect you just like this shell protects the animal inside.'"

Dad stares off into the corner, glassy-eyed. "Hmm. I haven't thought of that in a long while."

He leans down to kiss my forehead through his prickly beard. "Does that help?"

"I don't know. Maybe."

"Well, it's all I got for now." He pats my foot again and stands to leave. "Love you, Katie-Did."

I search his face for a clue to what he's talking about, but he's too well-practiced at hiding his thoughts. "Love you, too, Dad."

I lay there for a few minutes, fingering the pendant around my neck and digesting Dad's words. Protection and long life.

Maybe it was a message after all.

· ·

TWENTY THREE

GENERATIONAL ADVICE

SITTING IN MICAH'S HOSPITAL room a few days after he was admitted seems wrong somehow, considering I am the one who put him here. But after all these weeks of knowing him, I feel it's the least I can do. I brought flowers with me and leave them sitting on the bedside table in case he wakes up when I'm not here. It's a pitiful way to apologize, but it's all I have so far. I feel horrible leaving him here alone when no one else knows he's even hurt. It's then I realize I don't know what Micah does with his spare time, not that he has much. His family is gone, killed in that crash. He told me that a long time ago, but what about friends? Have I ever seen him hanging out at Meg's Café or downtown at any of the local restaurants? Except that one time I ran into him on my date with Saul, but he was alone then.

Being the cause of his injuries, it seems like I'm mocking him as I watch the nurses bandage his head again. Thankfully, he's sleeping, so he won't even know I'm here.

It isn't long after I've been here that a pair of young soldiers walks in.

"Can I help you?" I say, hoping to sound like I should be here instead of just assuaging my guilt.

"We were told to come speak to the girl who was with Mr. Pennington at the time of his accident." The way the guy says 'accident' makes it sound like he knows it's not an accident. "I'm assuming that would be you."

"What would you like to know?" I stand and cross to a small table near the window, hoping our voices won't wake Micah. The two men follow me.

"We'd like to hear what happened. From your perspective. It's for the accident report."

I wring my hands, trying to remember what I told the doctor and the guys on the back of the truck. Best to keep my story straight. "Not much to tell," I say. "We were out there doing research for the lab, and Mr. Pennington fell, hitting his head on a rock."

"You were in the Outer Lands for research?"

Gulp. "Yes."

"Do you have the paperwork to allow you passage beyond the borders?" the stockier man asks, looking from his compact to me and back again. These sound like normal questions they might ask, but I can't help but wonder if they're fishing for something else.

"Mr. Pennington must have it. I'm sure he'd taken care of that sort of thing. I was assisting him."

The taller of the two spoke up. "No Outer Lands Pass was found on Mr. Pennington when his clothes were discarded. Can you explain that?"

"No. I can't. Perhaps they were lost in the chaos of bringing Mr. Pennington in?" I try to sound confident, but I'm sure they sense the apprehension in my voice. I hope they don't find out the truth.

At the same time, they both look at me as if I've said something horrible. Which I have. No one accuses The Institute of making an error as small as losing paperwork. It doesn't happen. And I realize I've made a grave mistake. "I mean, perhaps Micah left it at home or at the lab. There has to be some explanation."

"I'm sure," the one says. "We'll be returning shortly to speak with Mr. Pennington once he awakes. Miss ..."

"Dennard. Kate Dennard."

"Miss Dennard." As he says my name, he jots something in his compact with the stylus. Immediately after, they leave.

I can't stay here anymore. I need a break, so I head to the cafeteria for another cup of coffee. By the time the elevator doors open up to the third floor again, I can hear her voice coming from the hallway. Great, just what I need. More confusion. I must be imagining things, so I peek my head around the corner. What I see loosens the grip on my coffee. The whole cup falls to the floor in a whoosh, sending the milky brown liquid splattering across the tiles. Holding only a few napkins, I sop up what I can. In that moment, I'm brought back to a time long ago. She's standing over me with a towel in one hand, cleaning up my spilled cup of juice. I'm crying, sure that I'll be punished, but she takes my chin in her hands and says, "No use crying over spilled milk." "It's juice," I say. She smiles, and we both laugh. Then she tells me to go play outside. And just like that, everything is right as rain.

Bringing myself back to the present, I toss the soggy mess into the garbage. The floor is still slick with coffee, but I don't care. I have to get back to Micah's room. Now.

With each step, her voice grows louder. She's still trying to speak in whispers, but with her hearing the way it is, her whispers aren't exactly quiet. Thankfully, the nurses' station is empty and the family walking down the hall doesn't seem to be interested.

"You need to be more careful," she says. "Ending up here isn't exactly a good way to *not* draw attention to yourself. What were you thinking?" She's not even being careful. Not worried about sounding out of it.

He lowers his voice. "It's not like I planned it this way, Emma. I didn't have another choice. They never got my message. I tried to explain, but Kate didn't take the news very well. Though, I can't say I blame her."

My name. They're talking about me! Suddenly a sickening feeling clenches my stomach into a tight knot. Barging in would obviously stop their conversation, but maybe if I lag near the door for a minute, I might learn something else. Like whatever the heck they're talking about.

"Sounds like my Katie-Did. She's pretty good at being distrustful of everyone. I think I taught her that. Apparently, a little too well."

"So this is your fault." Micah lets out a low chuckle. "She reminds me so much of my mom. Strong-headed. Intelligent. Beautiful … suspicious."

"You were sucked in the moment you met her, weren't you?"

"Do you blame me, Emma?"

"Not in the least. And don't worry, you'll snag her eventually. Just keep up that Pennington charm you've shown me."

"Can't read it in books; can't buy it in stores."

Gran laughs.

"I just wish I could convince her."

"You will, my dear. You will."

Micah changes the subject. "Have you found out anything new?"

"Nothing yet, but I hear the nurses talking about *him* so it won't be long before they drop a name. All I know is he's a big wig in The Institute's research center. So, be careful, Micah. Watch your back as you're working there."

That's it. I've heard enough. In another step, I enter the room.

"Gran, what are you doing up here? Let me get you down to your room," I say, putting on our senile-grandmother/concerned-grand-daughter act. "She must not be feeling well," I say to Micah as I put a hand on either side of her shoulders.

She's sitting in her wheelchair on the far side of the bed, leaning close to his head to talk. Smart move if she doesn't want anyone to hear, but not careful enough. I look toward the video camera installed in every room and hope this one doesn't record sound. It must not. Gran would be more careful than that. She knows what The Institute is like. To them, it would look like she was wandering the halls again, talking to the neighbors.

"Katie-Did," she whispers, looking at the chain around my neck with a wry smile, "I like this one. Don't you worry." She nods toward Micah, and smiles, scrunching up her nose. It makes her eyes twinkle lightly before they disappear into her wrinkles. Suddenly, her shoulders slump and her voice changes. It's louder and more distant. "This one, he's handsome. Very handsome. A good boy. Handsome boy. Looks a little black around the eyes, though." She wheels up closer to his face and yells, "How'd you get so black around yer eyes, boy?" Her frail hand gently slaps his forearm. "You get those eyes healed up so you can see better, okay boy? Maybe you can see my Katie-Did. She's a pretty girl. Nice, too. Very pretty. She doesn't have black eyes, but I think you'd like her."

When she backs away, I notice a young, frazzled nurse rushing through the doorway.

"Ms. Dennard, what're you doing up here? If they find you here, Dr. Matthews will have my head."

Must be a nursing student. They're the only ones who'd make mistakes like this.

Gran smiles at the girl. "Needed to stretch my legs. Go for a little walk." Laughing, she pats her withered legs sitting snugly in her wheelchair. She turns to Micah. "I saw this boy in here. He needed some company. All alone. Very handsome, though, don't you think?" Her face flashes the truth for a moment, but she quickly masks it with an empty grin and a far-off look. She pinches his cheek and pats his arm with her bony hand. "Poor boy. Wanted to talk. I told him to be careful. Don't talk to strangers. Strangers are bad." Gran waggles her finger at the nurse as she repeats those last instructions. The gesture only adds to her act.

Gran is a great actress. When she gets going on one of her "dementia rants," no one would ever know she knows what's going on.

Micah speaks up. "I don't know what happened, nurse. I woke up to this woman chattering beside my bed. She's been going on about strangers and letting my eyes heal and being handsome. I figured it'd just be better to let her go. She wasn't doing any harm."

"She's one of the Wombers. Must've wandered out and up a floor. Sorry about that." The nurse grabs the wheelchair handles and speaks to my gran again. She obviously doesn't know who I am. Maybe she's new. "Let's get you back to your room, shall we, Ms. Dennard?"

"My room. Yes. I like my room very much. It's purple, you know. Lilac, we used to call it. Pretty flowers they are. Sweet smelling. Makes my allergies go crazy."

Gran's voice, still going on about flowers or some such thing, disappears down the hallway as the nurse returns her to her room. I turn to Micah, who sports a sheepish grin and an I-told-you-so look.

"So ... protection and long life, huh?"

"What are you talking about?"

"The turtle. All folded up, like the fish at the library and the butterfly at the lab. I figured it out. Long life ... protection. You were trying to tell me I could trust you."

His eyebrows squish together. "I didn't send you a turtle. How would I have done that when I was bleeding and unconscious?"

Inhaling deeply calms my instantly agitated nerves. "I don't know. I figured you set it up beforehand or something."

If Micah didn't send it, who did? And does it still mean what I think it means?

"When did you get it?"

"When those men dropped you off here. One of them helped me out of the truck and slipped it into my hand."

The blood rushes from Micah's face, and he looks about ready to throw up.

"What's wrong? I thought it had to be a message from you."

"It was a message, but it wasn't from me. It was *for* me."

I eye him. I want to trust him, but honestly, I don't even know why I'm here. The guy tried to abduct me. There's no reason I should be anywhere near him. But my gut tells me there's more to this story. Maybe it was the turtle. Granted, I thought it was from him, but either way, if it really means I'll be protected, then there's nothing to worry about.

Micah nods and tries to smile, but the motion must hit a nerve because his eyes clench shut and he's silent for a second before regaining his composure. His voice turns to a whisper. "Apparently the bounty is off your head now."

"Good to know. Save someone from bleeding to death, avoid rotting in a prison for the rest of my life."

"No. It was called off before you saved me."

Beads of sweat pop onto my skin, and I can't stop my hands from trembling. If I was safe from the rebels before Micah and I went to the

Outer Lands, then why did he try to capture me? I back toward the door one step at a time.

"Kate, please. Let me explain. They were too late."

Too late. That sounds familiar. The man in the truck flashes into my head. *"Sorry we weren't quicker."* He wasn't speaking to me. It was a message for Micah.

Every breath seems too thick to inhale. I'm trying to hold myself together while I finagle the pieces of this ever deepening puzzle. "Micah, I need some serious answers."

"You'll get them. I promise. Let me get out of this place, and I'll tell you everything." Micah's hand covers mine. The movement surprises me, and all I can do is look down at his hand resting on mine. He squeezes it gently and lets go.

"It's going to be okay, Kate. Right as rain."

Gran's voice enters my thoughts. *"I like this one. Don't you worry."* Gran wouldn't lie to me. I know I can trust her. And because she says Micah is okay, I'll take her word for it and give him a chance to explain.

As if he knows I'm thinking about Gran, he says, "Your gran is remarkable. You didn't have to make her do the pretending thing, you know, but it was amazing how she just switched back into her ranting as soon as she saw that nurse. She's really quite creative. And quick!"

I play along with this new cheerful topic only because I don't think I can handle anything else right now. Only this isn't much better. "Yeah, she's been doing that for years. I guess it's become a habit for me, too." I don't know what to say after that. In the few minutes I've been watching the sight playing out in front of me, my entire belief that I was the only one Gran trusted with her secret has been blown to bits.

"I'm really sorry, Micah. You know, for trying to beat your head in with a rock."

This makes him smile. "Well, I suppose I deserved it." He touches his forehead where the stitches form a line to his temple. "You pack a hell of a punch."

This time it's my turn to smile. "Gran always told me to put my all into whatever I was doing." I look everywhere but Micah's face. But then I can't stand it any longer. I stare right into the swollen bubbles that still surround his eyes. The skin has turned from black to a purplish hue with traces of yellow around the edges where it's started to heal. "How long have you known my gran?"

"Since I came onto this job." And that's it. Apology over. If that exchange can count for an apology in the first place.

"And what job is that exactly?"

"Like I said, let's not talk about that here."

"Then it looks like we have a lot of talking to do when you're released," I say.

"Yes, we do. In the meantime, you're going to be getting a visit from the soldiers in charge of the incident report." I lower my voice as quiet as I can with him still being able to hear me. "Please tell me you have the day pass allowing us to be in the Outer Lands."

"Of course. The paperwork has been filed already. Well, at least it will be by the time they look for it in the data system. I have people covering our tracks."

"Now we just have to hope they don't inquire with my family."

"Why's that?"

"Because I told them I was picnicking with you. I didn't realize we had to have an alibi for our alibi."

"Don't worry. I'll cover it. I know people, remember?"

"So you say."

Before I can pull away, Micah's hand covers mine again, and his serious look urges me to believe him. "I'll explain everything. Soon."

I nod, not knowing how to respond. "I have to go."

"Kate?" Micah calls as I near the door. "Thanks for coming to check on me."

I nod again because it's the only thing that seems right. "Sorry about your face."

He tries to smile, but it makes him wince again.

Walking out the door, my mind is a whir of thoughts. *I'll explain everything*, he'd said. I'm not sure I want to know it all.

TWENTY FOUR

....

PRIDE

THE FOLLOWING WEDNESDAY AFTER my humanities class, I head to the hospital to visit Micah. I want some answers, and the quicker he recovers, the faster I'll get them. Every day he's improving though the concussion I gave him has been giving him nasty headaches. The first few days he slept most of the time. Dr. Rosenberg, who treated him, told me that Micah was to have no stimulation. Not even reading—nothing visual at all. Which pretty much means no thinking. How do you get a guy who works in a research lab practically all hours in the day to not think? Being in the hospital is good for him because there is absolutely nothing for him to do except stare at the walls.

When I get to his room, he's sitting on the edge of the bed, and Dr. Rosenberg is giving him instructions. "Your shirt was too stained to be any good, so we had it destroyed. You've been given some loaner clothing since we couldn't reach anyone at your home to bring you something to wear."

"I live alone, Doctor."

Dr. Rosenberg jots a note in his compact. "Do you have someone to assist you home?"

Micah gives him a sarcastic look. "I figured if you were releasing me I'd be okay to go on my own."

The doctor looks up with a straight face. "It would be beneficial to you if you had some help. You're fine to leave now, but you are still restricted from activities for another week. Activities like driving."

"I'll walk," Micah says.

I step up and tap the doctor on the shoulder. "I can help."

He barely glances at me. "And you are?"

"A friend," Micah says. "It's okay, Doc. I trust her." His eyes, when he says that, are soft and almost pleading. I don't argue.

"Very well, then," the doctor says as he backs out of the room. "You're free to go, Mr. Pennington. As long as your friend assists you." His head rises from his work to actually look at me. Then he leaves.

Micah leans forward and stands up. "I don't need any—" His hand shoots toward his forehead and his other arm steadies himself on the bed. "Whoa."

"Right, you don't need *any* help." I grab his arm to help him stand again.

"Just got up too fast. I'm fine." He blinks a few times and heads toward the door. But when he reaches the doorway, he closes his eyes again. "Okay, maybe a little help getting home would be good."

"Nurse!" When she arrives, I ask for a wheelchair to wheel Micah out of the hospital. Once we're in the parking lot, I realize his truck won't be here. We drove it to the Outer Lands and returned in someone else's vehicle.

"Micah, your truck?"

"Over there." He points to the middle of the lot with the keys he holds in his hand. Seeing the confusion on my face he adds, "I'll explain later."

As I wheel him toward the vehicle and help him into the passenger seat, my eyes grow big, and I try to comprehend how his truck ended up here. He directs as I drive him to his house.

Once I've helped Micah to his couch, I take a seat in the chair across the room.

"You don't have to stay. I'm fine now."

I don't move. "Mind telling me how your truck came to be at the hospital parking lot when we left it at the picnic grounds?"

His eyes avoid mine as he shifts into a more comfortable position. "It's a long story. One I'm not at liberty to tell."

"Why not? What happened to, 'You can trust me, Kate'? If I can trust you, you should be able to trust me, don't you think? And you told me you'd explain things."

He fidgets with his hands. "Kate, I want to tell you, I do, but I don't want to put you in any danger."

"How could telling me how your truck got back possibly put me in any danger?" I roll my eyes. "It's not like you have a secret group of friends living in some underground city or something, ready to do your bidding."

His eyes widen, but he says nothing.

"Oh. My. Goodness. You have a secret group of friends living in an underground city."

He nods, finally speaking. "Pretty much."

"All those stories I heard as a kid about the Natural Born? The rebels?"

"True."

"And that stuff you told me in the forest just after I cracked your head open?"

"Also true."

"So, what? You live in some secret community and sneak into our town like little fairies or trolls or something?"

"Kind of. Only without the wings or warts." He smiles, but seeing my shock and confusion at his confession, it fades. Then he shakes his head. "I shouldn't even be telling you this." Our eyes meet, and he sighs. "We have a few entrances to the city. When we need to go back and forth, we use them, but visitations have to stay at a minimum so The Institute doesn't find out. They're desperate to find us and wipe us out."

"So, they don't know about you? Being a Natural Born, I mean."

"Nope. And I'd like to keep it that way." He shifts again on the couch, stuffing a pillow behind his head.

"Those guys you called?"

"Yeah?"

"They were NBRs, weren't they?"

He nods. "As soon as I was conscious, I sent a message to them telling them to get my truck."

"How'd you send a message?"

"That I won't tell you. I won't compromise anyone else."

"So, if you're really from some secret village, is this even your house? Do you even live here?"

There's the look again. The guilty-as-charged look.

Now I'm getting irritated and cross my hands over my chest. "Seriously? You need to spill."

He sighs. "Okay, here's the shortened version: remember when we were talking about the accident that mangled my face and stuff?"

"Yeah. Our first date."

"Well, it wasn't me."

Now I'm thoroughly confused. "What do you mean it wasn't you?"

"The kid in that accident died. I took his place." He pauses, letting the words sink in.

"Wha—? You replaced him? So, if you're not Micah Pennington, who are you and how did you get here without being noticed? It's not like you can just take over someone's life without any complications."

"Remember, the kid was mangled beyond recognition. My people were able to slip me in, after battering my face up pretty good." He grimaces at the memory. "Had a few friends who enjoyed that. Anyway, we have NBRs and sympathizers all over, Kate. Even in the hospital. Micah's death was the perfect opportunity to plant another Natural Born in the society. My only regret is that no one knew the kid died. No one was able to mourn his passing because, in their eyes, I *am* him."

"But don't you look different? How is it possible that no one noticed? It's not like he was your twin or anything."

He points to his face. "Messed up, remember. I guess I sort of looked like him. When they put me back together, of course I was going to look a little different, but we were similar enough that people believed it. The Penningtons don't have any extended family around here. So the only ones we had to worry about were some friends. But since I was under the care of Sector 4 for over a year, the friendships kind of dwindled. The real Micah's friends had been assigned to study elsewhere."

"So who are you then? What's your name?"

"I'm Micah Pennington. That's all you need to know right now. I'm not going to compromise what's going on here. Not now. But I promise I'll tell you someday."

It all starts to come together in my mind. "And the park? That first night I ran into you? You were following me weren't you?"

"Yes, but once I saw you were assigned to my lab unit, there was no need for that. I could keep my eyes on you without making you paranoid. The problem was the more time I spent with you, the more I liked you. I ... I ... mean. That's not a problem for me, but it was for the original plan." He shakes his head a little and laughs at himself. "As soon as I realized it, I sent word to my superiors canceling the order on you. It was a long shot, but I hoped to convince them you could be an asset. There was still no response the day we went to the Outer Lands, the day I had planned to ... well, you know. So I had to go through with it. Now I know they not only got my message, but relented."

"The turtle?"

"Yeah. Unfortunately, I didn't get their response in time. Hence the botched abduction. I'm sorry. I didn't know what else to do. Sometimes even our best intentions fail miserably."

Micah's shoulders slump, and he has a blank look on his face. For the first time since I met him, he seems broken. Here is a guy who is more intelligent than most, keeping secrets, and putting himself in harm's way in order to be a liaison for the resistance; and he's bested by an ancient and slow communication system. It would be comical if it weren't so dangerous.

"So the turtle really does mean what I think it does?"

"Yes. It's my people's way of saying that a person will be protected by the resistance. If it's found, people will only see a folded turtle, but anyone associated with the resistance knows what it means."

This is all too overwhelming. If Micah replaced someone in our community, and he was originally sent to abduct me, then someone was out there waiting to replace me. I don't think I can hear any more of this. It's a lot to take in all at once.

"Look, Kate," Micah says. "I know this is a lot, but when I'm feeling better, I'd like to take you somewhere and explain some things. I think it'll ease your mind a bit."

"Take me where?"

"To the Hidden City."

· ·

TWENTY FIVE

MORE UNVIABLE

THE NEXT TIME I see Micah is on my break between classes a week later. He was home with strict hospital orders to rest, so he didn't return to work for a few days, but I called him every few hours to apologize; he did the same. I can't help it if my crazy, impulsive side got the better of me that day in the woods. He *did* try to capture me, so I figure I at least had a good reason to defend myself.

I'm headed to the library to work when I see him waiting for me inside the main doors.

"Hey, your face looks better."

He touches his forehead where the purpled specks still show through the yellowed blotch on his head. "Feels better. A little tender still, but better. You're a great shot. I swear that rock was the size of my head." He manages a small smile, but there's something wrong. He's not himself.

"Thanks for rubbing it in."

His hand trembles as he takes mine. "Come here. I need to show you something." Glancing around as we enter the stacks, he leads me to the back corner near my favorite study spot, but we don't stay there. Around the stacks at the far end, tucked just behind my corner is a door leading to a storage room. Putting a finger to his lips to shush me, he turns the handle and pulls me inside.

"Micah, what's going on? What's wrong?"

"Shhh. Just let me—"

Without warning, his lips crush mine, and we're entangled in each other's arms, barely breathing, searching for the sense of reality that comes from each other's touch. The questions about his obvious fear evaporate in our embrace.

Then he pulls back and rests his forehead against mine, leaving his hands resting on either side of my neck.

"What was that for?"

"To say I'm sorry one more time. I needed to feel you in my arms and prove to myself that you're safe."

Now I'm confused. "You saw me just the other day. Why wouldn't I be safe? Other than you and your friends trying to get rid of me."

He offers me a sarcastic look. "I'm never going to live this down, am I?"

"Nope."

His eyes meet mine as he gathers his breath and brushes my hair away from my face. His hands are warm and rough, but his touch is tender as he runs his thumb over my cheek. "They made the decision to dispose of an adult today."

I'd back away if the door weren't holding me in place. "What? What are you talking about? The Institute only disposes of unviable infants and the few Wombers left."

"Not anymore."

He steps next to me, and we both slide down the wall until we're sitting on the cold cement floor of the storage room. "Today was my first day back at work, and I was prepping the lab when one of the doctors from the long-term care facility came in. He was looking for Professor Donovan. Said he had an order straight from Fishgold. When I heard that name, I knew something was up, so after I brought the guy to Donovan, I eavesdropped."

"Micah, are you crazy? If they'd caught you listening, they could have …" I don't need to say it. We both know.

He ignores me. "Anyway, the guy tells Donovan that an order has just passed by Fishgold and the Council stating that injured adults who don't show improvement in a matter of weeks or those whose healing is not completed in a yet undetermined amount of time will be subject to disposal, decision made by the Committee itself."

I stare at the far wall in disbelief. "So, they're going to start disposing any adult who gets injured?"

"Pretty much. If they can't fix it right away. Something about over-crowding at the facility, but I think it's more than that."

"But they haven't actually done it yet, right? I mean, they didn't dispose of anyone yet. Maybe they're just putting the idea out there."

"I wish, Kate, but the guy said it was a direct order. Must be Donovan needed to know since he's in charge of the disposal unit. Besides, I heard something else ... They've already scheduled one."

I'm sure my heart just stopped.

The wall scratches at my shirt as I stand up and look around for any sort of monitoring device. "We need to get out of here. What if someone catches us? Who knows what could happen." Jitters take over my body, and suddenly I'm shaking. "Do you know what this means, Micah? They could get rid of anyone for any reason. Heck, they could even cause an accident if they wanted to."

"I know," he says, getting up. His arms wrap around my waist, and he kisses me again. "I'm sorry. I shouldn't have said anything. It was just ... I freaked out when I heard it and needed to tell someone. Now I've got you all upset."

I take a deep breath and smooth my hands over my pants. "I'm okay. But it could've been you."

"I've thought of that."

"We need to get out of here."

"Good idea. It's time I tell the leaders in the Hidden City about this." Micah eases the door open a crack and peeks out to make sure no one's there before letting me slide through and into the brightly lit library again. He follows and closes the door silently behind him.

....

TWENTY SIX

A TREK THROUGH THE UNDERGROUND

"**Y**OU SURE YOU WANT to do this?" A set of keys dangle from Micah's hand.

"Yeah. I'm ready."

He twists the key, and the old truck revs to life. "I don't want to make you uncomfortable. We've been through a lot lately, so if you need more time, I'm okay with that. I know there's not really a good reason to trust me yet."

"I know, Micah. It's fine. You forgave me for cracking your head open with a rock; I think I can offer you this." I crank the heat up as high as it will go to ward off the nervous chill that settles on my bones.

"And you forgave me for your botched abduction."

"Call us even. Now let's get this over with."

Suddenly, his hands are on either side of my face. He pulls me closer and kisses my nose. "You are an amazing woman, you know that?"

"What I am is giving you a second chance."

According to Micah, the elders of the Hidden City have agreed to give me a chance to become a sympathizer instead of letting me rot in an underground prison. I'm not sure what possesses me to take him at his word. But Gran told me once that sometimes all the evidence will point one way and your gut will point another, and you have to decide which you're going to follow. Today, I'm following my gut and hoping it knows what it's doing.

Twisting sideways, Micah faces me. "I'm sorry you even have to give me a second chance."

"Okay, enough with the apologizing."

"How many times did you apologize for the afternoon in the Outer Lands?"

"That's totally different! You were bleeding. And passed out. And needed stitches. Remember the hospital stay?"

"And I zip tied your hands and was planning on having you thrown into prison to rot. I think I win."

"Okay. You win."

He lets out a hearty laugh as he fingers the scars along his temple. He throws the truck into gear. In my head, I try to keep track of the turns, but after ten minutes, I'm totally lost. I swear he's circled the city at least twice before I notice the birds chirping through my open window and the sounds of other vehicles quieting down. We've crossed over the hills on the edge of town. Somewhere buried among the trees and dirt is an entire city of NBRs. A Natural Born community subsisting all on its own. A group of people the rest of the world doesn't even know exists.

Once I lose track of where we are, I spend the time asking about the gran I thought I knew.

"You already know your gran's opinions about The Institute, but what you don't know is that she's one of our main sources of information. The whole dementia thing she puts on is the perfect ruse because many times the doctors and administrators talk in front of her. She sets herself up in a busy hallway or near the nurse's station, allowing her to lift sensitive material. She's even helped to thwart a few scientific experiments."

"Like what?" I ask, now thoroughly fascinated with this side of my gran.

"Well, a few years ago, the research department wanted to increase the microchip abilities before implantation at birth. Suppress any physical pleasure of any kind. They've already eliminated the need to procreate, so why not eliminate all forms of physical pleasure? As soon as your gran overheard their plans, she informed our Institute plant. It allowed us to work with our contacts and sympathizers in the designated areas to overturn such decisions. That's not to say The Institute workers won't try again, but we were able to at least put it off for a while."

My gran, an underground spy. How cool is that? Knowing this makes me prouder of her.

"How many people do you have in the community?"

"Not as many as we'd like. That's why we're getting more and more rash with abductions. We need more people and waiting for an accident like the one I used to enter topside takes too long. The point is they aren't people you'd notice. We have to blend in or our entire existence is at stake." He downshifts as he talks, and the truck tilts as we climb a hill. "I can't tell you numbers. Honestly, I have no idea how many of us there are. We don't even know each other half the time unless it affects our personal assignments. Then we're informed of the people we can trust."

I turn my head toward him. "So who else is a spy? Is that what you call them?"

"Call them what you will. You already know about your gran, but the others, I can't reveal. For their own safety and yours. That way, if something goes wrong, we can't implicate everyone. As for this little trip we're taking, I'm anxious to see what my superiors say when they've found out what I've learned."

Me, too.

With each turn of the road, my stomach lurches. I swear I didn't know Micah drove like this. "Geesh, take it easy on the bumps, would you?"

"Sorry, they're kind of inevitable. No paving where I'm from."

"Right, well, try to warn me or something next time."

"No need." He lets out a sigh as we come to a stop. "We're here."

Rubbing my eyes, I look around. There's nothing. Well, not nothing. Trees are everywhere. And fallen branches. And a few rocks jutting out of the side of the hill. "Wow, this is—" I'm lost for words. Is he losing it? There's no city here. I expected some abandoned, broken down ghost town or something. A place the people could take over and revitalize, but there's nothing here.

Suddenly, tension seizes my body, and I can't move. This place looks like the forest we picnicked in the day I put him in the hospital. Flashbacks flood my mind, and for a moment I wonder if I'm safe here with Micah.

"Kate?" Micah's voice is smooth and deep. Like a soft rumbling of thunder in the distance.

"Huh? What?" I don't even look at him, instead, gathering information from my surroundings. Branches, trees, rocks. That's about it. No city. No people.

"Hop out of the truck." He's standing next to my door. How did I not notice him getting out of his side and rounding the truck? "Watch your step. It's a bit of a jump here." He offers me a hand, and I take it, hopping onto the needle-covered ground. My feet press into the soft dirt, but the dry pine needles still crunch with every step.

A branch I eyed earlier is a few steps away, and when we pass it, he bends down to pick it up and props it against the truck.

"Kate, I need some help here. Search around a bit and try to find branches with the needles still on them. We need to hide the truck as much as possible. At least until I can send someone to get it."

But I just stand there, contemplating if I can fend him off if, by chance, he decides to complete what he started our previous time in the Outer Lands. After all we've been through. All he's told me. Part of me just wants to give in. Stop fighting that instinct telling me to trust no one. It'll be easier and probably less painful. But I *want* to trust him, to trust my gut that told me only hours ago that this would be okay.

Apparently, he doesn't notice my hesitation because he's busied himself gathering fallen branches lying a few yards away, propping them gently against his truck, trying not to let them scratch the paint. Soon, it's mostly covered. You can still tell there's something large and metal there, but from a distance, with just a glance, one might not notice against the backdrop of trees. That must be what he was going for because when he steps away to examine his handiwork, he nods. "Just a few more."

I hand him a branch. No need for him to think I'm not being help-ful. When he's done, he brushes his hands together and wipes them on his pants. "Kate? Are you okay?"

Suddenly, his hands are on my arms, holding tight, and I'm wrench-ing my body from his grasp. "Kate!" He shakes me. "Move!" There's a cracking sound above me, but I can't process it. It's like I'm in a daze. Practically picking me right off my feet, he moves me an arm's length away as a crashing branch careens downward. Where I stood, a huge tree limb lays.

I stare at it for a minute then look at Micah, whose breaths are heavy from the work he's done. He looks at me with a face I can't interpret.

Shaking my head, I say, "Sorry, I'm disoriented from the drive."

He lets out a soft chuckle. "You thought I brought you out here to hurt you, didn't you?"

My eyes grow wide with disbelief.

My muscles relax, and I blush. "It crossed my mind."

Micah's smile widens as he hooks his arm around my waist. "Kate, if I wanted to do that, I had many opportunities before now." He kisses my cheek.

I glare at him. "Gee, that's so comforting."

But his hearty laughter eases my nerves, and I fall into step at his side.

Okay, so he's right. He's had many opportunities before now, even this past week. If he wanted to finish what he started, he could have several times. But I can't help my paranoia. It flares up whenever I get nervous. It's been practically beaten into me by Dad. Be careful of ev-erything and everyone. Never fully trust anyone, no matter how much you may want to. I can't help it. It's part of who I am. But I want to trust Micah more than anything.

Up ahead is a patch of boulders set into the side of the hill. They look totally natural, and when Micah leads us there, I expect he's stopping for a rest. But I nearly jump out of my skin when he reaches down into the soil, searching for something. Then he stands, having seemingly found whatever he was looking for, and the rock in the center of the patch pulls back to reveal a long, dark tunnel.

I look at him, feeling my skin crawl at the thought of being enclosed under the earth, but he just smiles and takes my hand as he steps his foot into the passageway. "It's okay. You don't have to freak. I'm not going to bury you alive." He chuckles. "This leads to the Hidden City."

Maybe it's the creep-factor of entering a damp, musty underground tunnel. Or it could be my heightened everyone's-trying-to-hurt-me in-tuition, but taking those first steps into the darkness behind Micah sets off my danger beacon like fireworks at the Parade of Values celebration.

The dampness doesn't bother me, though I can't say I'm fond of the sticky feeling that pastes my clothing tight to my body. I don't even mind the musty, earthy smell that grows stronger with each step deeper into the tunnel. What does totally freak me out are the sounds or lack thereof.

At first, it's the utter silence. A strange quiet that shocks my core. Even the sound of my footsteps disappears into the blackness. But as I listen closer, I hear Micah's breath, heavy but even. In the distance, drizzling water echoes as it trickles over the rock walls.

We travel for what seems like hours, though I'm sure it's only been a few minutes. With Micah's hand in mine, my sense of time is slightly skewed. I'm more focused on my surroundings and the feel of his palm grasping mine.

His voice breaks through the dark. "Almost there."

Once he speaks, I find myself squinting through the shadows for any indication of where "there" might be. A few more sloshy steps and we round a corner, which gives way to a tiny beam of light. From what I can see, it's the end of the tunnel. A rock wall. But to Micah, it must be more.

Reaching the wall of rock, I see shreds of light breaking through holes in the earth. Like a child's drawing of sunbeams shining over a simple landscape.

"Stand over here," Micah instructs as he pushes me gently against the wall and moves to the rocks at the end of the cavern.

I stay still as I watch him heave on a huge boulder, knocking it to its side. I have to shield my eyes as the light pours in, and when I look up, he's standing there, one arm offered to me and the other motioning toward the opening.

"The Hidden City," he says.

TWENTY SEVEN

·····························

THE HIDDEN CITY

A FEW MOMENTS AGO, I thought the light bursting through the walls of the tunnel was sunlight. Now I see it's from a whole underground network of electrical lines. We must be pretty deep underground because the buildings I see are as tall as any in Sector 4, and the sky is dark in most places, save for the street lamps. Eternal nighttime.

Micah sees my astonishment and answers my unasked question. "The tops of the buildings are disguised as the forest floor. Some of them are inside the trees; others brush the forest floor, which is held up by thick panes of glass, allowing a little natural sunlight into the town."

I'm speechless as we walk down the main street, inhaling the scent of fresh earth. The buildings are much more primitive than what The Institute would build. The dingy metal shingles are pieced together, some giving way to the rot of rust, but considering they must have been scavenged and brought here piece by piece and put together entirely underground, this place is amazing.

"It started off as a safety bunker a few of our founders discovered long before the first raid years ago. But the population grew," Micah explains. "They had to branch out. So, they began scavenging and dig-ging tunnels away from the core of the bunker. When people came here, they brought what they could, but now we have a whole group of people whose job it is to create or scavenge building supplies. They cut lumber from the forest, and we even have metal workers to create nails and screws. We confiscate what we can, and with technology, we have most of the conveniences you have above."

"This must be my history tour," I say.

I can see the pride on Micah's face. Or maybe it's relief. Like the secret he's kept from everyone he knows is finally out. He can be himself.

It's amazing. There's a school, restaurant, and coffee shop scattered down the main street. Off to the sides, I see smaller brick streets lined with tiny suburban looking houses. Pots of flowers decorate an occasional corner. It's eclectic. No two buildings looking like the next, but that brings out the personality of this city. A city of diversity.

I point to the flowers and turn to Micah, "How do they—"

"Fake," he interrupts. "Most of the plants are silk except the giant tree roots that support some of the building structures. We do have a few in the greenhouses, but the fake ones look just as nice."

That makes sense. No sunlight means few flowers can grow. But the splash of color and the smell of the dirt make it seem like spring.

"There's a girl here who is in charge of the flowers," Micah explains. "She changes the pots all around town depending on the season. Notice they're mostly mums right now? That's because it's fall. Come winter, it'll be pines and poinsettias and in spring, she goes a little crazy with variety."

The street is long and bustling with people of every shape and color. Shop owners, I presume, but every few people we pass, I notice something unusual. One guy walks with a limp. Another woman sits in a wheelchair, her legs atrophied from lack of use. A little boy with braces on his legs plays in a group of kids his age, and they don't even seem to notice that he's different. The amount of people with handicaps here is astounding. On the outside, we might have one or two, resultant from an injury or something, but now with that new law approving disposals of such people, soon there'll be none. And the different skin colors. At The Institute, at least in Sector 4, everyone has white skin. But here, I see sprinklings of every color. Down the street, I notice a girl about my age with something I can't identify. A mental disorder of some sort.

She approaches me with her wide face and pinched eyes and shows me a thick-lipped smile as she hands me a flower between her stubby fingers. "For you," she says with a slight lisp,

"That's Meagan," Micah informs me, seeing the look of shock on my face. "She has what they used to call Down Syndrome. She might not be able to have her own business or raise a family, but her positive attitude spreads cheer to everyone she meets. Everyone here loves her, and she loves them right back. But whatever you do, don't hug her."

"Why's that?"

"Because she's as strong as an ox and can crack a rib if she's not careful."

"So, who takes care of her?"

"Her parents do. And the rest of us. Kate, don't you see? No matter what The Institute says is *wrong* with people, they have something to give. We shouldn't destroy that. It's why we refuse to kill to replace people. All life is precious." The main street curves, and when we turn the corner, he grabs my hand again. "Here, I want to show you something." His gray eyes are duller here, like the sunlight lightens them when we're above ground, but I see a spark as he guides me through the doorway of a shop front. A little bell dings as we open the door, and an old man with wire-rimmed glasses greets us.

"Micah! Long time no see."

"Hey, Silas. Brought a friend today."

"I can see that. Pretty one." He smiles at me, and the wrinkles near his eyes crease. Grabbing a cane that hangs on the edge of the counter, he limps around in an effort to be helpful. "What're you looking for?"

"Classics. Don't bother getting up. I know where to find them."

The walls are lined with shelves and covered with books, and I wonder why Micah brought me to a library. But as we're passing the shelves, I reach out my hand like I so often do in our above-ground library, letting the books slip under my fingertips. I gasp at the touch.

Micah looks at me and smiles as the realization sinks in. "These are real books!" I say, almost not believing my own eyes.

"Sure are." A contented smile settles on his face. "Silas saved most of them when The Institute planned on getting rid of them all and replacing everything with technology. That's another thing your gran discovered for us, from what I hear. I wasn't around then. Long before my time here."

My hands drift back to the cool, smooth spines. I can feel the imprint of the lettering, and feel the bumpy texture of a leather-bound anthology. I wonder which of these very same books my great-grandmother has read. Which stories she told me as a child came from the pages that line these shelves. My fingers clasp around a worn binding frayed at the edge, and I pull it off the shelf. Its pages crack lightly as I pry them apart and breathe in the most unusual scent. Like trees and sunshine. I inhale again, not wanting to forget the smell that reminds me of her.

"I knew you'd like this place," Micah says.

"This is amazing! Can you take these books out, like at a real library?"

"Not only that," Micah says, "you can keep them."

When my eyes grow wide, he continues, "It's a bookstore, Kate. You purchase these to keep."

I'm silent for a moment, taking in what he just said. It's incomprehensible to have a treasure like this in my own home, so I don't try to understand. Instead, I turn back to the books. "Have you read all these?"

Micah shakes his head. "Not all, but some."

I hold the book in my hands out to him. "This one?"

His fingers brush mine as he takes it from my hand, and I'm sure they linger a little longer than necessary.

"*Fahrenheit 451*" He reads the title. "Good choice."

"What happens?"

"The government uses firemen to set fire to all the books in a society, and they punish anyone who reads."

This piques my interest, and a story Dad told me years ago pops into my mind. The leaders of our town did the same thing when they chose technology over these pages.

Micah sees the look on my face, and his head cocks in recognition.

"At least we're still allowed to read," I say, knowing he knows what I'm thinking.

A sigh escapes his lips. "Only what they want us to read."

I suppose this is true since these titles are unfamiliar to me, but our leaders couldn't possibly want to control us like that. Even if their methods are unconventional and they do want to keep the people in line, what possible purpose could they have by restricting our reading? Even if I don't agree with The Institute's methods, they're only trying to do what it takes to create a safe community. "So what happens?"

Micah hands the worn pages back to me. "Read it and find out," he says.

I drop the book on the counter and reach into my pocket to dig out a few bills, but Silas raises his hand and shakes his head, his loose gray hair falling into his eyes. "No, young lady. No charge for the first one." He flashes me a crooked smile as I thank him and tuck the novel into my back pocket. Then he notices the pendant around my neck. "Where'd you get that necklace? It's unique."

"My great grandmother gave it to me. Used to be hers."

"Ah," he says.

Just then the bells above the door clink, and a breathless guy barges through. "Micah!" he yells. "I've been looking everywhere for you. You were supposed to be back hours ago." His hair is matted to his forehead with sweat. As he reaches up, he slicks the hair back, revealing concerned eyes.

"My meeting with the elders isn't till later."

The guy shakes his head. Micah's smile disappears, and his stone face returns.

"It's Ally," the boy says.

Micah's entire body tenses as he looks at me then back to the boy. "She's going early."

Without hesitation, Micah's through the door followed by his friend. I look to Silas, who says, "You better hurry or you'll get lost around here."

I push through the door just in time to see Micah round the corner of the block and rush down a dark alley. He's forgotten me. I feel lost and out of place as I hurry after him. I shouldn't be here. Now, with Micah rushing off, I'm like the third wheel.

In the distance, I see Micah glance back. We make eye contact, and he shouts something to the boy and points to me. At least he hasn't entirely forgotten I exist.

In a huff, the guy jogs back to me and grabs my hand. "Come on," he says before I have time to protest. "Micah's going on ahead. I'll show you the way."

"And you are?" I tug my hand away. It's not that I want to be rude, but I try not to make a habit of holding hands with strange guys, and, this friend of Micah's certainly fits into that category. Heck, anyone who lives in this underground city fits into that category.

"Jaxon Salinger." He thrusts out his hand in an official greeting. "No relation to J. D." His smile is wide, but the obvious confusion on my face ends his joking. "Never mind," he says. "Let's go."

Tentatively, I follow him down the alley. We rush through a maze of streets, occasionally cutting through a building to reach our destination. Much like at The Institute, many of these buildings are interconnected. This one's made of whitewashed bricks, and I wonder where they found the materials to build such a massive structure, much less build it underground. It sure would be difficult to smuggle this many cement blocks. In a way, it reminds me of The Institute, which makes sense when I read the *Hospital* sign hanging over the doorway. The further we venture into the building, the more primitive the surroundings become. The front is clean and white—sanitary looking—but the back rooms are separated by wooden planks instead of the cement bricks I saw up front. Obviously, the people building this hospital ran out of materials halfway through. They probably couldn't find enough to finish it.

Jaxon is still a few steps away from me, but every few minutes he turns to make sure I'm right behind him. "It's just around the corner," he states, turning to the left.

When I round the corner, he's there holding a door open for me. Down the dimly lit hallway, Micah paces. The sign on the wall makes my heart drop.

Maternity Ward.

"Wait here," Jaxon says. He motions to a rickety chair in the corner. A makeshift waiting room. "I'll see what's going on." He starts to go, but I stop him.

"Wait, Jaxon."

He looks at me, and I stare back, silent. I can't formulate a thought much less a sentence. There's too much to take in here. Hidden pathways, real books, underground buildings, and Micah in a maternity ward.

"Sorry we had to meet in such rushed circumstances." He shrugs and puts his hands up as if to say, *there's nothing I could do about it.*

***

It's odd sitting in a hospital maternity ward, and I wonder if this is what it'll be like to wait for my own son to be born if the circumstances were different. At first, I'm relaxed. However, Jaxon and Micah's voices echo down the hallway.

"How's she doing?" Jaxon asks.

"Not well." Micah's trying to stay calm, but the shaking in his voice gives way to his fear. "The doctor says there are complications with the baby. If they don't figure it out soon, Ally could die, too."

I stand up and move to the edge of the alcove. I don't want to intrude, but I have to see what's going on.

The moment I peek my head around to catch a glimpse of Micah, I see him slink to the floor and rest his head in his hands. Jaxon stands above him looking like he doesn't know what to do. I'm about to rush to Micah, to tell him it will be okay and put my arms around him. I'll let him grieve.

Jaxon leans down and places a hand on Micah's shoulder. "Hey, man. Ally's going to be fine. She's a tough girl."

"Micah?" I want to ask if everything is okay, but clearly, it isn't. I slog toward him, cautious of the unknown.

He scampers up and rushes to me before I can say another word. "Kate. I'm so sorry. I didn't mean to leave you alone."

"Who's Ally?"

"My sister. She's having a baby and something's wrong."

"Having a baby?"

He shakes his head and guides me by the elbow toward the door. "Yes, only something's wrong. The doctors are working now."

He points toward the door with the glass window. All I can see is the glint of the light off of a scalpel in the doctor's hand. It's moving toward a distended belly exposed through hospital sheeting.

"What are they going to do to her?"

"They're going to get the baby out."

TWENTY EIGHT

JUST LIKE BATCH 4

Code of Conduct and Ethics: The Institute—Sector 4, USA
Section 3 Article 1.0: Each individual shall conduct him or herself with the
utmost modesty. Proper attire is required at all times. Clothing shall cover
all intimate parts of the body. Only arms and legs (below the knees) are al-
lowed to be visible.

"WHAT DO YOU MEAN 'get the baby out'?"

"Right. I forget you've never seen a pregnant woman. The baby was inside Ally, Kate. The way things used to be before The Institute's birthing practices rendered women barren and took over the life-building process with science and test tubes."

"You mean she's actually birthing a baby from her own body?"

"Well, sort of. The doctors are removing it from her."

"They can do that?"

"Let's hope so."

Minutes slip by into hours. Micah, Jaxon, and I take turns keeping post outside the operating room doors. Even when it's Jaxon's or my turn and we insist Micah get some rest, he refuses to leave. Instead, he pulls a rickety chair into the hallway and sits sideways, half curled, nodding in and out of sleep.

In the wee hours of the morning—I know only because I've been watching the clock on the wall tick by second by second—a doctor exits the room. The dark circles under his eyes are evidence of a long night, and his slumped shoulders give away his exhaustion.

"She's going to be okay," he says.

Micah perks up. "And the baby?"

"Is fine."

Letting out a huge breath, Micah finally relaxes. "When can we see her?"

"Ally's resting now. She'll probably be pretty sore for a while, but you can visit after she sleeps. Come back this afternoon."

"I'll wait here." Micah sits in the chair he's leaned against the wall.

Jaxon crosses his arms. "Micah, really? There's nothing more you can do. Go back to Silas's and get some rest. We can come back in the morning."

Jaxon's voice of reason breaks through Micah's overprotective-brother-barrier, and he relents.

"Tell Silas we're coming."

Jaxon shakes the doctor's hand and is off in a flash. Micah looks at me.

"Not exactly the homecoming celebration I was hoping for. If you need, I'll get you back to The Institute."

"Micah, I'm not going anywhere. It's the weekend. No one will be looking for me."

"We hope. In that case, let's get a little rest."

****

I sleep on a guest bed in a tiny house attached to the back of the bookshop. Micah takes a couch in the reception area, so I don't notice when he leaves.

Silas wakes me after what seems like only minutes. He pushes his glasses up on his nose with his middle finger and leans against his cane. "Micah went on ahead. He's sending his friend, Jaxon to get you and bring you to the hospital to meet his sister. Jaxon will be here soon, so you should get ready. I'll get you something to drink. How does a latte sound?"

"Great. Thanks," I manage to whisper through my morning grogginess.

He turns and walks back to the front of the store. I brush my hair into submission with my fingers and run my tongue over my teeth. What I wouldn't give for a toothbrush right now. Splashing water on my face wakes me up a bit. My clothes are wrinkled from sleeping in them, but I don't have any other options at this point.

In the distance, Silas is making a clatter. Meanwhile, I find my way back to the bookshop and settle down into a ratty old chair with huge, threadbare cushions and wait for Jaxon. I kinda like it here. It's quaint and homey.

I flip open the pages of *Fahrenheit 451*, the book I got from Silas yesterday. Soon, I'm so engrossed in the story, I don't even notice Silas's voice from around the stacks. "You can't go over there, Jessica."

"Why not, Silas? I deserve to know if it would have worked."

"It's not right. She shouldn't know. Not now. She's been through a lot, and Micah's not here with her."

"That's because Micah's an idiot who doesn't know what he's doing. I do."

When I hear Micah's name, my ears perk up. Silas offers one last ditch effort when he says, "Jessica, don't!" but it's not before I see her standing at the end of the row of bookshelves. She's only there a second before she rushes out of the building, sending the bell above the doorway into a fit of rage, but it's long enough to see what I needed to see. She is me. Down to the hair style, and height and even the high cheekbones I swear only my family has. It was like looking in a mirror. But then she disappeared. Mirror shattered.

Minutes later, I'm still trying to piece together what I saw when Silas returns with a latte and a blueberry muffin. "Thought you might be hungry. Hope you like blueberries."

"Blueberries are great."

As he hands me the drink, I watch his face. Its wrinkles carve deep lines into his cheeks and forehead, and the crow's feet around his eyes soften what were once angry eyes. Sure, he's the sweet old bookshop guy now, but hidden beneath his withered features, lays a man with passion and fortitude. In his younger days, I'll bet he was one to be reckoned with. I'm not sure how I know this, but deep inside me, I'm convinced it's true.

Silas lowers himself into the seat next to me and hangs the cane over the arm of the chair.

"Who was that?"

"*That* was Jessica."

"Seems like a peach."

A loud chuckle bursts through Silas's lips. "Something like that."

Before he can explain any more, the bell rings again, announcing another visitor. This one I know.

"Morning! Micah's waiting for you at the hospital. I'm his lackey, sent to rescue you from the clutches of the old man." Jaxon grins.

Shaking his head, Silas stands, balancing on his cane. "In case you're wondering, yes, he is always like this." As he passes Jaxon, he pats him on the shoulder.

I stuff the last of the muffin in my mouth and chase it with a hot swig of latte. "Let's go."

We're barely out the door when I ask him about the girl. "What do you know about someone named Jessica?"

Jaxon licks his lips and casts me a sideways glance. "Jessica. Um, she's headstrong and gorgeous and slightly psychotic and gorgeous and a little frightening and gorgeous and—"

"My replacement."

"Right. Yep. That, too." He slows our pace to a crawl.

My lips press together, and I touch my cheekbones, wondering what he thinks when he looks at me because, in my one quick glance, I swore I was looking in a mirror. I wonder what she looked like before and how many surgeries she had to go through to look just like me.

It must be strange for him seeing me look like her, a girl he's obviously in love with. But when he looks at me, even though I know I should feel uncomfortable, I don't. I'm still a stranger to him.

"You two *do* look a lot alike. But her nose is different, and her eyes are a different shade of brown. You're not her … or she's not you … or whatever. If I were on the surface, I'd be able to tell you two apart faster than a rabbit can … well, never mind."

After a few more streets, we reach the hospital, and Jaxon shows me to Ally's hospital room. Micah's waiting, coffee in hand.

"Looks like Jax didn't scare you off yet." He hands me the drink and leans in to kiss my forehead.

"I tried," Jaxon says, "but like most women, she finds me charming."

"I'll bet."

"Speaking of charming, I think I'll go find Jessica. See if she's still immune to my advances."

In seconds, Jaxon is gone, and I turn to Micah. "I've never known anyone like him."

"And you never will."

We hasten to a waiting area and settle. "How's your sister?"

"Doing better today. Still sore, but she's awake."

"What were the complications? Is she going to be okay?"

"Her blood pressure had dropped. She'd been pushing for hours with no success. The baby was stuck. If they didn't do something, the baby's oxygen could be cut off, resulting in all sorts of problems. The doctors could tell the baby was in distress, but couldn't get it out."

The look on my face must clue him in that I still don't understand.

"Like the Cesarean we learned about in class?" The whole birth process was foreign to me other than what I read in my medical books under the history section. I recognized the term, but couldn't remember what it meant.

"It's where they cut into the mother's stomach and uterus and pull the baby out. Come to find out, Ally's birth canal wasn't large enough to birth a baby. She would have died if she'd continued to try. So would the baby."

"I can't believe they cut her open to take it out." I know I sound ignorant, but these things just don't happen at the Institute. Besides, it was practices like Cesareans that led to The Institute forming the Creation Unit and to move away from primitive practices that exposed women in such ways. Modesty is more important. What happened last night was downright barbaric.

Micah and I move toward the door to Ally's room. I hear the quiet beeping of monitors as we push the wooden door aside. Micah peeks his head in first. "Stay here for a second. Let me see if she's up for visitors."

I wait alone in the hallway staring at the plain square tiles until Micah comes to the door again.

"Come on in," he says slowly pushing the door aside and allowing me to pass.

I'm taken aback by the youth of the girl in the dilapidated hospital bed and am surprised at how different she is from Micah. His stature and dark features are the contrast to her tiny, frail-looking frame. Her thick, blonde hair is pulled back in a messy ponytail. Her face is still freckled with light acne, but she's pretty, nonetheless. Despite these differences, I can tell they're brother and sister. It's in the eyes. Hers sparkle in the same shade of his: gray, almost silver. And there's a defiance in her look that Micah has as well. Determination.

I stand as far back in the corner as I can; I don't want to be a bother. Maybe the shadows will hide my apprehension to meet this girl who's lived so much more of life than I'll ever know. But it doesn't work. Micah turns to me and reaches out for my hand, pulling me to him and next to the metal framed bed.

"Ally, this is Kate." His smile widens like he's showing off a prized possession.

The girl scoots up in the bed and rearranges the thin sheets to cover her legs, wincing at the motion. "So this is Kate," she says as a tiny smile perks up on her lips. "THE Kate. We've heard a lot about you."

I try to smile. "When did he tell you about me?"

"The last time he was here. When was that?" she turns to Micah, who's standing next to me. "About a month ago?"

"Yep."

Just before our fated date in the Outer Lands that landed Micah in the hospital. Wonder what he would have told her if he'd visited her after I whacked him on the head.

Micah clears the air with his hand. "Where's Hunter?"

Ally shakes her head. "I'm the one who just had a baby and major surgery, and you're worried about Hunter?"

I like Micah's sister more and more with every passing minute.

"I see sarcasm runs in the family," I say.

"Hello? Wasn't I talking here? Hunter? Where's the proud poppa?"

Ally smacks Micah's arm. "Sure you were talking, but half of what you say isn't that important, so we try to ignore you as much as possible." She giggles like a child. "He'll be back. He went to grab some dinner."

Just then, the door opens again. A young man about Micah's age enters with arms full of grease covered bags. His brown hair is disheveled, and he nearly drops the bags into Micah's lap as he settles himself into the tiny room. Feeling cramped, I push myself as far into the wall as possible.

"I had a hankering for burgers." Ally grins. "The nurse said it was okay for Hunter to bring me some."

Hunter rounds the bed and stands next to Ally's side. His lanky arms reach around her shoulders, and he has to lean over to kiss her cheek. "You eat. I'm going to go get the baby from the nursery."

"Wait," she stops him. "You have to meet Kate first." She looks at me and does the formal introduction. "Kate, this is my husband, Hunter. Hunter, Kate—Micah's girlfriend."

He looks flustered, but he composes himself enough to extend a long-fingered hand in greeting. "Nice to meet you. Now, if you'll excuse me, I'm going to go get my son." He smiles and exits.

Since Hunter bought enough to feed the entire hospital, we all busy ourselves unwrapping and munching on burgers and fries until Hunter pushes the door open with a wheeled cart. On top is a plastic tub holding a tightly wrapped, screaming baby.

"Bring him here," Ally says, wiping her hands on a napkin. But Micah steps in front.

"No way, I've got him." Without hesitation, he scoops up the little cocoon and cradles him in his arms. In seconds, the little one quiets and settles into a rhythmic breathing. Soon, he's asleep again.

"Wow, impressive," says Hunter. "I haven't figured out how to do that."

Micah smiles at Hunter. "It's the new father nerves. The little man can sense it. Besides, I've worked in the Creation Lab long enough to have handled a few infants." He moves next to me to ask if I want to hold the child.

"No, it's okay. I shouldn't."

"It's okay, Kate," Ally says with an encouraging nod of her head. "He won't break."

Glancing back at Micah, I see he's already holding the child out to me. Denying the baby again would be rude, so I reach out and take the bundle into my arms. It's surprising how much he looks like the fetuses in batch four back home. A little bigger maybe, but all the features are developed and his tiny movements are the same as the babies still in lab tubes. He smells new and fresh, and his skin is pink and smooth. My finger softly traces his little features. As I do, his face scrunches in response to my touch. When I look up, I see Ally and Hunter smiling at me, but the look on Micah's face takes me by surprise. He leans into me and kisses my cheek.

"You're going to make an amazing mother someday."

His words hit my heart like a sharp arrow. I'm already a mother, but no one knows. Suddenly, overwhelming emotions push to the surface. This is what holding my son would be like. I can't take it any longer, so I sniff the tears away and hand the baby back to his mother. "What's his name?"

"Benjamin."

For the first time in my life, I wonder what it's like to have a squirming creature living inside me. I'll never understand what it's like to carry a child like that. All my eggs are frozen in storage in some back room of The Institute. That way, the Institute can control who has children. No criminals, no delinquents, no irresponsible people are ever allowed to have kids. And certainly not teenagers. Except I do.

I look back at Ally's lightly freckled face and wonder what made her choose to get married and have a baby when she's barely seventeen.

Perhaps Micah sees the strange look on my face because he says, "We'd better be getting back before anyone realizes we've been gone as long as we have." He takes my hand in his. "Ready for the trip home?"

"What happened to your meeting with the elders?"

"It got waylaid after I found out about Ally. But don't worry, I took care of it. Jaxon knows all about it. Told him this morning before he came to get you. He'll make sure the right people know what's going on."

"So that's it then? We can leave?" The stress and surprises of this day have taken their toll, and I feel like I could fall asleep in an instant even though I just woke up a few hours ago.

"Yep."

We say our good-byes and Micah kisses the baby once more before we head out the door. When we finally make it back to the truck, I'm exhausted, but there's still something I have to know. It's been gnawing at me since I saw the baby. So as we uncover the vehicle, I build my courage.

"Micah, can I ask you something?"

"Anything."

"Why was she pregnant? I mean, she must only be seventeen. It's a little young, don't you think?"

Micah grins widely and laughs. "In the Hidden City, in order for the Natural Born to survive, we need to start reproducing early."

"So, they implant fertilized embryos while the girls are still teenagers?"

"No, Kate. Here we do things the old-fashioned way." His wry smile and twinkling eyes say enough, but the wink he throws at me removes any remaining doubt.

"You mean, she and Hunter ... you know ..."

"Had sex?" he whispers like it's a huge secret no one should ever find out then breaks into a hearty laugh. "Yeah, he *is* her husband. And it's not like the teenagers above ground are abstaining, by any means."

"Well, I get that, but they won't get pregnant by doing it." Things are so different here.

"You forget, Kate, we don't live by your rules. We don't have to be thirty before we marry, we don't remove eggs at birth, and we don't have to apply to The Institute for children. We have our own ... the fun way."

My face immediately flushes, and I decide to keep any further questions to myself. One can only handle so much embarrassment in a day, and I've definitely reached my quota.

TWENTY NINE

THE BURNING

W E ARRIVE BACK HOME late Sunday evening, but when I come into class on Monday, Micah is nowhere to be seen. His normal presence at Professor Limbert's side for lab days has become commonplace, and I've found myself looking forward to the time I'll get to see him for a few extra moments.

Now, as my icy fingers fumble with the buttons of my heavy coat, Professor displays a few instructions on the board. There's only a few of us in class. On lab days, the rest of my classmates meet at different times according to their specialties. Less chaos is good.

"Please get these notes down quickly. We're headed straight to the labs, but you'll need this information first."

"Hey, where's Micah?" Taryn asks while flipping open her compact and typing in the notes, glancing occasionally to the board as she sketches the drawing the professor has placed there.

I shrug and file my own drawings away into the appropriate folders.

"Don't shut down your notes," Professor Limbert interrupts. "You'll need them once we get into the lab." He zips his briefcase slowly while he continues giving instructions.

I glance at Taryn, who stuffs her compact under one arm and throws her coat over the other. She smirks at me. "We're observing a chemical disposal today."

I whisper back. "Haven't we already done that? The first one with the embryos was a chemical disposal, right?"

"Same idea. Older fetus."

My stomach turns, and my leg muscles freeze. I hope it's not my son. *Oh, please don't let it be my son.* No, it can't be. He's been marked, but they observe any fetuses older than sixteen weeks for a while to make sure their records are correct. So he's got a little while longer. It'd be a travesty to dispose of a perfectly good fetus.

"Oh, okay." I fall into line behind Taryn like this is just another day in the lab, but deep inside myself, I know it's not. Thankfully, Taryn takes everything in stride. She's steady, and I find myself following her footsteps and staring at the back of her head to keep myself moving forward.

"I hope this doesn't take longer than our normal lab time," she says. "I have a date with Devin."

"Whoa, wait, what?"

"You'd know this if you were ever away from Micah enough to hang out anymore." She's teasing, but I hear the hint of exasperation in her voice, so I make a mental note to give her a call after class to see if she wants to hang at the café.

"What happened to Cam?"

"Cam?"

"Yeah, Saul's friend? We doubled that night."

"Oh, right. That was just a one night fling, Kate. Devin and I have been seeing each other for a few weeks now. We've even recorded it in the data system."

"Wow, that's true commitment."

"I guess we all have to grow up sometime, right?"

I'm distracted by our conversation, but entering the lab for what seems like the millionth time this school year affords no surprises. There's no more nervous anticipation or revelations. We've pretty much seen and practiced everything there is to do, but despite its familiarity, nothing can prepare me for what I'm about to see.

***

"All right, ladies and gentlemen. Today you're going to observe a chemical disposal, so if you would please gather around and take a seat." Professor Limbert heads to the far end of the lab, and we all follow like trained dogs. Only this time, we pull chairs around and place our compacts on our laps, all clicking them open at the same time.

A lab technician—not Micah—rolls a cart with a capsule sitting on top through the far doorway and into the room next to Professor Limbert. He thanks the assistant and pulls the blue paper covering off revealing a container about two feet tall by a foot wide. Inside is a twenty-six week old fetus. A girl. Breathing a sigh of relief it isn't my son slated for disposal, I click open a file and ready myself for the lecture that will accompany this procedure.

The baby is squirming, and it's then that I see her foot. It's slightly deformed, bent over with a tiny growth that's not supposed to be there. Probably would end up with a club foot if left to develop.

But she won't.

Other than that, I see no signs of improper development. And when Professor Limbert begins his explanation, my theories are confirmed. It's the club foot. All other developments and tests have come back normal. Strong and healthy in every other way. He reads off some technical lingo about gender, deformity and the choice to dispose, which apparently is voted on by a committee of scientists at The Institute. There's no need to operate on a child so young after birth. It's too much of a risk, so disposal is the only viable option.

It's crazy how a group of ten or so people have the fate of the future in their hands.

The professor, head sunk into the file in his hands, reads the instructions while the lab technician follows them. Apparently, the committee also leaves the dirty work to the technicians.

How convenient.

Finally, he looks up, "We stress the use of gloves to prevent contamination though, at this point, it won't matter to the fetus. However, you can still be contaminated, so please follow protocol." Limbert's head dips again, a contrast to the tiny smile on the face of the lab technician as he snaps gloves over his wrists. Like he's enjoying what he considers a private joke or something. It sickens me, and I find myself turning away for a moment. "So just as with any other lab, wear your gloves."

Taryn is leaning forward, engrossed in what's happening and only relaxes when she sees me looking at her. "You okay," she asks.

"Yep," I say as I turn back. No need to give anyone any indication that my stomach is starting to churn, and I can feel my skin turning green. I don't know what it is that's causing this because the process hasn't started yet. I've never gotten sick during a procedure yet, and I don't plan on starting now. I'm strong enough to endure this even though I have my doubts.

The professor's voice breaks my haze. "The first step is measuring the right amount of saline. It will vary depending on the age of the fetus involved, so please refer to your charts whenever you're assigned to this type of disposal. Once this is done, about half of the amniotic fluid needs to be drained."

A young man from class raises his hand. "What about the weight of the fetus? Is that taken into account?"

"At this age, no. Most fetuses are very similar in length and weight. It's not enough of a difference to affect the saline measurement."

The guy nods and types the fact into his compact.

Meanwhile, the technician plugs in a hose to the bottom of the capsule and flips a switch. The fluid slowly drains and as it does, the baby tightens itself into a ball and sinks as low as it can into the remaining fluid. A natural response.

"Then simply replace the fluid with the salt solution."

Raising the lid on the top of the capsule, the technician injects a huge amount of saline into the container.

"This is where I'd like you to begin your observations."

Simultaneously, fifteen compacts hum and the constant click of fingers on keyboards is the only sound in the room.

Before I look at the baby, I watch Professor Limbert. He's turned his head and is burying himself in the paperwork in front of him, not even watching what's happening. He's witnessed countless disposals, so he must be used to it by now. But I wonder if it's something you can ever quite get used to.

I turn my attention back to the capsule. The lights are still low for the other fetuses, and it's a little difficult to see the details, but within minutes, the fetus's reactions to the chemical become obvious.

Seeing the child struggle in front of me is too much to bear, so I turn my eyes away. I want to be able to watch, to give this tiny life the respect it deserves. To see what happens to these babies who are deemed unviable. But I can't.

Around me, only the sound of fingers against keyboards breaks the air, and words like, "fascinating," and "unbelievable" hit my ears. They're right. It is unbelievable. Unbelievable that I'm forced to watch this. Unbelievable that no one but me seems to care about the life they're destroying. I'm numb to the professor's lecture as he describes what's happening, barely looking at the child in front of him. He can say it from memory. My classmates furiously type their observations while my compact sits open on my lap, empty. My arms barely holding on to the computer screen on my lap. Frozen. Like the rest of me.

All eyes are pasted to the capsule in front of us. All, but mine. And Professor Limbert's. He's still flipping through papers as he waits out the time it takes to complete the process. I'm watching him. He must sense this because his gaze meets mine. I can hardly see him through the watery glaze in my vision.

It's only when I turn back to the capsule after it's all over that I allow myself to wipe away the tear hanging on the edge of my eyelid.

It's over. Finished.

She's dead.

The professor knows this, too, and moves to continue his lecture. Setting his paperwork down, he straightens his back and takes a deep breath, lifting the child from the case in front of us. With care, he wipes the fluid from her body and rolls her from one of his hands to the other, checking for any signs of life. There's a heaviness in the surrounding air. No one speaks. Each face in the room reveals something different. Interest. Fascination. Indifference. But mine reveals the horror, which I can't erase from my mind.

The bile rises in the back of my throat, and I swallow to keep it down.

Professor Limbert continues. "The last part of the procedure is to place the body into the hazardous waste bins that will be brought to the incinerator." As he says this, he wraps the child in the blue cloth that covered the growth capsule, tucking it around like a cocoon, and then reaches for a small bag labeled *hazardous waste*. Cradling it in his arms, he moves to the cabinet and pulls open the trash can. Placing the bundle inside, he closes it.

I'm revolted by the sound of the lid locking on tight. Garbage. We just threw out a life like leftovers on my dinner plate.

I can't stand it any longer. I don't care if it's rude or irresponsible, I have to leave. Standing, my chair scrapes against the floor making a horrific screech. Much like the sound of the silent scream aching to tear out of my throat.

I don't answer Taryn when she asks what I'm doing, nor do I pay any attention to the room full of stares that are boring holes into my back. And I don't look to see if Professor Limbert is upset at my leaving. It doesn't matter. I'm gone.

***

I open the front door of The Institute to see Micah leaning against the steps. Not stopping, I rush past him, but he ignores me when I brush my hand through the air, gesturing for him to leave me alone and follows me down the sidewalk anyway.

"You okay?" His fists press into the pockets of his jacket, stretching the material taut. It digs into his neck, leaving a striped mark from the fabric on his skin.

I wrap my arms around myself, but it does nothing to stop the shaking that's taken over my body. I can't hold myself together. Pointing toward the building, I ask, "Is that why you weren't in class today?"

He doesn't speak, and I know my suspicions are true. "Have you done a saline disposal before?" I prod. "Is that why you skipped the class?"

He nods, slipping his coat from his shoulders and places it around mine. "Last year was my first one as the technician in the room. I swore I'd do anything I could to not have to witness that again, so when

Professor Donovan had some paperwork to finish, I jumped at the chance, and they scheduled the new tech in my place."

"You could have warned me." My hand runs over the cement barrier, cold and hard. I grasp it like it's the only thing that's real because, at that moment, it is. Walking does nothing to steady my trembling legs though I'm determined to keep moving. I have to get as far from that lab as I can.

"Sorry."

"Did you think that was something I had to experience to make me a better person or something?" His face is sad, and I know he wants to erase what I've seen because he's seen it, too. And I can tell by the look in his eye that he's seen much more. But for some reason, he had to let me see it. Without warning me beforehand. He had to let me see for myself what The Institute is capable of. Until now, I wouldn't have fully understood.

"Something like that."

My feet stop moving, and my body crumples to the ground. But before I hit the snow-covered earth, Micah's arms wrap around me, and he pulls me into an alley in between two buildings. Once in his arms, I collapse. My body shivers with sobs, and if it weren't for his arms, I'd curl into a ball on the cold asphalt and wait for death to come.

"They killed it, Micah. And I watched."

"I know."

"I watched that little baby die. And I didn't do anything about it. I couldn't."

"I know. I'm so sorry, Kate. I'm so sorry."

I cry until I can barely breathe. But thankfully, Micah picks me up and puts me back together. "Come on," he says. "Let's go somewhere private."

. . . .

THIRTY

DR. FRANKENSTEIN ... ALMOST

O PENING THE DOOR TO Micah's home, I remember I've only been here once before. It seems a bit odd, considering our relationship, that we haven't spent more time here. After living in a state run facility until he was sixteen, he was given back the house his parents had before they died in the crash. Well, not his parents. How strange it must have been for him to take over a home that wasn't his. To step into someone else's life. Despite the strangeness of the situation, there's a peace about this place, and somehow, just stepping through the doorway, I know Micah's going to make things better.

"Here," he says leading me to the living room. "Sit down. I'll get you something to eat."

I don't protest, even though I'm not sure if I'll be able to keep anything down.

The living room is sparse. A few pieces of matching furniture—quite comfortable, I might add—fill the space, but the walls are nearly bare save for a few photographs leaning against the mantle. No frames, no tacks. Straining to see from my seat, I immediately recognize the subject.

Me.

The green scarf Gran crocheted is wrapped around my neck, and I'm standing in what looks like a field of snow. It was taken in the park.

I'm staring into the distance with a look of wonderment on my face. I'm surprised at how nice the picture is. Normally, I avoid having my picture taken, but this one makes me look … pretty.

In minutes, Micah returns with a homemade turkey sandwich. He explains when he sees the confused look on my face.

"I keep the leftovers in a small cooler. There's no need to waste anything I don't eat one day when I might eat it the next. With as many advances as The Institute has made, waste management is not one of them."

This doesn't make any sense to me. When Mom makes dinner, she unwraps the prepackaged meals designed specifically for our individual body types.

Micah clarifies further. "Remember, Kate, I'm not from around here." His soft smile eases my tension. "We don't get meals delivered. We have to make our own."

Taking the plate from his outstretched hand, I grab the sandwich and take a bite. Despite my lack of appetite, it tastes amazing.

"Sorry about the house," he says as he sits next to me. "Scratch that, I'm not going to be one of those people who apologizes for my house. You've seen the worst and best of me. There's no need to apologize."

Licking my finger, I manage a smile. "You're right. Besides, you have a nice place."

His face lights up when he laughs. "Well, it's not really home if you know what I mean. I consider it my temporary lodging."

For a moment, I wonder if he's referring to the fact that this house belongs to the strangers whose son he replaced, but then I realize he's talking about the Hidden City. Our above ground society is foreign to him. No matter how long he's lived here, his heart is in another place. "Like a hotel, only without the room service."

"Something like that," he snickers.

The sandwich calms my nervous stomach, and when I finish, I lean back on his couch and pull a pillow in front of me. "So what was it like? When you had to see that kind of disposal?"

Micah's cheekbones drop, and a sharp crease between his eyes appears. I mentally kick myself. We were having a nice time; he'd finally gotten my mind off what I'd seen earlier in class, and I pull us right back there. Why would I ask such a stupid question?

For a second, his lips stiffen, and his hands ball into fists, but he soon relaxes and leans back next to me. Staring off at the ceiling, he relates that day to me.

"I'm sure it was much like what you saw today," he begins. "The professor doesn't do any of the actual procedure. He leaves that up to the techs. It was my first week as a graduated tech. I'd seen the procedure a few times before, each more sickening than the last, but that day, I wasn't expecting to actually have to do the procedure myself." He sighs. "I'm not sure why. I should have known. Having seen it happen, I knew the techs did the duty. But for some reason, I thought I had more time to prepare."

Micah's hands must be sweating because he continues to rub them up and down his thighs, ever so slowly, eliminating every crease in his jeans. "After the procedure was done, I excused myself and spent the next hour in the bathroom throwing up. I thought I'd never get over that sight. Knowing that child's life was in my hands, and I took it away. A perfectly good life, gone because of me. It didn't matter to me that it was smaller than the rest or had some sort of a disease; it was still a living human being. To this day, I have nightmares."

"It wasn't your fault." My hand covers his.

"Kate, I wish that were true. I wish I could say I never had to do it again. I avoid it as much as possible, yes, but there are some days I can't steer clear of it. Those days bring back every detail of the first, and my dreams turn to nightmares. It's worse every time around, and it never goes away." His hand combs through his black hair, pushing it back from his face. "That first day, however, changed my life."

"What do you mean?"

"I was sent here by the officials of the Hidden City to glean as much information as possible from The Institute by just living a normal life and listening to what people might say. After that day, I went to the leaders and told them I had to do more. Just waiting around for information to fall into my lap was maddening. I needed something more tangible. So they gave me a more advanced assignment. Something I could wrap my hands around."

I raise my eyebrows at him, and I know he's about to reveal something big.

"Let me show you something." Standing, he reaches out his hand and pulls me off the couch.

My stomach flips, and the knot in the pit of my gut tells me that whatever he's going to show me is going to change my life forever. Weeks ago, it would have set off my freak-o-meter to be headed down a rickety set of steps into his basement, but after all we've been through together, this just seems normal.

From the light of the room above us that sends a stream of light through the cracked door and down the steps, I see a weight set and old couch, now musty smelling after spending months in the damp recesses of the basement. I try not to think of the mold spores filling my lungs. In the middle of the floor is a rug covering the poured cement. It must be to make this place like a family room or something, not that anyone would spend much time here, but hey, you never know. Maybe the rug was meant to make it look a little comfortable, but when Micah pulls it back, I see its real purpose.

To hide a door.

Micah moves the slab covering and turns to me. "Wanna see my secret lab?"

"What are you, a mad scientist?"

"I'm working on it." He grins and winks at me. "You can be my assistant." We step into the darkness. "But you're much more attractive than Igor."

"Igor?"

"Right," he says, "I forget you haven't heard some of those stories. Igor was the hunchbacked assistant to the mad scientist who used dead bodies to create new life."

"That's disgusting."

"Perhaps, but it makes for a great story as long as you get the evil laugh down pat."

"Evil laugh?"

"Mwa-ha-ha-ha-ah!"

I'm practically rolling in laughter when he says, "I've been practicing."

We descend another set of steps that lead deep into the earth beneath Micah's home.

"How long did it take you to build this?" I ask. Because there's no way an Institute-built home would allow plans for a secret lab underneath.

"The whole first year I lived here. It's only been operational for a year now. Some of my contacts helped dig it out and got things ready."

At the bottom of the steps, Micah flicks on a black light and the room glows with a purple haze. At the same time, my jaw drops open.

This room is identical to the lab at The Institute except for the dirt walls held up by beams made of two-by-fours. It's complete with Petri dishes along one side and larger capsules connected to the ceiling in the middle. Tubes run along the rafters to a generator in the corner that's hooked up to some sort of filtration system. But that's not what has my attention.

As I scan the walls where the Petri dishes sit, I realize they're not empty.

My eyes wide, I turn to Micah, who's stepped back and let me examine at my own pace. I don't even have to ask the question. He answers it as though he's reading my mind.

"That night you caught me in the lab a few weeks ago—"

"Your keys."

"Yeah, um, not my keys."

My mind is drawn back to that night, and I can see him standing in front of me that night in the lab, slipping something in his pockets.

"You stole these from The Institute?"

He nods.

Now, I'm confused. "Why? What do you do to them here?"

"Kate, it's not what I do to them here, it's what they do to them there."

"So these were all marked Unviable?"

"I can't take them all," he says, "they'd notice so many missing, especially with as many as they dispose of in these early stages, but when one or two disappear, they don't care. Especially if they were labeled

Unviable. I figure it actually makes their jobs easier. One or two less to dispose of. With my job as the lab assistant, I have access to the database. A quick change of a number in the system, and it's pretty easy to take a few."

"But Micah, what are you going to do with them?" I run my fingertips along the edge of the glass, looking at what seems like an empty dish. I know better. Its contents are microscopic at this point. But it's not like it will remain that way for long. They'll grow. Quickly. And as I look around, I see a few specimens that are bigger, older. Ready to be transferred into the next pod.

"I take them back to the Hidden City. We implant them in surrogates."

"What?"

"We implant them into women who are willing to carry a life that's not their own."

"Are you crazy?"

"Yes, most likely," he says, smiling again. All I can see are the whites of his eyes and his brilliant teeth glowing in the dim light. It does make him look like a mad scientist.

"You can do that? Implant them, I mean?"

"Yep."

"And they survive?"

"Some of the time. It's not an exact science. It's an old one, actually. They used to do the procedure years ago before places like The Institute began their own breeding procedures and made women's wombs obsolete." He moves toward me and places one of the Petri dishes under a microscope. "If a woman couldn't have children of her own, doctors would implant fertilized eggs inside her. To make sure one took, they'd often use many eggs. The problem was that doing this many times led to multiple births, which could cause complications for the mother and the babies." He leans in, presses his eyes against the microscope, and examines the embryo under the scope.

"So why are you doing this?" I feel like I'm yelling. The hum of the generator is loud, and I have to raise my voice to speak over it. No wonder it's in the basement. Scratch that. Beneath the basement. If it were any higher, the sound would alert someone.

Pulling his face from the microscope, he turns and leans against the counter, placing a hand on either side of his hips on the table. "Don't you get it yet, Kate? Even after what you saw today? We do this to save the unborn."

"Even when they're deformed or diseased?"

"Even then. They're still human, Kate. They still deserve a chance at life. And sometimes, when these people grow old, they'll even tell you they wouldn't have changed a thing about their lives. Not even their disabilities. They are just as viable as the rest of us." He pauses. "Remember the woman in the Hidden City who was responsible for changing out the flowers?"

"Mmm hmm."

"I told you she had a disorder called Down Syndrome."

"Yeah."

"She was one of the first successful implants in The Hidden City. Just think of what our village would be like if she weren't allowed to live. Colorless."

"What do you plan to do with the larger capsules?" I say, eyeing the other table across the room.

"I figure we won't be able to get all these embryos implanted soon enough. It's a delicate procedure transporting them to the Hidden City, much less implanting them. So I stole some of the capsules in case they need to be moved from the dishes. Stole is a harsh word. I borrowed them from the discarded pile and fixed them up. As long as we're not caught, I can raise them here, and when they're born, we can assign them to a couple in the Hidden City. An old-fashioned adoption."

"Adoption?"

"When a couple takes a child that's not their own to raise as their own."

I'm shaking my head, eyes wide in disbelief. They have this plan all figured out. I just wonder who *they* are. In my time with Micah, I've come to realize that there are a lot of Natural Born hidden in my own community. Still, he won't say who he knows. It's a safety issue, he says.

But if they are able to hide among our people, unnoticed, then The Institute also has to have spies undercover, too.

The thought makes me shudder.

"So what happens next?" I ask.

"If you're up for it, you help me."

"Me?" I shake my head. "Why?"

"You may not realize it yet, Kate, but you have the makings of a true rebel. Just think. Instead of destroying life through the disposal techniques, you could be saving them, giving them a chance to survive. I've already discussed it with my superiors. They think someone officially from the other side, another person like your great grandmother, is a fantastic idea. We have sympathizers who help on occasion, but someone of your knowledge and placement would be perfect."

My head is swirling. Saving lives at the risk of my own. I know this is the case because if any of us were ever caught, we'd disappear from society, never to be heard from again. The Institute would never allow such treason to go unpunished. Suddenly, my mind wanders back to a conversation I had with the soldier I dated once. Saul. The way he described being the one to invent the idea to strip the rebel of his own skin was disturbing enough as it was, but thinking that sympathizer might be me sends the bile at the back of my throat into my mouth. I swallow to keep it down. To the citizens, the person just drops off the face of the earth, but I suspect what really happens. Torture. Long, painful, unimaginable torture.

"So, what do you think?" Micah asks.

A fluttering in me soars. "Count me in."

Without hesitation, I am in his arms, his lips crushing against mine. When he pulls away, he says, "I knew you'd do it."

....

THIRTY ONE

INTRODUCTIONS

ACH NIGHT I SPEND in the lab, I find a reason to stay a few minutes longer. Once everyone else leaves, I head to the back storage room where the unviable are kept until their scheduled disposals. It's here that I spend time with my son.

I know I shouldn't allow myself to get attached, but I can't help it. It's different knowing which child is yours, even if you didn't authorize it. Watching him grow and change little by little. Placing my hands on the pod in which he's growing to feel his tiny movements. He's real. Alive.

So, any time Professor Limbert or any of the other professors need paperwork filed, I volunteer. Any excuse that can get me into this room is okay with me. If I don't have an excuse like filing for my teachers, I still come, pretending to file papers or take notes on a few fetuses to get even a single glimpse of my baby. Most times, I can only spare a few minutes before one of the scientists or professors comes in to do work, but other times I lose track of time, and when I finally leave, I find I've been there for an hour or more. I don't even have to be standing next to him; just being in the same room is good enough. Besides, with the cameras planted everywhere, I have to look like I'm here on official business for the professors.

I've named him. My son. Seems to me that he needed more than a number. Brody. Maybe I'll change it later, but that's what I call him when I talk to him. Tonight, I tell him what happened with Micah. What he showed me. The words I say don't matter, it's the mere sound of my voice that Brody responds to. His eyes open in the purple light, and I wonder if he can see me. If somehow, on a deep level, he knows I'm his mother. When I smile, he stares. And when I tell him about Micah, his arms and legs move frantically like he's excited. Maybe I'm just imagining things.

Since the day I discovered him, I've been gathering information. Papers. Conversations spoken in whispers. Brody is marked for a lack of lung development. They'll do more tests to determine whether he'll survive. Tests I haven't learned about yet. But if he's marked now, the chances of him being unmarked are slim to none. There's some sort of marker in his blood, too, but from what I can understand of the reports from the database, it isn't anything life threatening. Just not what they want. Not perfect. But that doesn't matter to me. He may be unviable according to scientific standards, but to me, he's just how he should be. Now I understand what Micah was talking about.

"I have an idea, Brody," I whisper. "I can't tell you about it yet because I don't have it all planned, but I have an idea that might save you. I'm going to promise you something." I place my hand against the flexible capsule where his hand rests. "I'm not going to let them get rid of you. I'll find a way, somehow, to get you out of here. And no matter what, you'll someday know that you were wanted."

Like he hears me, his legs kick out in response.

Tonight it's only been a few minutes before I hear the inevitable creak of the door telling me I need to pack up or look like I'm filing something in order to seem like I belong here. I grab the spare stack of folders I keep in my pack for moments when someone enters. It buys me a few extra seconds without suspicion. Opening my compact helps, too. That way I can look like I'm entering information into the system.

My compact is open, and I yank a seat over to the counter next to Brody. His presence, even encapsulated, brings me comfort. I tilt my head in close to the screen. Usually, this stance tells intruders that I'm involved in my work. But tonight it doesn't work.

"Come here often?" His voice pulls me into an upright position, and even in the darkness, I can see his brilliant, imperfect smile.

"Micah. I didn't expect to see you."

He places his own compact on the table beside mine and pulls out a stack of files. "What are you doing here?"

"Filing?" I fake a smile. I could tell him the truth, but I'd hate for him to get in trouble for something I did. Sometimes the less a person knows, the better, and Micah and I already know too much about what really goes on around here.

Laughing, he shakes his head. "Since I'm here filing for Professor Limbert, I kind of doubt that's the case with you. Wanna try again?"

"Okay," I say. "Can I tell you a secret?"

I see a tiny eye roll before he answers. "Now don't you think that's kind of a silly thing to ask at this point in our relationship? I mean, you know every deep dark secret about me and more."

He's right. I know enough about him to destroy his life if I so choose—not that I would. He trusts me with that information, so there's no reason I can't do the same. I lower my voice to barely a whisper, so there's no way the recording devices can record what I say. "I'd like to introduce you to someone." My hand falls on Brody's back and the touch makes him squirm. "This is Brody." I stare at the tiny creature in the capsule in front of me before gathering enough courage to look Micah in the eyes again. "My son."

A nervous smile appears on his face, and his head cocks in bewilderment. "Your son?"

"Okay," I sigh, "I'll give you the shortened version." I don't even look at Micah. Brody has my full attention. It's the first time I've told him the story of how I discovered him, and immediately, he seems engrossed. As engrossed as any preborn could possibly be. His eyes even seem to meet mine as I talk. "Professor Limbert sent me in here a few weeks ago to file paperwork on the upcoming Unviables. When I was recording the DNA numbers, I noticed something strange." I glance at Micah for a brief second. "My number. I looked it up again just to be sure. That's when I discovered that this is my son. At first I was angry and confused. There's no way I would have approved such a thing, even if it were in accordance with Institute policy. I didn't look for him and tried to avoid this room, but after a while, I had to see him for myself. The first time I looked at him it was like I knew he was mine. After that, I couldn't stay away. I've been sneaking in here to spend time with him as much as I can. He's mine, Micah. My own flesh and blood." The smile I give Brody holds as I look at Micah, but when I see his face, it disappears.

"Kate, don't you realize what this means?"

"That I have a son marked as Unviable."

"Besides that?"

I shake my head. "No."

"What's the only reason The Institute could possibly have for creating more humans?"

"I don't know. I haven't figured it out yet. Limited population has always been a key to the success of our society. Why would they want to create more?"

"There's only one reason I can think of." Micah reaches his hand out in an attempt to touch Brody through the capsule. "They're using them for medical experimentation."

The thought makes my stomach sick. Clenching my eyes doesn't do anything to rid the pictures of experimental operations from my head. I lower my voice so the cameras can't pick up what I'm saying. "This is why I need to discuss my plan with you."

"Plan?"

"I'm going to steal my son before they dispose of him."

································

THIRTY TWO

THE END OF A LEGEND

A FLASH OF HORROR crosses Micah's face before it's replaced with a sexy grin. Without having to explain, I can see the wheels turning in his head. "My lab."

I nod. "Might not even need it. He's only got nine weeks left in gestation. Depending on the timing, we may be able to birth him here."

"Birthing him is one thing, Kate. Getting him out of here unnoticed is quite another. It's why I've only been taking the embryos. I can hide them easily, and they don't make any noise."

Right. A baby. Crying, hungry, naked. I hadn't thought of that. And transferring Brody to Micah's lab any time from now until his birth is sure to be noticed by someone. The look on Micah's face says he's thinking the same thing.

"And reproducing his amniotic fluid at this point in his development will be a challenge. I can recreate the fluid, but it's better if he's not transferred from one capsule to the next. He's already adjusted to the chemical balance in his own capsule. It would be difficult to duplicate without complications. We could steal the whole pod, but a missing pod would definitely be noticed by the other technicians. Kate, I don't know how this could possibly work. It's why I take the ones early before they've developed."

Of course, it's not going to be easy. Just getting him out of here unnoticed will be a miracle. And if someone does notice, then it'll be even worse.

"So you're not going to help me?"

"I didn't say that. I just said it'd be difficult. You know I'll help," he says as he leans over to kiss me. "I have to say, you coming up with this idea is brilliant." His thumbs hook into my belt loops and pull my hips into his. "You're such a rebel."

"Apparently, it runs in the family." That gives me an idea. It's a crazy long shot, but it just might work. "My dad."

"What about him?"

"He works at the data collections agency. He has access to all sorts of classified stuff. Maybe he'll help me hide Brody from the people in charge. At least any record of him. That way, when we get him out of here, there'll be no record that he ever existed."

Micah doesn't respond to me. Instead, he leans in close to Brody, his nose almost touching the capsule. "You've got an incredible mother, little man. I hope someday you'll realize just how special."

***

We're getting ready to leave the lab when I check my phone. Six messages, all from my mother. As soon as I turn my ringer back on, it rings. "Mom, what do you want?"

"Where the heck have you been, Katherine? I've been trying to get a hold of you for hours."

"Sorry." I glance at Micah, who's zipping up his bag. I mouth silently that it's my mother as I point to the phone against my ear. "I had to file some paperwork for the professors."

"Well, turn on your phone then." I glance at Micah and roll my eyes.

"It was on, Mom, but I can't bring it into the lab. Interference and all that." Mom's obviously upset, but yelling at me and my lack of phone service isn't going to help. "What do you need?"

"It's not me. It's your father. Actually, it's about your great gran."

By this time, Micah's at my side, and we're hustling down the hallway hand-in-hand. But when I hear Gran's name, I stiffen and drop his grasp. His face is immediately fraught with concern. We keep walking, but I can see his head turn to gauge my reactions to what my mother is saying.

"What's wrong with Gran?"

Micah knew Gran before I knew him, so his quick intake of breath is of no surprise to me. The sound makes me look at him. He's shaking his head, and the crease in between his eyes has deepened into a dark chasm. It's like he knows something I don't.

We're outside, having walked through the swirling snow, and I'm reaching for the door handle of his truck. He's stark still, standing beside me, awaiting whatever news my mother is about to tell me.

"She's dead."

I've been hit by a wrecking ball, I'm sure of it. I can't move; my vision blurs, painting swirls in front of my eyes, and every bone in my body is ready to collapse. Luckily, the wall behind me steadies me when I lean out my hand for support.

"Why? How?" Should I be surprised? She was old for Natural Born standards, but she was so healthy. And her discharge wasn't scheduled for another two months.

"When The Institute informed your dad, they said she'd taken a turn for the worse, and her discharge had to be moved up."

Gran knew something. She discovered something valuable, I'm sure of it. But now, no one will ever know. I'm shaking all over and can't keep my grip on the phone. It slips out of my hands and lands with a crash on the icy pavement.

It's a good thing the door handle is so close to my hands because, at this moment, it's the only thing holding me up, at least until Micah's arm wraps around my waist. He opens the door with his other hand and helps me into the truck, shutting it behind me.

It's so cold in the cab, I can see my breath. I can't think. I'm staring out the frosty windshield, and suddenly it seems like I'm looking at my entire life through ice covered glass. Nothing is clear.

There's movement outside, but I don't realize what it is until Micah is sitting in the driver's seat next to me. He rubs his hands together, blows on them before inserting the keys into the ignition. Then he starts the truck and cranks the heater before addressing me.

"They discharged her, didn't they?"

I can't answer. I'm silent even though on the inside I'm screaming obscenities at The Institute.

"Drive," I command.

"Where to?"

"The Home. I've got to see for myself."

Since The Institute is a village of its own, we don't have far to go before the truck whips into a parking spot in front of the section where Gran lives. Lived.

The bastards.

The walk to the reception counter takes years, and once I'm there, I'm terse with the receptionist. "I want to see my gran's body."

"I'm sorry," she replies, tapping a stack of papers to straighten them. "Who would you be speaking of?"

"My gran! Emma Dennard. If you paid attention to your visitors, you might know this by now. How many times have I been in here visiting with her? How many hours have I spent in her room by her side or pacing these halls? Do you pay attention to anything around here?"

The woman looks shocked, and Micah's cool hand rests on my arm, pulling me back from the reception desk. "I'm so sorry," he says. "We just received news that Ms. Dennard was discharged. We'd like to know if we can speak to someone in charge or at least pay our respects."

"And you are?"

"Micah Pennington." He flashes his lab badge, which gives him clearance in most parts of The Institute that aren't highly restricted. "I'm a friend of the family." The smile he flashes the brunette behind the counter makes me cringe, especially when she blushes in return.

"Of course, Mr. Pennington. Just let me look it up for you." She smiles back, and I swear she starts batting her eyelashes at him. To me, on the other hand, she gives an icy glare before switching back to her peachy-sweet smile for Micah.

I'm about ready to wipe the stupid grin off her face with my boot heel when Micah slips the clearance notice into his back pocket, thanks her, and takes my hand gently in his. "Let's go," he says as he leads me down the hallway to the morgue. "They haven't completed the procedure yet." Thank goodness.

**

The pungent smell accosts me long before I reach the door. Putting one foot in front of the other suddenly becomes a challenge. Like I have cement feet. But trudging through the muck of dread and anger is nothing. I'm determined to see Gran one last time before they destroy her body.

The metal door is cold against my palms as I push into the room. A row of silver cabinets lines one wall, and I wonder which one holds Gran's body. I shudder at the thought of her being locked inside. Metal slabs on wheels are strewn around and covered with that disgusting blue paper gauze used in anything medical. An urge to crumple every piece of it I can get my hands on and to send the scalpels and other instruments flying across the room with the sweep of one hand nearly overwhelms me, but that's not what I'm here for. Perhaps another time.

A middle-aged man steps out from a back room. He's dressed in the signature white lab coat of nearly everyone who works here. A set of black wire-rimmed glasses sits on the end of his ruddy nose, and when he sees us standing there near the door, he takes them off, folds them, and places them in the pocket of his lab coat. How odd that my gran is disposed of because of old age and a few aches and pains, yet they keep this man around, whose vision is obviously not perfect.

"May I help you?" The tenor of his voice is calm and friendly, but the look in his eyes shows he's not impressed with visitors in *his* morgue.

Micah unfolds a piece of paper the receptionist gave him before he dragged me away from ripping her apart. "We have permission to view the body of Ms. Emma Dennard."

The man steps forward, takes the glasses out of his pocket, unfolds them and places them on his face to read the document. "Who granted this permission?" Dr. B. Johnson is embroidered into his coat in dark blue thread.

"This is Kate, her great-granddaughter."

"Who granted the permission?" he repeats.

"The signature is on the bottom of the paper."

"Dr. Rosenberg." Dr. Johnson purses his lips then lets out a thin puff of air. "Fine. Box thirty-two." Without another word, he retreats to the back room.

I look at Micah. "Thanks."

"Any time."

Box thirty-two is located near the end of the middle row. Micah's hand rests on the handle. "You sure you want to see this?"

No. But I swallow the lump in my throat and wait for him to pull her out of that metal cage.

The sharp click of the handle against steel echoes in my ears, as does the clacking of the rollers as Micah yanks the slab out from the wall. I'm sure I'll be haunted by the sounds for as long as I live. The shape of her body is covered with a blue sheet. At least it isn't the papery stuff that covers everything else around here. I'm glad they have the decency to use fabric. But I have to admit, I'm beginning to hate the color blue.

My shaking fingers won't let me uncover her. They hover above the top of the sheet, trembling. I bite my lip to stop the quivering that's spread there from my hands.

"Here, let me." Micah's long fingers gently grasp the sheet above Gran's head and carefully fold it just beneath her face. One naked shoulder sticks out from under the cloth.

Her soft, wrinkled skin has a plastic look to it. And her hair, normally combed and smoothed back behind her ears is lying wildly across the silver beneath her. Reaching out, I tuck a lock around her ear and hold my palm to her face, just like I used to when she sat next to me. Somewhere deep inside of me I expect her to move, to lean her cheek into my hand and tell me I'm the only one who touches her like that, but she's still. Frozen.

I want to be strong, but when the tears well up on my eyelids, I can't stop them from spilling over. "I'm so sorry, Gran." A single tear falls onto the sheet, turning it a deep blue.

She knew this day was coming. Warned me of it, even. Told me they were trying to get rid of them early. The last of the Wombers. I should have seen the signs when the others were taken away, but I was too busy to notice.

With all the other Wombers, an announcement of death was given shortly after. I'd have recognized that for sure. Now that I think about it, I remember reading a few death notices. But I brushed them off. Gran said they were going to be releasing the Wombers once a month until they were gone. But Gran wasn't scheduled for another few months. That meant one thing: She either died of natural causes or they killed her to keep her quiet.

My bet is on the latter.

"Kate," Micah whispers. "You've got that look on your face. What're you thinking?"

"She knew something, Micah. Something big. And we have to figure out what it was."

I lean down and kiss her forehead. "I'll figure it out, Gran. Promise."

We cover her up and seal the door tight.

"You know what this means, don't you, Micah?"

"What?"

"We have to get Brody out of The Institute as soon as possible."

"I know."

THIRTY THREE

·······························

SECRET MESSAGES AND GIFTS FROM BEYOND

O
PENING THE DOOR TO my house is like entering the morgue all over again. Only I feel the heat of fury rising from my father's frame instead of the cold morgue air. It's hard to determine how my dad will react. When he's really upset, the rage barrels out of him like a torrent of waves crashing on the ocean shore. It just takes a lot for him to get to that point. "Where the hell have you been?"

Ocean wave. He never speaks to me like this.

"At the morgue," I reply. "Giving my respects."

My answer catches him by surprise, but he's still angry. "You should have told us where you were going. Your mother and I have been worried sick."

My mother's silence is her way of cussing me out. Not as effective as she thinks.

I decide not to antagonize him further. "Sorry, Dad. When Mom called, I freaked. I had to see for myself." I slide into a chair next to my mother. "Had to see if it was true."

He softens, knowing I loved her, too. "Sorry. I'm upset."

I nod. "I know." Right now, the last thing I want to do is have some sentimental family moment. Gran is dead and never coming back, and I'm pretty sure The Institute got rid of her because she knew something.

All I want to do at this moment is have some time alone to think. "Can I take dinner in my room?"

"Sure, honey," my mother says to my father's disapproval. But I've already heard her approval and responded, my feet hitting the stairs in a matter of seconds.

"I just need some time to myself," I say as I head to the stairs. Explaining isn't necessary; they are going through the same loss. But I feel the need anyway.

***

In my room, I curl up on my bed and click on the lamp on the bedside table. Reaching up to the pendant on my neck, I roll it under my fingers over and over, turning it from one side to the other. My mind wanders back to the recent times I spent with Gran, and I snicker as I remember her arguing with Micah about the messages in the stars. It was just after her *Starry Night* picture was taken away. The day she gave me this necklace. She was so insistent that there were words in the stars and not pictures. It was almost comical.

I spring upright in bed. Words in the stars. She gave it to me right after her painting was taken away for being … what did she say? Broken.

That's it! She was trying to tell me way back then, but I didn't listen. With fumbling fingers, I unhook the clasp and pull it from around my neck. Flipping it over and over, I find nothing unusual. It's a small turtle with a jade shell and four tiny feet sticking out from the corners. But there has to be something more to it. A secret compartment somewhere. It makes sense, really. A person her age would have no use for something like paper and pens. Personal notes are all but obsolete. Besides, with her mind the way The Institute believes it was, she would have no need to write a letter or make contact with any remaining relatives. Which is why she had to make do with what she had. The paper from the *Starry Night* print.

I finger the pendant again. Its long oval shape is raised in the middle, but I can't see an opening. There's no clasp or edge to indicate it's anything more than a pendant. But I know it's here somewhere. Maybe there's a hidden message in the shell. Letters woven so intricately into the lines that to the naked eye, one might not notice. No. That doesn't make any sense. She used the paper from the painting. I'm positive.

I move closer to the light and hold the metal nearer to its beams, squinting to see if anything stands out, and that's when I see it. A darker shadow creases along the under edge of the shell right next to the turtle's right front foot. At first I figure it's just dirt. This thing is probably a hundred years old, and it's bound to collect a bit of grime here and there, but scratching at it with my thumbnail doesn't loosen anything so it must be a shadow. I scratch again then press in on the edge of the shell. Nothing.

There's a pin on the bed stand, which I grab to scratch any excess dirt around the creases. It's a bit more successful, and I manage to remove a small glob of petrified goo. Picking away at the filth makes each section of the turtle shell stand out, but when I press each lightly, still nothing happens.

Even pressing each of the feet does nothing. *How on earth does this thing open? Or maybe it doesn't. Turtle … turtle … That's it!* Turtles pull their heads into their shells for protection. With a press of its nose, the head sinks into the shell and the oval shell cracks open at the neck.

I was right. It is a locket.

Two fingernails on either side should do the trick. In seconds, I've pried the locket open. Onto my lap falls a tiny paper folded to fit inside. It's not yellowed or worn as I might have expected, being in such an old locket. No. It's new paper. Crisp and neatly folded.

A secret message.

Unfolding the paper gently, I smooth it out over the tabletop, rubbing out the wrinkles. One edge is torn around while the other two are straight and come to a point on one side. I was right. It's been ripped from the corner of something.

There's no ink. Gran would have had no access to a pen of any sort, but I can see she scratched the letters with something. A fingernail, maybe. In the depressed lines, it's a little darker like she attempted to smudge the lines with some sort of dirt to make it easier to read.

Written in my gran's scratches are these words:

Bring the little one there.

I hear myself gasp. Gran knew. She knew about my son. How is that possible? Did she see some paperwork? Hear a conversation? I hadn't talked to her in weeks, so I knew it wasn't me. This was what she found out. That I had a son, and The Institute was using unapproved DNA. It had to be.

"I told her." My dad stands in the doorway, his voice choked with emotion. "She found out about the unapproved DNA use and confided in me. Wanted to get a message back to … so I told her what I knew."

My dad and I have shared things, suspicions, in the past, but something about this moment is different. It's a chain reaction that can't be stopped. We're on the verge of something big, and I'm stuck in the middle of it.

"How did they find out? Are you okay? Has anyone questioned you?"

He clears his throat and sniffs lightly. "I'm fine. I told her I couldn't get a message out right then, but I'd do it as soon as I could. Pretty sure she found someone else to take her message, but she chose the wrong person."

"Do you know who?" My stomach churns at the thought of Gran desperate enough to trust someone she didn't know.

"No. But because of it, I'm off the hook. No one knows she asked me."

Gasping, I feel in my spirit it's true. All the details come together. She found out and wanted to send me a message, so she ripped the only thing she could find to write on. They discovered it, which is why they took the painting. They just didn't know where to find what she'd written. That's why she gave me the necklace that day. She had to get rid of the evidence. But she had to let the elders of the Hidden City know, too. She trusted someone to carry a message, and they betrayed her. My son's existence is the secret that caused Gran's death. The guilt rushes over me, forcing the air from my lungs.

And suddenly, the realization hits me in the pit of my stomach.

It will cause my death as well.

"Dad, we can't let them get away with this."

"It's too late, Katie-Did. She's gone."

"Then let's do something about it. Honor her memory."

"What do you propose? I already buried your ID beneath several layers of encryption. No one will know you're the mother."

"When the time comes, I need you to delete his entire existence."

"What are you planning, Kate?"

My whole life, my dad has been my hero. Now, as I think back on all the stories he used to tell, I realize he's been preparing me for something like this. Something big that will change my whole life.

"I'm going to take him to the Hidden City."

Dad doesn't even look surprised. "Can you do it?" he asks.

"I hope so."

"Me, too."

THIRTY FOUR

....

ASSIGNMENTS

TARYN PLOPS DOWN NEXT to me and scans her ID card to order lunch.

Pulling her compact out of her bag, she places it on the table. "I hear we get our late gestation disposal assignments today."

Oh Yippie! "Where'd you hear that?" I ask, sipping my coffee in an attempt to hide the contempt I feel through silent sarcasm.

"Overheard Professor Donovan and Limbert talking. Exciting, don't you think?"

"Yeah." I try to act it by pasting a fake smile on my face, but how can I possibly be excited about disposing of an innocent child? Not exactly my idea of a fun time. And since I discovered the message in the locket Gran gave me, I've been trying to figure out just how my life's ambition of being a creation scientist is supposed to play out now. I can't save every child marked for disposal like I plan to save my son. Sure I can try to avoid disposal days like Micah does, but if I'm going to be doing this the rest of my life, the chances are someone will notice my odd avoidance techniques. Why couldn't they have separated the job into creation scientists and disposal technicians? That way, the sick and twisted who like to destroy things could have their enjoyment.

"So, who'd you get?" I ask, not thinking.

"Who?"

"When, I mean when."

"Three weeks from Thursday. And, your Micah's going to be there, too."

"Cool."

"It's going to be so incredible to be doing these procedures. I mean, it's kind of gross when you think about it, but it means we're moving up, you know. One step closer to Creation Engineer. Once we learn these procedures, they'll move on to the actual creation part of the Creation Unit. I bet they weed out the weaklings by doing all the gross stuff like disposals first. Whoever can withstand that is sure to do well with the rest of it." She laughs.

I must look like I'm not paying attention because she gives me a funny look. "You gonna check yours?"

Act normal. Don't be scared or freaked out, Kate, I tell myself, opening my compact on the table in front of us. I scan through the memo I've received in my inbox, noting names and dates. "I have the day after you. With Professor Donovan."

"Who's the lab assistant? Is it Micah?"

"No, Tom Stonemill." I crinkle my nose. "Who's that?"

"New guy. Just received his promotion a few weeks ago. Don't you remember? Limbert introduced us in class."

"Oh, that guy." I fake a response because I have no idea what she's talking about. Taryn smiles lightly.

"So, how old is the fetus in yours?" I slide my compact next to hers and compare data. "Let's see."

Then as I'm making comparisons, Taryn asks a question that catches me off guard. "Ever wonder who they belong to?"

"Whaddya mean?"

"Well, they have to use someone's DNA to create the suckers. And those poor saps don't even know they have a kid up for disposal. They're only informed when there's a viable kid." She finishes off her sandwich and wipes the corners of her mouth with a napkin. "The couples must know it's a possibility when they apply, but imagine what it would be like if they had to be informed every time there was a mistake."

"Heh. Yeah. That'd be crazy." It's times like this when I wonder if Taryn isn't a sympathizer. How many times have I heard her talk about the way we all look alike and how boring that is or about how they treat my gran is unfair. Even some of her reactions during the different disposals have made me wonder. I want to tell her what I know. Tell her about Micah's fake tattoo and his secret lab and our plan to steal the unviable and my son, but I hold back. If she knew, even if she is a sympathizer, it'd make things more difficult for her. I'd hate myself if I put her in a dangerous position.

We're silent for a moment as we scan each other's assignment. Date, time, blah, blah. *Procedural assistants: Taryn Black, Micah Pennington, Dr. Dane Donovan.* There are some other names I don't recognize. Probably lab rats hoping to observe.

"You're with Micah," I say.

"Yeah, I already mentioned that. Too bad I don't have the hots for him like you do."

Laughing, I keep reading. *Age of fetus: thirty-six weeks.* Wow, that's late. Maybe they were hoping for a viable. No, The Institute wouldn't have assigned the disposal to a student already if they weren't sure. *Reason to dispose: Low birth weight. Poor lung development. Blood markers. Identification number: 1298732.*

I gasp and then cough.

"What?" Taryn asks.

"Nothing." I cough as I look at her inquisitive eyes. "I just swallowed wrong."

"You okay?"

"Mmm hmm," I lie. But nothing is going to be okay.

In a little over three weeks, my best friend is going to kill my son.

THIRTY FIVE

LISTENING

"T, CAN YOU LET Professor Limbert know I won't be in class today? I'm suddenly not feeling well." I'm packing my compact back into my bag as I stand up. Taryn gives me a funny look.

"O-kay," she draws out the word like she's never heard it before. "You were fine just a minute ago. What's wrong now?"

Nothing like pointing out the obvious. I brush off the crumbs stuck to my hands. "Insta-headache. And I think whatever I ate this morning must have been bad. My stomach is doing flips. I'd like to use the bathroom and lie down."

Taryn stands, packs her own bag, swings it over her shoulder, and crumples her napkin into a tiny ball to throw away. "I can walk you home. Get you tucked in."

"No." It's a sharp response, and I can see the hurt on her face even when half of it is hidden by the light streaks that line her hair. "No, really, you don't have to bother. It's okay. I'll be fine. Just need to rest a bit. And I don't want to make you late for class." Yeah, nothing like sounding suspicious. *Good job, Kate.*

She must know this is a total lie. Taryn's known me forever. She's able to see through my terrible attempt at covering up what I really want to do, which is to find Micah. I have to talk to him. Maybe there's a chance he'll know what to do. I hope.

"I'll tell him, but you know how Prof is when it's a last minute thing. He gets all grouchy and takes it out on the rest of us. Thanks for letting me do your dirty work," she adds as a passing joke. But she's not joking.

I allow a pout to settle on my lips and attempt to look sick. "I know. Sorry about that. I just don't feel well." By this time, I'm walking out the door with Taryn right behind me. She squints her eyes against the sun-kissed snow and stands, probably waiting for me to explain further. But I don't. She'll have to wonder. Maybe between now and when she questions me about it—which she's bound to do—I'll have come up with a better excuse. Probably not.

On my way home, my mind is whirling in an attempt to figure out how to halt my son's imminent death. Half of me wants to run in there screaming and steal him away, but I can't. It's not that easy. I need a plan. I don't care if it's three weeks away; I need to do something now. By the time I reach my front door, I've come up with a huge bucket-load of squat. Every idea I have leads to trouble. Mostly, for me. But for my family as well. And for Micah. And even Taryn. While trouble for someone is inevitable, I want to minimize the damage as much as possible.

Thankfully, no one's home. Mom's at work, busy putting bad guys away using her human lie-detector abilities. Hopefully, she won't have to use that talent on me ever, but with the way I'm going, I wouldn't be surprised if she did. Dad won't be home till late. Data collections work. I know how that goes. And with the new assignment I gave him, he'll be sneaking in some overtime. Seems like that research center is our second home these days.

I'm thankful for the empty house because it means I can talk to Micah in private. I dig my phone out of my pocket and dial his number.

"Hello?"

"Micah! I need to talk to you."

"I assume that's why you called," he jokes, but he must recognize the anxiety in my voice because his tone turns serious. "You okay? What's wrong?"

His concern is comforting, and I find myself slouching into the overstuffed chair in the living room instead of pacing back and forth across the kitchen tiles like I did a moment ago. "I just found out that Taryn is assigned to my—"

"—Your lab work? Of course, I'll be over as soon as I can. Just wait for me, okay?"

"Okay. Micah, what's going on?"

"Don't worry, I'll be there in a few minutes, and we'll figure everything out."

His response totally freaks me out, but I agree and hang up. Then I spend the next few minutes working myself into an absolute tizzy trying not to worry. Not that it takes long. I'm already frazzled about Brody. So much for lounging in a cushy chair while I wait; I'm back to pacing, tapping my phone against my leg to ease the nerves.

I glance to the object in my hand. *The phone! Of course.* No wonder Micah won't talk.

It's like my entire world is crumbling one lonely stone at a time. I find out about the Natural Born, nearly get abducted, discover I have a son, my grandmother dies, and now my son is about to be killed in a procedure I'm attempting to learn in order to earn a living for the next sixty years. Um, yeah, not really a pleasant few months. My life is so twisted.

Ten minutes later, Micah knocks on my door.

I open the door to his dark face. There's no vehicle in the driveway, but there's no way he could have run fast enough to make it to my home in ten minutes. "How'd you get here so fast?"

"Drove. Parked around the corner. Didn't want anyone to suspect you of anything with my truck sitting in your driveway."

I move to the side as Micah steps past me and shut the door behind him, but not before a freezing gust sweeps into the house sending a chill over my skin. He shrugs off his coat and scarf and curls them over his arm as he enters the house. Swinging his head around, like he's looking for someone, he says, "Your parents home?" Frantic, he rushes through the house, opening doors and glancing in closets.

"Uh uh." I cross my arms around myself. Suddenly, I'm freezing, but I can't tell if it was from the wind that followed Micah inside or the strange vibe he's giving off.

"It's my phone, isn't it? They're tracking or recording or something." I offer it to him.

He doesn't say anything but takes it from my outstretched hand. The lack of confirmation is confirmation enough.

He pops the back off and starts rooting through the mechanics. Pinching something between his thumb and forefinger, he holds it up for me to see. "Look." It's a tiny square chip. "Recording device."

"They've been recording my phone calls. I should have known. How stupid of me."

Finally, he calms down and places his coat over the back of a chair at the dining room table. "Sorry." He crosses the room to me and takes my face in his hands. "I'm so sorry. I didn't mean to scare you," he says, gently meeting my lips with his own. They're cold from the icy walk around the block, but they're still soft and welcoming.

"All phones have them. The Institute likes to keep track of the community."

"The Institute." Inside my blood boils. With each passing moment, my hatred for this place grows, but it's countered by the pleasant memories, by my hope for the future. The internal tug of war is sometimes too much to bear.

Micah shakes his head and taps the chip back into my phone before snapping the cover on again. "I should have told you before, when you first found out about the Hidden City, but I knew you weren't going to say anything, so I didn't bother." Pulling out a chair, he takes a seat and crosses his arms on the table. "It's not like you use your phone a lot anyway. It's basically this: The Institute follows your every move. They record your phone conversations, they have spies everywhere observing your activity, and when you do something unusual, it's noted. Too many notations mean you get your very own personal spy to track your every conversation, every e-mail, and any unusual activity. And you already know about the surveillance."

"How do you manage to do the things you do?" I ask. After all, he's got a freakin' secret lab in his basement. Surely someone noticed something while he set the thing up. They must have noticed parts go missing just after he was on duty.

"I've been doing this for a long time, Kate. I know how to cover my tracks. You've already seen the origami messages. We use that as often as possible. And," he reaches into his pocket and pulls out a phone and hands it to me. "I have a phone without a listening device. This one is for you. But you can only call me on it. If you call anyone else, it will be recorded on their end, but not on yours, which would obviously send up warnings to the heads of the detection unit at The Institute. So if you're going to call your mom or Taryn, use your regular phone. To contact me, use the one I gave you."

I'm staring at the phone in disbelief. I knew The Institute was strict, but I'm only beginning to realize the lengths it will go to watch the people it's supposed to be protecting. "Why don't you use these to call your people? Seems more effective than folded paper notes."

"The above ground-to-underground calls can get a little sketchy. Don't always work and those signals might be intercepted. On the surface, it won't be questioned as much. Besides, you'd be surprised how effective the origami messages are."

"I'm still trying to wrap my head around how you do all the things you do."

"Like how I get all the lab equipment to my house without being noticed."

"Yes, like that."

"It's not just me. I might take something, but I'm not stupid enough to have stolen every piece of equipment that's in my basement. *And* I know what to look for."

"Like with my phone."

He agrees. "Like with your phone. And I obey the rules. Not drawing attention to myself is essential." His hands flatten out on the surface of the table. "That's basically it. Just be careful. Trust no one, even the people you've known forever." His gaze is intense as it holds mine like he's imparting the importance of his statement through his stare. But then his eyes soften and crinkle into a smile. "So, what's this news I'm supposed to hear?"

Right! After his strange behavior, I almost forgot the reason for his presence in my house.

"It's Brody."

"Brody?"

"My son."

"Oh yeah. I forgot you named him. What's the problem?"

Just thinking about my conversation with Taryn earlier today sends the shiver up my spine again. I can't sit still, so I push away from the table and pace. It helps me think, but judging by the look on Micah's face, it makes him nervous. I told Micah about my conversation with Taryn. "But then I happen to see the ID number. It's Brody's number. Taryn's been assigned to kill him." Having unloaded my stress for the day, I plop down next to Micah, who takes my hand in his and covers it with his other. It's a gesture my gran used to do. *The hand sandwich* I used to call it.

"I'm going to kill whom?"

The warming comfort from the hand sandwich wilts away, and I nearly fall out of my chair when I hear her voice. "Taryn! What are you doing here?" Sweat breaks out on my palms, so I rub them on my pants as I stand. Dang, the phone Micah gave me is still on the table, so I grab it quickly and shove it into my pocket, hoping Taryn doesn't notice that it isn't the one I've carried for months.

"I came to check up on you. You know. See how you were feeling since you were *too sick* to be in class today." Her jaw is clenched, and she's eyeing me suspiciously.

My face flushes, and I'm searching for an explanation, but my mind doesn't work well under pressure, and the only thing I can think to say is, "*My son! You're going to kill my son!*" Obviously, that won't go over well, so I purse my lips and close my eyes, hoping something will come to me in the next few seconds.

"Who am I going to kill, Kate?"

Micah rescues me from my vocal mumbling. "Kate's just a little nervous about the third trimester disposals. She's been doing a lot of work for Professor Limbert after hours and became kind of attached to the fetus you're assigned to dispose of." He stands, steps behind me, and puts his hands on my shoulders.

"That's exactly what we're not supposed to do, Kate," Taryn says as she sets her bag by the front door. "Get all attached. You know that. Besides, it's not really killing. They aren't even born yet."

"She was just saying if anyone were to dispose of him, she wanted to do it." Micah kisses my cheek lightly. "Right Kate? Besides, it's not killing when they're unviable. We're just helping to create a better community by disposing of stuff that will harm us in the future."

"Mmm hmm." He obviously pulled that from some lecture or textbook. I glance over my shoulder at his steady steely eyes, and mentally project a silent, "thank you." I hope he can read my look. "That's right. I wanted to check with Micah to see if he could arrange a switch for me."

Taryn crinkles her nose at me, and her shoulders drop, relaxing a bit. "Why didn't you just say so in the café?"

I clear my throat. "Um, I didn't think it was possible, so I thought I'd check with Micah first before I said anything to you." *Oh, please believe this pack of lies I'm feeding you.*

"Oh." Taryn's response seeps slowly out of her. "You could have confided in me. You can trust me, you know."

"I know." Suddenly Micah's recent words run through my mind. *Trust no one.* "Sorry. I just didn't want to make a big deal out of it without knowing if it was a possibility or not. I suppose I could have waited until I saw Micah again, but it surprised me a bit, and I panicked." At least that part wasn't a lie.

"I don't mind switching if you'd like," she says. "I mean, if they'll let us. I don't care which one I'm assigned as long as I get to do the procedure. It's the last major procedure before we get to attempt the creation of an embryo."

"Really? That'll be great," I mumble. "I mean, if they let us."

Micah grabs his coat. "Let me see if I can arrange something. I'll talk to Professor Limbert and Donovan today and let you both know."

"Thanks," I whisper.

He nods silently, and I know he understands I'm thanking him for covering for me.

THIRTY SIX

....

IT'S TIME

THREE WEEKS PASS IN an instant, and the next thing I know, it's D-day.

Disposal day.

Professors Limbert and Donovan agreed to the switch of Taryn and me. Not sure what Micah said to convince them, but I know he had to enlist the help of someone else he knew to get the change to pass. Another Natural Born hidden in our society. Sometimes I wish I knew who these people were, but Micah refuses to name names. No arguing that I might need to know who these people are sometime in the future has convinced him yet.

I know I can't get out of this disposal. I shouldn't even want to, seeing as how it's Brody. But if something goes wrong with our plan, and I have to watch him die, I won't be able to live with myself. I just hope Micah's plan is actually going to work and not get us both arrested or killed or taken captive to some underground torture chamber. My mind has been reeling with torment-filled possibilities for my future.

Micah, on the other hand, has taken on an everything-is-going-to-be-fine persona with an underlying nervous current of it's-going-to-take-a-freakin'-miracle-to-make-this-work. He's trying to hide his fear from me the best he can, but I can tell he doubts the plan.

The worst part of this day is I know very little about what will happen. Well, I guess that's not entirely true. I know my dad's timing with the data systems has to be perfect. I know exactly how the procedure will work and the physical reactions the child will have to the drug, but as for Micah's part and actually getting Brody out, I know very little. That way, I can't be blamed if something goes wrong. So he's kept his part in the plan secret. It'd be a nice gesture if it didn't set me on edge. Besides, if something does happen, what would I do? Go back to my house and pretend everything is normal? I think not. How would I possibly be able to hide the fact that my boyfriend is gone or that I'd be an absolute wreck and would not be able to continue on with my career choice? No. This plan has to work. There's no other option.

Micah told me that if we aren't able to get Brody to his lab, I'd have to take him directly to the Hidden City. He'll end up there eventually, but we'd rather not risk it now. Micah even drove me there once in the weeks awaiting Brody's disposal in case I needed to know how to get there, and I hope to anything holy that I can remember the way. Especially when the entrance to that place is hidden in snow covered woods. I keep running over the turns in my head, but it becomes a blur somewhere after the back alley behind Main Street. And I don't want to think about entering the woods where there aren't any trails. So I'm hoping it won't be necessary. I'd ask for Micah to write down the directions, but any paper trail leading the soldiers right to the rebels wouldn't paint me in a very good light with the rebels.

"If anything goes wrong, anything at all, meet me at the Hidden City."

I hope it won't come to that. Instead, I'm counting on Micah being at my side the entire time.

Basically, my job during the procedure is to do what the professor says. Act normal, like I know nothing. Shouldn't be too hard, since I know nothing. I'm also supposed to pay attention to any opportunities, whatever that means.

After hours for the last few days, I've wandered the halls memorizing all the back exits, just in case I have to get out quickly. I'm hoping I'll walk right out of here looking as normal as I do every day, but that means leaving the hard part—carrying Brody out of here unharmed and unnoticed—to Micah.

I know he's willing. More than that. He's trying to protect me and Brody, but he's the one who has to put himself at horrible risk. I don't like it, but it doesn't matter. None of my protests have had any effect on changing his mind and letting me in on a few details.

"I'm not going to put you at any more risk than you already are, Kate. You know too much as it is. I'd rather not put you in any more danger than you are already."

"But this is my son, Micah!"

"It doesn't matter. You've never done this before, and I'm not going to let your first time be with a screaming newborn in your arms to alert anyone who passes us. You'll just need to follow my lead."

So as I'm standing next to Micah, scrubbing in, my hands shake.

"You ready?" he whispers.

"No."

"It'll be fine. Trust me." But when his eyes shift toward the window of the door, I know he's hoping all parts of his plan fall into place.

***

Pressing his back to the door, his arms bent and raised at the elbows, we enter the prep room where we put on rubber gloves and meet the professors who are already waiting, compacts in hand, ready to record our progress. The procedure itself is left up to me and Micah.

Professor Donovan begins with his motivational speech. "You'll be fine. You know the procedure. And remember, if you measure or administer the saline solution incorrectly, you'll have to proceed using the forceps on the brain. It's the only alternative at that point."

Great motivational speech. Makes me want to run away screaming. Stick to your day job, Professor.

Professor Limbert, on the other hand, looks as if he wants to hug me. Instead, he tosses a curt nod, making his gray hair quiver on his forehead and says, "You'll be fine, Katherine. Micah will help you." He leads us to the table in the middle of the room where Brody is being kept. "Just keep your eyes open, and you'll know how to do it right."

His eyes are kind, and I can't help but find myself smiling in reassurance. Something about his serene presence eases my mind. My brain is clear, and I'm checking everything around me.

The back door of this room leads to a hallway that's only used by the research scientists, and if I can sneak through the classroom at the end of the hall, there's a door that leads to a back alley. But I won't have to use that because everything will go according to Micah's plan. If I keep telling myself this, maybe I'll begin to believe it.

Beside me on the table is a tray covered with that horrific blue paper. Underneath, the syringes and scalpels and forceps are laid out in a neat row. A bottle of salt solution sits on the corner.

Micah stands to my left while the professors sit opposite me. It's Micah's voice that guides me through.

"What's the first step, Kate?" he asks.

"Checking the fetus's weight and measuring the appropriate amount of saline solution."

"Yes, go ahead."

Taking a deep breath, I look at Brody one more time, hoping this isn't the last I'll see of him. He opens his eyes and looks right at me as if to cheer me on. Or maybe he's saying good-bye.

"Kate."

"Huh?" A minute has passed since I uncovered the capsule and all three men are staring at me.

"Katherine, are you all right?" Professor Limbert asks.

"Yes, sorry, I was just walking through the procedure in my mind first."

"Very well," he says with a glance at his compact. "Continue."

Taking the weight measurements, I write down my findings. "Five pounds, eleven ounces."

"Low birth weight," Professor Donovan pipes in. "Tests have already confirmed lack of lung development and markers have been found in his blood. All this combined confirms what?"

"The need for disposal of the fetus," I hear myself saying.

He nods and makes a notation in his compact.

"Go ahead and measure the saline, Kate." Micah's shaking voice sends a surge of fear through me. Is his plan not working? I look at him, eyes wide, but he's got all his features under control and won't meet my gaze.

I do as he says, pulling the plunger slowly to make it look like I'm measuring exactly, and I lay the syringe alongside the capsule. "Now, I have to drain the fluid inside the capsule to at least half and replace it with the saline." I speak matter-of-factly, but my heart is racing.

"Go ahead and hook up the drainage tube."

Inserting the tube is easy, but actually allowing the vital liquid to flow out makes my breathing stagger and my heart pump faster. I watch as Brody curls smaller, trying to stay within the liquid, and I swear I see fear on his face, too.

I'm draining it slowly, trying to buy another minute of time. Another second. Glancing at Micah, occasionally, does me no good. He refuses to look at me, but I do catch him glimpse at the clock every few seconds. The crinkle on his forehead deepens as the second hand ticks by. And when his hand reaches to run through his hair and stops short—the rubber gloves probably—and his shoulders rise with the calming breath he's trying to inhale, I know he's wondering if we can pull this off.

"The syringe, Ms. Dennard." Professor Donovan looks irritated. He twists his wrist to get a good look at his watch. Must have something more important to do than kill my son.

"Sorry," I say. "I'm nervous."

Professor Limbert speaks up, "Nothing to be nervous about, Katherine. Everything is going to be just fine."

My fingers wrap around the large syringe, cold and hard. I lift it to the top of the capsule and unlock the barrier separating Brody from the world. It's how we'd birth him if he were deemed viable. Just lift him out. The bile in the back of my throat rises as I begin to squeeze. Slowly. A few drops at a time.

Micah, I silently plead. *Please do something! I can't go through with this.* My hands tremble, and I'm sweating in the sweltering heat of this room. Closing my eyes, I'm holding back tears.

Micah, do something.

The knock on the door makes me jump, and I have to catch myself before I depress the entire salt solution into the capsule. *Thank you!*

All the men in the room swing their faces toward the door. Donovan looks irate as he kicks his chair back and gets up to answer the call. From where he stands, I can't hear what he's saying, but his stance, with crossed arms and constant head shaking, add to his irritation. I take the few moments of reprieve to look at Micah. Finally, he meets my eyes and flicks his hair off his forehead with a tiny twist of his neck.

I'm not expecting it when he leans into me and whispers in my ear.

Turning back to Donovan, I see Professor Limbert has joined him and is growing increasingly agitated. They're both arguing with whoever is behind the door, but finally, Limbert steps aside and holds the door for the group of men who enter.

There are six of them, all well over six feet, and with heavily muscled arms they carry rifles in their hands. More guns are strapped to their hips along with handcuffs and stun guns and an array of other unidentifiable weapons. A raid. At the back of the pack stands Saul Goodman. He lifts his eyes to meet mine, and I'm sure I see pity in them.

"Micah Pennington?" one of the men says.

"I'm Micah." He steps forward, a look of confusion on his face. "What's going on?"

"You're under arrest."

I gasp. Micah looks shocked. "What? Why?"

Saul's staring at me, gauging my reaction. But I don't know what's going on, so if he's here to spy on me, there's nothing to learn.

"Micah?" I ask.

"It'll be easier if you don't put up a fight." The man in front stands with his hand on his holster, ready to draw at any moment.

Micah's peeling off his gloves now, turning them inside out. "I'm not going anywhere until I know what this is about."

I can't tell if the bewilderment he's portraying is part of his ruse or if this is just as much a surprise to him as it is to me. What have they found out? Then it hits me. They know he's a Natural Born, and they know about the lab and the underground city and Brody. The Hidden

City will be destroyed. They'll raid it as soon as they can get men over there.

"Sir," the man in the center says. The others flank Micah on either side as if readying themselves for a potential disaster. "If you'd come with us." Their eyes are ready, and their guns raised.

Now Micah's raising his voice, and he crouches his legs ever so slightly and puts his hands out in front of him. It looks like he's about to surrender, but there's a tiny bounce in his legs. He's expecting a fight, and I'm watching the scene with horror. This is not part of the plan. Getting arrested is *definitely* not part of the plan.

"Not until you tell me what's going on. Why am I being arrested?"

The head police officer pulls a paper out of his pocket and unfolds it. "Micah Pennington," he reads, "a warrant for your arrest has been issued due to the following infractions: Improper use of disposal devices. Lack of attendance at mandatory procedures. Suspicions of stolen property. And public misbehavior."

Micah shakes his head. "This is ludicrous. I haven't done anything. What have I stolen? What have I done that's improper? Huh? Tell me!" He looks at the two teachers in the room. "Tell them, Professor Limbert. I haven't done any of this."

But Professor Limbert retreats sheepishly into the corner. "I know, Micah, but it's our word against theirs. Maybe if you go with them peacefully, you can get this all figured out."

The band of men slowly surrounds Micah. "I haven't done anything!" he shouts again, and when one of the giant men takes hold of his arm, he yanks it away and throws a punch into the man's nose. "Keep your hands off me! I haven't done anything wrong."

"You have now," says the head police officer. "Add assaulting an officer to that list."

In seconds, all six men are on top of him, holding him down and yanking his arms behind his back. He's on the floor struggling against the weight of the men, but it's no use. Saul has his knee on Micah's head, pressing it to the floor.

I catch Micah's gaze through the tears in my eyes. "Go!" he mouths.

The men jerk him from the floor and push him out the door, stumbling over his own feet. Through my haze, I hear Donovan telling Limbert he'll accompany Micah to the station. "You have Kate finish the procedure," he says. Professor Limbert agrees.

Finish the procedure! Are you kidding? They've just arrested my boyfriend, and they're going to make me go through with this? These people are freaking insane. If I can get Professor Limbert out of the way, I can grab Brody and run away. But when I allow myself one more look toward the door the police just dragged Micah through, I see my teacher walking toward me.

He passes me and reaches high on the wall behind me. I hear a snap, and when I turn, I see a crack through the lens of the recording device programmed for this room. Then he rushes around, grabbing things I don't recognize and throws them into a shoulder bag he takes from the supply closet.

"Kate!" he yells. "Snap out of it!"

His face is right in front of mine, and he's grabbing more things off the table and shoving them into the bag. "Take the baby out of the capsule, Kate."

I stand there, numb. What is going on? "Kate! Grab the baby. Hurry, we don't have much time."

It's like I'm hearing everything he says through a thick fog. It's muffled and foreign, and I don't understand. This isn't the professor I know.

He's pulling open a cupboard in the back of the room and removing items I haven't been taught to use.

Finally, his instructions reach the synapses of my mind, and I do as he says. I reach my hands into the sticky fluid and pull Brody out of the top of the capsule. Professor Limbert is at my side in an instant with blankets ready to wrap the tiny body. He grabs a small rubber syringe and clears Brody's nose and mouth, and snips the umbilical cord, disconnecting my son from the synthetic placenta at the bottom of the pod.

"Come on," he says, rubbing Brody's skin vigorously. He's not talking to me. Brody's skin has a red tint to it, but not like that of a normal newborn. He's been burned by the little bit of saline in the fluid. The few drops I had to administer.

I stand in shock, watching Professor Limbert work. Another minute passes before the child lets out a cry. The professor sighs and drops his shoulders in relief. "Good. Good boy," he coos. Turning to meet my gaze, he speaks quickly but in hushed whispers. "He'll be okay, Kate, you just have to keep him warm. Watch his breathing. His lungs may have been affected, but hopefully it'll clear out on its own." Professor Limbert takes more blankets and wraps the baby in one, then another, tucking the ends behind the child.

"I have to keep him warm?" I'm in a daze, and I can't grasp what's happening. Everything's moving so fast.

Pushing the baby into my arms, Professor Limbert slides a small hat over Brody's head and takes a step away from me. "Yes, Kate. You need to get out of here. Quickly. Your father will see to the ID change. They'll think he's been disposed of, but you have to get him out."

"My dad? You know about my dad?" I cry.

"You'll need this." The strap of the bag he filled tugs on my shoulder. "It's got some supplies in it. Formula and baby needs, but it won't last long."

"I have to take him to Micah's lab."

"No, it's too dangerous."

"What do I do with him, then?"

"Take him to the Hidden City, Kate. He'll be fine there."

I stare at him. Professor Limbert? The man who taught me all the disposal techniques, the one who walked me through my first chemical disposal firsthand knows about the Hidden City. Is he a sympathizer or a Natural Born?

He throws another bag at me. "These supplies will get you there, but you'll need to go now."

The bundle in my arms squirms as I look at the face of my baby. He's breathing and snuggled into the warmth of the blankets. But what do I do if he starts crying? Or if he needs medical attention? Or if he needs to eat or be changed? I know nothing about caring for a newborn. I'm instantly regretting not having prepared more for this day. It wasn't supposed to happen this way. We were supposed to have more time. To take Brody to Micah's lab. To birth him there. It wasn't supposed to happen this way.

Professor Limbert pushes me along, but my feet feel as if they've grown roots into the floor. "Kate, if you don't go now, they'll suspect something. Then we'll all be in trouble. You need to leave. Now."

I'm at the back door. Limbert opens it for me. "Welcome to your new life of hiding, Katherine Dennard. Good luck." With that, he pushes me through the door, bundles and all, and tosses my coat and scarf at me.

"But—" I don't have a chance to finish my statement before he shuts the heavy door in my face as I'm sliding my arms into my coat and wrapping my scarf around my neck with one hand.

"I don't know the way to the Hidden City. I don't remember how to get there." I'm sobbing to the cement walls. Tears stream down my cheeks when I realize Professor Limbert is gone. Micah is gone, and I'm on my own with a newborn I don't know how to take care of. On my way to a place I don't know how to get to.

....

THIRTY SEVEN

NOTHING HAPPENS ACCORDING TO PLAN

THE EVENING AIR IN early March bites my skin as I press my back against the door leading to the back alley. Clutching Brody to my chest, I pray he doesn't cry out until we're beyond The Institute's borders and away from the city. A harsh wind whips through the alley, pinning me to the wall and slipping under my coat as if to say, "You won't survive against me."

The gust must have reached Brody because he inhales a tiny breath and lets out a pathetic whine.

"Shhh," I whisper into the collar of my coat where I've nestled him, holding him with one hand. "It's okay, little man." The sound of my voice quiets him, and his fluttering eyes settle.

I want to pause. To have a moment to take in the magnitude of what's just happened. To lay this little creature down in front of me and examine every tiny part like a normal mother would. I want to know if he has long fingers and toes and if his ears are shaped like mine. I want to feel his breath on my skin and rub my cheek against his silky hair.

But I can't. Not now. Not ever if I don't get moving this instant.

I turn down another alley. Standing there, I give myself a moment to gather my thoughts. I'm on my own. Micah's been arrested. There's no way he can help. *Shake it off, Kate. He'll find a way out. Focus. Get to the Hidden City.*

"Get to the Hidden City," I reiterate. I'm hoping hearing my own voice will motivate me to move. "Step one: Get away from The Institute." Easier said than done since The Institute spans most of the city. It's the hub of the whole community. Only home residences lay outside its fenced borders. And beyond that, the entire community is surrounded by high chain link fences. But I can't let myself focus on that. One step at a time. If I can at least get away from the research center and school, that'll be a start.

"Step two: Back alleys only." Isn't this what Micah told me? Following his directions, I turn down the dark alley and make a left at the end. Of course, it's blocked off by a seven foot tall fence. Okay, so the fence problem came a little earlier than I thought. Climbing it wouldn't be a problem if I weren't laden down with two bags of supplies and an infant in my arms. But there's no choice. Taking the main streets isn't an option. Anyone could see that I'm escaping dressed like I am.

The alley is fairly clean. Must be the garbage has recently been removed. The Institute makes sure that within its borders, everything is cleaned up quickly. It's all about precision and cleanliness. A great philosophy if you're just going about your business, but they don't take into consideration those who are breaking the rules and trying to escape with a stolen infant in their arms. Obviously.

Luckily, I spot one lone crate sitting upside down by a doorway. I rush over, grab it, and place it down next to the fence. It'll give me one less foot I have to climb on my own. But I can't let go of Brody and climb at the same time. *Think! Now's not the time to be slow on your feet. You need to get out of here, now!* Unwrapping the green scarf Gran knitted me so many years ago, I slink out of my coat.

Brody whines against the icy air. "Sorry, buddy. It'll just be a second." I wrap the scarf around my chest and Brody, strapping him to the front of me like a papoose. *Thank you for making this scarf so long.* Then I tie the ends together and bounce once or twice, holding my hands underneath, just in case he might fall. Nothing. He's not going anywhere. I won't run without holding him, but I can at least get over the fence with two hands. Shaking the snow off my coat, I sling it over my shoulders and button it around both of us and grab the supply bags, wishing I didn't have to carry them. I'm not used to being so bogged down, but I can't afford to leave them behind either. And I don't know how long I'll be traveling on foot.

With gloved hands, it's hard to get a handhold on the fence, but I'm afraid to take them off. Stepping on the crate, I reach as high as I can, yanking myself upward and trying not to squish Brody against the clanking metal. My toe presses into a crevice, and I hoist myself up a little higher. *Again.* I tell myself. A few more times and I can clear this fence.

One more. My hand can almost reach the top of the fence. I shove my toe between the tiny criss-crossings and set my weight on it. But the squeak of a door breaks my concentration. Twisting to see, I catch a glimmer of light and a tall form creeping out from one of the doorways to my right.

"Hey!" a deep voice breaks through the darkness. "What're you doing?"

Crap!

Just then, my toe loses its grasp, and I slip. My fingers grip the metal, and somehow, I manage to hang on, but not before slamming my chest into the fence. Brody gives out a horrific screech.

"Hey, you!" the man yells again, this time taking wide strides toward me. No taking my time or being careful now. I have to move. Brody crying or not. So I hoist us up with one last effort and swing my leg over the fence. For a second, I pause, sitting on the bar at the top of the fence before I turn and grind my toes into the crevices again. One or two steps down and we're on solid ground just as the man reaches the fence. Brody screams again. "Stop!" the man yells.

It's like I'm suspended in time. I know I can't stop, but everything swirls around me. All I can see is the man's face pressed against the fence and his fingers like claws, sticking through the metal. It's not a face I recognize other than the angry, determined look on it.

"Get back here!"

As I turn to run, Brody lets out another cry. The man's eyes explode in disbelief, and he's running toward the alleyway door yelling, "Stop her! Someone stop her! She's got an infant with her!"

Without hesitation, I turn and sprint—if that's what you can call running with two supply bags and a crying child—as fast as I can to the end of that alley. Running solely on instinct, every turn I take is only a chance I'm headed in the right direction. As long as it's farther from where I came, it's better than nothing.

At each twist and turn, I watch over my shoulder, but the man who saw me must have gotten lost in the maze of alleyways. It only took a few minutes of running before his voice faded into the distance as well.

This particular passageway looks incredibly familiar, and I'm convinced I've traveled it before. About twenty minutes ago. I've lost all sense of direction, and for all I know, I could be headed straight by the police station or even back to the study center of The Institute. Neither would be a good thing. How did I get so turned around?

Turn, run, run, run. Turn, run, run, run. Avoid people talking on the corner. Shush Brody every time he whimpers. At every intersecting alley, I carefully steal a look toward the street in an attempt to get my bearings. After what seems like hours, I recognize something under the light at the corner of the street. The café. At least I know where I am now, not that it does me any good. It's not like I can walk toward the main street and head out of town.

Keep your head, Kate! You can do this. I know I'm in for it when I realize how much I'm talking to myself. In my head, audibly, it doesn't matter; it's not a good sign. *Think. This alleyway follows the block to the corner.* I look to my right. There's another fence for me to climb. Wonderful! Picturing the main street in my head, I can see the café and the length of the block past the library. *Yes! The library.* Once I reach the end of the alley, I should be in the wooded area of the park that butts up against the library's western side. I can travel off the pathways and still know where I'm headed.

This is a great plan. And if I can make it through the park without being seen, I can stop at Micah's to warm up and rest.

***

This time, I'm up and over the fence with no surprise visitors to draw attention to us. To calm myself, I talk to Brody. He's whining again, and I'm sure he's hungry. "Just a little further, little guy, and we can stop for a rest. I'll get you something to eat and get a diaper on you, and we'll be off again. Patting him as I walk seems to calm him a little, so I keep it up as we criss-cross through the park, avoiding all the paved paths.

Walking to Micah's house will require me to take the main sidewalk down the street for two blocks. With the possibility of soldiers marching through the streets at the same time. There's a chance we might get caught, but at this point, I'm willing to take the risk. If I don't risk it, the chance is guaranteed. I mull over an excuse in case we're stopped by anyone, and as long as it's not the military, who I'm sure by this time have an announcement out to be on the lookout for a young girl with a baby, we should be okay. *"My parents were just assigned this newborn."* I practice in my head. *"They asked me to watch him, and I had to walk to a friend's house for some formula because we're out, and the new shipment won't come until tomorrow."* Yeah, that should work. I hope.

Brody and I step out onto the street. "Be confident," Micah once said to me, "and they'll not suspect a thing." So I do. I don't try to hide at this point, but walk directly to my destination. I pass one or two people on the sidewalk who give me quick glances before turning back to their own business. I hold my breath each time and wait until I've passed them to exhale.

Keeping my head down, I try to hurry, but hearing footsteps, I look up. Right into the face of a soldier. There are three more behind him all holding guns and standing in a straight line, waiting for more orders.

"Stop right there, Miss."

I'm stone still on the sidewalk, pulling my coat tighter around me. Maybe they won't notice the bulge of the baby underneath the thick wool.

"What have you got there?" he asks, pointing to my coat with the butt of his gun.

My brain races, trying to think of an excuse, but when Brody cries out again and squirms, there's no denying I'm holding a child.

"My baby brother," I spurt out. Then the rest of my rehearsed speech comes to my lips. "My parents were just given this infant. They asked me to watch him while they went out, but I needed some formula because our shipment doesn't come until tomorrow. I couldn't leave him alone, so I brought him with me."

"Show me your ID."

Crap! This is it. Once he sees my ID and enters my number in his screening device, I'm done.

It's in my back pocket where I always keep it, but I feign digging through my coat to buy time. Add to that the fact that I have to hold a squirming Brody with one hand and root around with the other, and I'm fumbling as I search. Mr. Officer is not happy about it. His jaw clenches, and he shifts his rifle from one hand to the other.

"Your ID, Miss."

"It was in my pocket earlier." A quick glance around reveals an empty street, which means no one can help me even if they know I need help. I'm trying to stall just one more moment, but the look on the officer's face is growing harsher by the second. Dipping my chin, I kiss Brody on the top of his head, knowing this will be the last moment we have together. Then I reach into my back pocket where I knew my ID has been all along and pull it out. "Here it is," I say, holding it out to the man.

He takes it and flips it over to see my picture. At the same time, his walkie-talkie goes off.

"Unit twenty-four, come in."

He turns his head to the side and clicks the button on the device attached to his shoulder. "This is unit twenty-four."

"Report to one twenty-nine West Avenue. Assistance with entrance into a residence is required immediately."

"Yes, sir," he says to the man giving instructions. Then he turns to the three soldiers standing behind him. "That's the dissenter's house. Move out."

They turn and head down the street while he hands me back my card without even examining it. "Get home immediately, Miss. These streets aren't safe for a young woman."

I nod silently and relax my tensed muscles. Slipping the card into my pocket, I wait until they're out of sight before I can convince my legs to start moving again. More than anything, I want to turn around and go the other direction, but the only way out of here is to follow the soldiers.

One more block to Micah's place. "Almost there," I whisper to Brody, who's settled for the moment. But when I turn the block, my heart sinks. Of course, I should have known when he said it. One twenty-nine West Avenue. That's Micah's house.

There aren't many, but I can make out a few soldiers hovering around the Pennington house. Some carry flashlights. Another one or two are in the house, lights on. An unmarked car sits in the driveway. Two of the soldiers who questioned me are guarding the front door. I assume the other two are either out back or in the house.

What if they find the lab? They'll never let Micah out of custody.

I should have known I couldn't go there. That they'd be watching the house. What do I do now? My house is out of the question. Mom and Dad might notice if I come in carrying Brody. My dad knows about him but trying to explain it to my mother would be next to impossible. She'd return him immediately to be destroyed. No. As much as I long to say good-bye, I can't. I have to find another way. Then a thought pops into my head. Maybe I *can* contact Dad. I pull the phone Micah gave me out of my pocket and dial Dad's number.

"Hello?"

"Daddy?" The sound of his voice brings the well of emotions I'd been pushing under to the surface. My voice quavers with the one word I've spoken.

He hears it, too. "Katie-Did? What's wrong? Where are you? Is everything okay?"

"No. I've got him, Dad." As if he knows I'm talking about him, Brody whimpers.

Dad hears him. "Is that the baby? Is he okay? Where are you?"

I speak fast, knowing there's not much time. "Yes. It's him. Stuff went all wrong at the lab, and I took him. I don't know what to do."

The sound of shuffling feet and a door closing echoes in the background. "You can't bring him here, Kate. Your mother's home."

"I know. I just wanted to say good-bye." By this time the tears have started, and I try to sniff them back.

"Good-bye? Kate, wait." He's whispering so my mother doesn't hear.

"I have to get Brody to the Hidden City, Dad. I have to get out of here."

"Kate, where are you? Don't go anywhere. I'll come and get you."

"No, Daddy. You can't. It's too dangerous. They'll come after you if you do." More soldiers march up the street toward Micah's house. I can't talk anymore. If I do, Dad'll convince me to stay, and I know that's not an option. "I have to go."

"Kate. No. Wait."

"Good-bye. I love you."

"Katheri—" I don't hear him finish my name because I've already hung up the phone. My face is streaked with tears that I wipe away with the back of my hand. Sniffing again, I glance around to get my bearings. I have to be fast. More than likely, Dad will come looking for me. Besides, I can't be out much longer. Even though the deep frost of winter has broken, the frigid wind and light snow storms of early March can be just as cold. My fingers are going numb, my cheeks are burning, and I have to find a warm place to feed and change Brody.

Only there's no one I can trust.

....

THIRTY EIGHT

NO ONE TO TRUST

A N IDEA POPS INTO my head, and before I have time to weigh the consequences, my feet are already putting my new plan into action. Maybe there *is* one person I can trust, even if I haven't told her all the details. I know where she stands when it comes to all things associated with The Institute. She'll listen. I'm sure of it.

It's another mile from Micah's house, and the biting cold has already frozen my toes. Climbing up the front steps is physically painful. I hope she's home. Alone. This is my only chance to get help before I have to confess everything to my parents. Before my cracked knuckles can bang on the door, it opens in front of me. She jumps back, surprised.

"Kate, what are you doing here?"

"Taryn, I need your help."

She backs into the house, letting me pass. "Kate, what happened? What is all this stuff?" she asks, pointing to my bundles.

"Are your parents here?"

She shakes her head. "Working late."

"I have something to show you, but you can't freak out."

Her foot taps frantically. "I'm already freaking out. You're acting all weird, Kate."

"I know. I'm sorry. But before I show you, I need you to promise you won't say anything. Ever."

She rests her hands on her hips and twists her one eyebrow at me in question. "What are you talking about?"

"I mean it, Taryn. This isn't just some teenage-love-story-please-don't-tell kind of secret. I need your word." I'm holding Brody with one hand, still under my coat. He's starting to squirm, but I won't show Brody unless she promises me.

"Fine, I won't say anything. Now, what's going on?"

"The Institute has been lying to us our entire lives," I say, pressing into her house as I unbutton my coat slowly. "But I've recently discovered something. They've been using unapproved DNA to create new embryos."

"What?"

"That's not all. Remember how I switched my third trimester disposal with you?"

"Uh huh. It was supposed to be tonight."

"Well, the real reason I wanted to switch is because he's my son. They used my DNA to create him."

"Kate, this is crazy! You're talking nonsense."

"No, I'm not. And here's my proof." I set the bags on the floor in the dining room and slip my coat off and reveal Brody, still strapped to my chest with my scarf. "Taryn, meet my son."

Taryn lets out an audible gasp and presses her fingertips to her lips. Her eyes widen and she stumbles backward before catching herself on a chair. Gathering her composure, she creeps forward as if she's afraid she might get hurt if she gets too close. "Kate, this is insane. You have to bring him back. Maybe they'll overlook the infraction or … You have to take him back there."

I shake my head. "No. You don't understand. He was set for disposal. They'll kill him if I take him back. I won't let that happen."

Her eyes are frenzied, and she keeps stepping closer to see then backs away. This must be a lot for her to take in all at once. I've at least had the past few weeks to get used to the idea. "But if he was supposed to be disposed, then there's something wrong with him. He won't survive either way. Why would you take him out and make him suffer? He's not right, Kate."

"Because I don't believe he's truly unviable. I've seen things, Taryn. Wonderful people living with disabilities and diseases. He doesn't have to be destroyed."

In her frantic state, she spouts the things we've heard all our lives. The things The Institute has taught us about the Unviable. "That's the whole point. We're trying to eradicate those things. By letting them live, it affects all of us. It's not like people can't live with medical problems. It's that we don't want to. Look at what you've done, Kate. He can't live here. They'll never let him. What are you going to do with a sick infant?" Her hand pushes back the hair that's fallen out of her ponytail and comes to rest on her opposite shoulder like she's half hugging herself.

Maybe this was wrong. I shouldn't have brought him here. It's too much for her to handle. I should leave.

I'm regretting my decision, when I look down at Brody. He's breathing rapidly, but at least he's breathing. I need to get him medical help as soon as I can. Then looking over his tiny ears and pouting lips boost my confidence that everything is going to work out. "I'm taking him to the Hidden City."

Taryn runs her finger and thumb over her eyebrows as if to press away the frustration. "Seriously? Kate, you know that place doesn't exist. It's a fairytale to keep the hopes of the sympathizers alive."

Of course she would think this. It's what we've been taught since we were in diapers, but I know better. "It's not."

"What? You've been there?" Her hands drop to her sides.

"Yes, I've been there. With Micah. It's where Brody belongs." I run my fingertips over the thin, silky hair that covers his head. "Where I belong."

"Where you belong? What kind of crazy talk is that? So, what? Your plan is to just up and disappear to live in some underground cavern or something? Gee, that sounds like a great life, especially with a baby to take care of." She takes a deep breath. "Listen to yourself, Kate."

"It's not like that. Okay, look, I'm not going to argue with you." So much for getting her help. "Can I just warm up and change and feed Brody? Then I'll be on my way. Will you at least help me with that?"

She exhales loudly. "Yeah, fine. I'll help you with your crazy plan, and when you wake up and realize how insane this idea is, I'll do my best to help you stay out of trouble, too." She gives me a weak smile. "Because that's the kind of gal I am. Just hurry before my parents get home."

I unwrap Brody and nuzzle him under my chin, feeling the warmth of his skin against my neck. "You realize they're going to dispose of him when they find him."

I shoot her a fierce look. "Which is why they won't find him."

Shrinking away from my protective mother glare, she heads toward the kitchen. "Do you need anything? You know, to feed him or something."

"Some warm water would be great." She nods and turns away. "Taryn?" Stopping, she glances back at me. "You aren't going to say anything, are you?"

"Kate, have I ever told any of your secrets to anyone?"

"Thanks."

"Yeah, yeah. That's what friends are for, right?"

While I lay Brody on the couch and scavenge through one bag for a diaper, Taryn disappears into the kitchen for some water.

By the time she returns with a glass, I've changed him and wrapped him back into his blankets, not as well as Professor Limbert did the first time, but enough to keep him warm, I think.

"Here." She hands me the glass, which I transfer into a plastic bottle, add formula according to the package, and shake it well. "So, you get to play mother for a while, huh?" Her tension seems to have eased, and she's fallen back into the supportive friend role again.

"Guess so." I smile at the tiny creature in front of me. I still can't believe all of this is real. Brody, alive. Me having to care for him. Correction, having to save him from The Institute's primitive practices. It's like something out of a story my gran used to read to me. Heck, maybe those stories weren't so far-fetched, after all.

The two of us sink into chairs in the living room while I feed Brody. He must be starving because he sucks down the bottle in record time. It's like a dream as I watch his tiny lips pucker into an O. His skin is soft and smooth, and I can't help running my fingers over it again and again. This seems to soothe him. He's a little miracle man. Not meant to survive.

Taryn watches him from the chair next to mine with a mixture of fear and amazement. Every once in a while I see her reach out her hand like she wants to touch him but then pulls back at the last second.

"You wanna hold him?" He's suspended in mid air as I offer him to her.

She shakes her head. "No. I'd break him, for sure."

Taking a few minutes to rest is heavenly. Soon, Brody settles into a comfortable sleep. "So how are you going get to this underground city?" she asks.

"Walk. I just hope I can remember the way."

She rolls her eyes and shakes her head and says, "That's insane, Kate."

"I need to get going," I say, getting up and gathering my things.

"Wait, your bag," she says, "Just one minute." She walks away. "I'll go get it."

"Thanks," I say. "For everything."

"No problem."

I'm tying Brody to my chest again, wishing I had something warmer to wrap him in, when I hear the doorbell. Taryn's footsteps approach the door, and she pulls it open. There's whispering, but I'm sure I hear Taryn's voice say, "Yes, she's in there."

My heart sinks as I swing the one bag over my shoulder and run for the back door. No time to get the other supplies. They're still sitting next to the front door. I have to get out of here fast. I'm across the yard before I dare to look back. It's just a glance, but I can see her clearly. Standing in the doorway to her back porch, scowling.

"You should've known, Kate!" she yells. "I can't let you get away with something like this! It's treason."

I may be committing treason, but in my mind, Taryn's the traitor.

THIRTY NINE

. . . .

RUNNING

L ITERALLY RUNNING FROM THE law is not how I wanted to start this journey. But with who-knows how many military chasing me, I can't stop. I have to reach the Outer Lands as fast as I can. It's my best bet at escape. When I see an alley, I take it as long as it's going in the same direction I am. Otherwise, I don't even bother hiding. I'm already an outlaw, so what's the sense of hiding now? What does matter now is speed. And with Brody, I can't move as fast as I'd like.

I try not to think as I travel, but it's impossible. With only an infant to talk to, my mind spins with the events of the last few days and hours. Taryn. My most trusted friend. A traitor. To think she not only could get me in trouble, but she could get Brody killed. My heart aches for the friend I've lost. Pressing through the harsh, snow-covered ground, I wipe the tear trail that trickles down my cheek. Why did it have to be her? It's still impossible to me that she would do such a thing. After all we've shared and her questions about The Institute's practices, it doesn't seem possible for her to be willing to turn me in.

Maybe it's more than that. Maybe she's more than what she seems, a friend who did what she thought was right in her own mind. Micah mentioned personal spies. Have I been tagged? I know I was being followed months ago, but Micah admitted it was him. What if it wasn't just him? Could Taryn have been my personal spy, determined to out me? She easily could have followed me, especially knowing pretty much every detail of my schedule. No. I can't allow myself to think like that. She just had to perform her civic duty. That's all. It has to be.

But I can't think of that now. Right now, I have to concentrate on getting out of The Institute's territory. Of getting to the Hidden City despite having no idea where I'm going. Every few blocks I check behind me, waiting to see cops at every corner, ready to surround me and Brody and take us into custody. But none show. It's strange. Eerie, almost.

As I tramp through the back streets of the residential area, I press my hands to his back in a constant rhythm. Brody's sleeping now, thankfully. The full belly and clean behind must be comforting. His warm breath kisses the skin of my chest as we weave between private residences and trees. Before long, I see it. The road leading out of town. It's surrounded by tall pines. The Outer Lands. I find myself sighing in relief as we travel the last block of civilization. It's within my grasp now. Reaching the edge, I turn to look at what had been my life, wishing I could have said good-bye to those I love or explain to them that I'll be okay. But there was no time. There's never enough time. So instead, I trust that they know.

Creeping closer to the fence that surrounds the grounds, I tense when I see the guard tower that looms next to the road. *Dang it!* How could I have forgotten something so important? Here I am, inches from escape, and I forget to factor in there'd be guards. *Stupid, Kate. So stupid.*

I press my back against a large sugar maple, now a bare skeleton covered in a thin frost. It'd be beautiful if I could stop to notice it. The single light from the tower beams onto the main road, and looking carefully from my hiding spot behind a tree, I can't quite see into the guard station. If I'm going to know what I'm up against here, I have to get closer.

A few more maples line the yard of the next house over. If I can get there without being seen, I might be able to get a good look at my options. The problem is that between me and the house lays a span of twenty feet of open yard. Then there's another thirty feet at least before I can reach the shadows of the trees. It's a risk with guards so close, but

I have to try. Three deep breaths, and I push off the rough bark of the tree and sprint to the corner of the house. *Please let no one be home right now.*

Safely in the shadows, I give myself a minute to catch my breath and do a quick check of Brody. He's still snuggled against my shirt. Thank goodness for this scarf. It's been my saving grace.

I haven't caught my breath when I hear a creak. Turning my head to the right, I see the door at the back of the house begin to open. I can't stand here. They'll see me for sure. Before the door opens further, I'm off again, holding Brody with one hand to keep him still as I run. In the safety of the trees, I see a figure standing in the doorway of the house where I just stood. "Who's out there?" the woman calls. She steps onto the back steps and peers into the darkness, and I wonder what she would have done if she'd seen me.

Now, only feet from the guard station, I have a good view of the road and fence. From the looks of things, two guards man the post. I'm almost close enough to hear what they're saying, but from here, it's only muffled noise. In the distance, a phone rings twice, and moments later, both guards rush out of the station, hop into a truck, and speed down the highway.

This is *way* too convenient, and I can't help but wonder if it isn't some sort of set up allowing me through the gates so easily. But I can't give up the opportunity to cross the border without being seen. So as the truck disappears into the distance, I rush toward the tower with a now squirming Brody. "Shh," I whisper, hoping he'll settle down long enough for us to get into the forest, but knowing he won't. I have to move faster. His breathing worries me. I have to get him help as soon as possible, and the Hidden City is my only hope of saving him.

Sliding my hands along the rough wood of the guard station, I raise my head enough to look through the window. It's empty. Without hesitation, I slink to the other side through the opening of the fence and head for the trees a hundred yards away.

This is way too easy. Something's wrong; I know it. But with no one in sight, I can't stop to ponder the ease of my escape, especially with Brody squirming more against my chest.

"Just a little farther, buddy. Then I'll get you out for a minute."

As soon as we're through the fence, I give a quick look over my shoulder. Nothing. No one. We're alone with nothing but the Outer Lands in front of us. And the hope of finding the Hidden City again.

∙∙∙∙∙∙∙∙∙∙∙∙∙∙∙∙∙∙∙∙∙∙∙∙∙∙∙∙∙∙∙∙∙∙

FORTY

OVER THE RIVER AND THROUGH THE WOODS

THE TREES SWALLOW BRODY and me up into the thick foliage, and within a few steps, I can't see the road anymore. It's disappeared just like my old life. It's colder in here amongst the shadows. Luckily, the snow is lighter, too, probably finding it hard to break through the tree branches that canopy overhead. I'm thankful. Moving through snow, no matter how deep, makes my progress minimal.

Once we're deeper into the forest, I stop to take a break. Removing Brody from my chest is such a huge relief. His tiny whimper indicates he's hungry, so I reach into the single bag of supplies I managed to take from Taryn's house and pull out a bottle filled with water. No longer warm, I'm hoping Brody will drink it anyway. I mix the formula, shake it together, and offer it to Brody, who again sucks it down. When he's done, I take a moment to search through the supplies.

At first sight, my heart is lightened. Lying on top of a blanket is a tiny paper frog. I have no idea what it means, but it gives me hope that we just might make it through this.

Then I keep digging further into the bag.

Crap.

Of course, I have the bag with blankets and diapers. There's one can of formula that's been opened already and another large one as well. My problem is that I have no more water to make another bottle. Maybe I can gather some snow to melt it? My heart tenses as I think of the possibility of no food for Brody. I don't even consider that there's no food for me here. There's nothing to eat except what I can find in the forest. I wouldn't even know where to begin looking when it is full of summer berries much less in the dead of winter.

It's no problem, I tell myself. A day or two without eating isn't bad. I just have to find the Hidden City quickly. I'm more worried about Brody and his lungs than I am my stomach.

I lay Brody on my coat on the forest floor and pack his now empty bottle with snow, avoiding the pine needles scattered on the ground. Blowing on it every once in a while will melt it as best I can. There's at least one more meal for him. I don't think of my own grumbling stomach.

After a check of his diaper—clean, thank goodness—I wrap Brody and switch him to the opposite side, hoping he'll be more comfortable. He nuzzles into a tiny ball and rests his head against my chest. I'm amazed at how much the little guy sleeps. Soon, we're off again, blazing a trail through the frosty forest floor.

How long did Micah and I travel through the Outer Lands before he stopped? I have no idea. I know I have to head north, basically following the road, but since I can't see the road from where I am, I'm guessing the direction. No matter. I keep moving, telling stories to Brody to keep my own sanity in the silence of the forest. I try not to think of Brody's lungs. It's not like I can do anything about it now anyway. As soon as I make it to the Hidden City, I'll get him help. It's the best I can do. Until then, I hope the damage is minimal.

It's dark. It has been since I left, and we must have been traveling for several hours by now. My feet hurt, I'm exhausted, and Brody needs to eat again. Must find a resting place soon, not that I'll actually be able to sleep outside … on the ground … in the cold snow of early March. I'd hoped it wouldn't take this long. Hoped that I'd step into the Outer Lands and see signs pointing to the Hidden City, knowing all the while it wouldn't happen. So much for wishful thinking.

Remembering what Micah told me about finding a place free from wind—somewhere against a rock or under a tree with low branches, I scan the area for a place meeting those standards. In the distance, I see a patch of trees with branches almost brushing the ground. Unwrapping Brody for what seems like the thousandth time, I settle him into a nest of blankets while I crawl under the branches to check out our bed for the night.

It's wide enough for me and Brody with a little extra wiggle room. Reaching out of the branches, I pull my son and his nest inside and grab the bag as well. There's no fire and no hope of me building one, so I pull Brody as close to me as I can, snuggling him into the crook of my stomach and tucking the blankets around his tiny body. Then I remember he needs to be changed. The foul smell filling the air is my first clue. How am I going to do this without freezing him in the icy air? I can't think of a way, so I go for it, trying for speed.

As soon as I pull the blankets away from his bottom, he lets out a stifled squeal. "I know buddy. I'm so sorry. I'm trying to be fast." But I'm not fast enough, and by the time I get him wrapped up again, he's all out screaming in between his shivers and coughs. No amount of me patting or cooing or whispering is helping at all.

I know how he feels. Lost, cold, hungry, as if no matter how hard we try, it won't matter. We'll both die out here, despite my valiant efforts. With Brody's cries piercing my ears and my efforts to calm him not making a difference, I curl up in a ball, pulling him closer into me and let my own shrieks of frustration blend with his amidst the silence of the forest. There's no one to hear. No one to help. Tears streaming down my face, I manage to fall into a pseudo-sleep.

***

I wake shivering and stiff, my arm tucked around my son. Prying my eyes open despite my tortured rest, I look at Brody, hoping for a jolt of renewal. But his skin is freezing to the touch and his tiny body quivers with the cold. I bolt upright, intending to sit up and focus on getting him warm, but I crack my head on a branch above me, forgetting I slept under a tree last night. The motion startles me, and I wrench back hard, losing my balance, and connect with a rock jutting out of the ground. I finger the bump and gasp when my hands pull away covered in warm, sticky blood. My head swirls, and passing out is a moment away. I squeeze my eyes shut. "No, I can't pass out." Grasping onto the branch, I wait for the dizziness to pass before I touch the wound again. More blood. It's crawling down my face now.

I use one of Brody's thinner blankets twisted into a rope to tie around my head. It hurts, but if it stops the bleeding, I should be okay to move on today. Gathering my wits about me, I turn my attention to Brody. Change, feed, wrap. Using the melted snow in the bottle, I fix the formula and thank whatever possessed me to tuck it between my legs so it wouldn't freeze overnight.

Moving will do us good. Overnight, the temperature dropped, and from the feel of the air, it hasn't risen at all. We have to get going if only to get the blood pumping. Once Brody has finished the bottle, I take a minute to gather what snow I can find into the bottle again. Every time I look at him, I find myself thankful that he's still alive. He's eating and breathing. I can't worry myself about anything else. Just keep him alive till we get there. I wrap Brody into the blankets and tie him to my chest again, hoping what little body heat we both have will rub off on each other.

I'm already weak from the loss of blood, and the lack of food certainly isn't helping, but I have no choice. Get up, get moving. The problem is that whenever I stand, I swear I'll pass out, so every few steps, I have to balance myself on a nearby tree branch.

Despite my injury, we manage to make progress, stopping frequently for rest. I wish Micah were here with me. He'd at least know which direction to go. I'm wandering, hurt and dizzy, hoping I'm headed in the right direction. Stumbling with nearly every step.

****

Another night and day of the same. Sleeping under trees, melting snow so at least one of us will be able to eat, but I eat some snow to stay hydrated. Traveling by daylight when I can. As much as I can. But by the third day, I'm so weak, I don't think I'll be able to move any longer.

Come on, Kate. You can make it. Don't give up now. It's too soon. My self-induced pep talk does nothing for me, but the thought of seeing Micah again and getting Brody to safety pushes me forward.

By this time, all the trees look the same. All the rocks look the same. The forest floor is covered with the same pine needles and the same branches, and I swear, I'm going in circles. My legs are weak beneath me, and with my eyes seeing double, I don't notice the branch in my path.

My toe catches, and my ankle twists and pops, sending me to the forest floor. I let out a scream and try to protect Brody by falling onto my side. It twists my ankle further, sending a stabbing pain from my foot to my knee. I can't stop the sudden urge in my throat, so I turn my head to the side and vomit.

Wiping my mouth, I manage to sit up and unwind the screaming Brody from his cocoon, and set him on the ground. I have to look at my injury. Untying my shoe, I peel back my sock and clench my teeth whenever the shooting pain races up my leg. There's a giant bulb forming on the side of my foot, already purple. Even the slightest touch of my fingertips to the spot sends stabs through my foot bad enough that I welcome the thought of passing out. My hands shake, and I don't even wipe away the tears and snot that mix as I sob over my condition. I'm a mess. Hungry, injured, still dizzy from my head injury, hardly able to see straight, having to take care of an innocent sickly infant who may or may not survive the next few days. And now this. With quivering fingers, I unwrap the bandage from my head and rip it in half, placing half over my still oozing head wound and wrapping the other tightly around my ankle. The action sends stars to my eyes, and I black out. When I wake to Brody's feeble cries, I have no idea how long I've been out, but the little light we had guiding our path has dissipated into a deep gray. Dusk is upon us.

Maybe if I can at least stand, I can still go on. Pulling my shoe on is excruciating, and I can't tie it up due to the swelling. I reach up to a branch for leverage. But when I put pressure on my foot, the pain shoots clear to my hip, and I topple over again. It must be broken.

Now I can't stop them. The sobs wrench from my body in deep spasms. I can't do it. I can't. A few feet away, I see a large rock tucked in between a few trees. At least there we'll be out of the wind. Pulling the screaming Brody to me, I drag us both across the ground until I can rest my back against the stone.

I can't move any further. Brody's whine has diminished to a pathetic whimper. With no food, my energy is sapped. I can't go on. All the dreams Micah and I had for reaching the Hidden City have melted away. They're gone along with all hope of survival. If only I didn't have to do this alone. We could have made it with Micah here.

My back to the icy rock, I pull Brody out from his ties and cradle him close to me. "I'm so sorry, little man. I tried. I tried, but I can't find it. We'll die out here, and it's all my fault. I'm so sorry." I weep, my tears freezing to my cheeks. "I never intended for this to happen," I tell him. "Please forgive me." But weakened by the cold weather, Brody can't respond.

This is it, I tell myself. I allow my eyes to close. I know there is no more for me. I've come to the end.

"Kate."

I'm even hearing voices. The blood loss must be causing hallucinations.

"Kate. Is that you?" It's a different voice now. Vaguely familiar. But in my semi-conscious state, I can't comprehend anything. Between fluttering eyelids, I see three forms hovering over my face. One of them is me, and I wonder if I'm having an out of body experience. I try to sit up, and when I do, I see another form out in the distance. A shadow among the trees. They must be the angels ready to take me away.

"Hold on. Take it easy," one voice says as I feel myself surrounded by strong arms. "Come here. Let's get you inside. You'll be safe there."

I don't hear anything else because I'm swallowed up by the darkness.

FORTY ONE

. . . .

HOME

"**K**ATE. WAKE UP."
The voice is distant as it seeps into my consciousness. Am I dead?

"You're safe now."

I try to pry my eyelids open, but it feels like I may need a crowbar to do so. Every bone in my body aches, and my feet still tingle from the cold. I'm in a bed with blankets covering my lower half. My head is propped up by pillows and wrapped in clean gauze. A fire crackles in the hearth against the far wall, and I know instantly—I'm not anywhere near The Institute. I've made it to the Hidden City. Only I have no idea how I got here.

"Kate," the soft voice says again.

I turn my head despite the pain in my neck to see a young blonde sitting beside my bed. She's holding my hand, rubbing her thumb over my wrist.

"Ally?"

"You remember me?"

"Brody? Where's Brody?" My throat is on fire. Dry and crackling. Talking hurts.

"The baby you came in with is fine. He's being looked after in the infant wing of the hospital. They didn't have room for you there, so I told them I'd nurse you here in my home. You had quite a trip. I'm just thankful Jess, Silas, and Hunter found you. They brought you back."

My brain is fuzzy and trying to comprehend what she's saying is difficult. But I caught the part where she said Brody's okay. That's all that matters. Then I remember. My eyes pop open, and I sit up straight, sending a spiking pain down my left leg and twinkling stars in front of my eyes.

"Whoa. Sit back. You need to relax. You messed up your leg pretty badly. It's broken. And that wound on your head was pretty nasty, too."

"Micah? Is Micah okay?" All the memories of the past few days have come rushing back like a tidal wave. "He made it here, right? He said he'd meet me here."

Ally shakes her head. "We don't know."

"But he said if we got separated he'd meet me here. He has to be in the Hidden City somewhere. The whole arrest thing had to be a ruse. That's why he told me to go when they had him pinned to the floor. He said he'd be here."

"I know, he told me your plan. But he's not here. We don't know where he is." She tries to sound reassuring. "But you're here, and you're safe. I'm sure Micah will find his way back. He has a way with that sort of thing."

It's a hopeful lie. I crumple back onto the bed and let all the bottled up emotions pour out of me. I'm bawling. Crying for the friend I've lost in Taryn. Sobbing for the family I've left behind. Weeping for the trouble, I know I've caused. But most of all, I'm aching because I know if Micah isn't here by now, he's gone forever. I'll never see him again. I'm forced to live this hidden life without him.

And I don't know if I can.

FORTY TWO

·······························

HOPE

I USED TO THINK that entering the natal wing of the hospital would become easier with time. Not so. In fact, each time seems to get harder. Brody should be doing better by now; his lungs should be improving. But he's still hooked up to tubes and medicine pumps through his veins. I'm just afraid that I caused irreparable damage by birthing him too soon and then traveling with him through the cold air.

Balancing my crutches under one arm, I press through the heavy doors and am greeted by a nurse. "Kate," she says. "You've got to come quickly."

"What's happened? Is Brody all right?" I rush along beside her through the maze of hallways.

"He's fine. Breathing better every day. The doctor wants to speak with you as soon as you get here." She leads me to a room next to the nursery where Brody is being kept. I can see him through the glass in his tiny plastic cradle, covered with tubes going in and out of his mouth and nose. He looks so miniscule next to the other baby in the nursery today.

"What's this about?" I ask her, looking around for some kind of clue.

A smile spreads across her face. "I'll let the doctor inform you. He should be here shortly."

She busies herself with some paperwork while I try to sit on the uncomfortable chair to wait. I hate waiting. Seems like that's all I ever do anymore. Wait for Brody to heal. Wait for my leg to get better. Wait for word about Micah.

In walks the doctor, carrying a small compact and stylus. He looks up from the screen, and his eyes soften. He offers me a brown skinned hand. "Ms. Dennard. So nice to see you again."

I stand and shake it. "Dr. Johnston. What's this about?" I'm trying to be polite, but the nurse has me all twitterpated.

"Please, have a seat."

"I think I'd rather stand." It doesn't matter that I have to lean on crutches for support, sitting makes my nerves stand on end.

"In that case, come over this way." He motions to the glass window separating this room from the nursery. Leaning against the heavy glass, he taps and points to my son. "I wanted to let you know that Brody is healthy enough to be taken off the breathing systems. The last test we did showed that his lung function is normal."

I breathe a sigh of relief. "So, he's okay? The cold air didn't hurt him?"

"Brody seems to be quite a little fighter, Kate. He's going to be just fine. We're going to keep him here for a while longer to monitor him, but hopefully soon, you can take him home."

I feel myself relax onto the crutch under my arm. "Thank you, Doctor."

He nods and turns to leave.

"Nurse, is it okay if I see Brody?"

"Certainly." She moves to open the door for me.

I'm the only one in the nursery besides the infants cradled here. Across the room, my little man is breathing steadily, wrapped tightly in blankets. I touch the top of his head with my fingertips and wrap his silky hair around my fingers. "Hey, little guy. You get to come home soon." As if he's heard me, his eyelids flutter, and he takes a deep sigh before opening them. He looks right at me with wide eyes. Lifting him out of the cradle, I cup his tiny head in my hands and pull him tight to my chest. My lips brush over his silky hair again and again, and I whisper, "I love you, little guy, and I'm so thankful you're okay. Pretty soon, we'll go home and start a new life in this place together. Just the two of us."

Made in the USA
San Bernardino, CA
15 September 2016